Christine is on the hunt to find out more about her great aunt, Rose, hoping to decipher their severed relationship and the murder Rose committed, for which June is in prison. With a stroke leaving Rose incapacitated, it's a rush against time to find the truth.

Things are doubly complicated when Christine's girlfriend Terrie is accused of assaulting someone. Nervous about what she might do next, Christine and her friends avoid Terrie. With everything at stake, Christine must stick to the cold hard facts, reminding herself not to let her emotions get in the way.

Christine must evaluate everything happening in her life. The weight of the events buried by her aunt so many years before and the shame of the actions of the love of her life rest squarely on her. If the eyes of the law are always 20/20, how do love, emotion, and insecurities distort fact?

CRIMINAL BY PROXY

S.E. Smyth

A NineStar Press Publication

www.ninestarpress.com

Criminal by Proxy

First Edition, October 2022

ISBN: 978-1-64890-551-3

Also available in eBook, ISBN: 978-1-64890-550-6

CONTENT WARNING:
This book contains sexual content, which may only be suitable for mature readers. Depictions of past abuse, bullying, death/deceased family member, domestic abuse, grief, guns, medical procedures, homophobia, incarceration, murder, past trauma, stalking, and workplace harassment.

To my wife, friends, editors, and primary sources

CHAPTER ONE

DEAR ROSE

"I LOVED HER... That's what I tell myself at least," June uttered. Her exertion, her plea, resonated. "I told her that...yelled across the courtroom...in 1968, the day I went to prison, and I've said it a thousand times since."

June had been a psychiatrist years ago, but Christine was the one listening now, decades later.

Christine was pretending to be a law student to get information, clarity on historical facts about the actions of her great-aunt Rose from the time she was in a mental hospital in the late 1950s. Her aunt, who was in her seventies, was not in Christine's direct blood line but rather the child of her grandmother's sister. She'd lived with Christine's aunts and uncles and family from a young age, nonetheless. Christine had gathered scattered details in bits and pieces all her life. Every other family holiday or so, some new bit of information would surface. But she never asked. It was something everyone quietly avoided to begin with.

June had been Rose's psychiatrist at one point while she was in a mental hospital. Sometime after she was released, she'd moved in with June, and they had developed a relationship. Rose had ended up shooting and killing a man, but Christine was confused about the chain of events and who was to blame. June was in prison, and Rose had been free since 1972.

Several letters followed the initial blunt hello letter to June. In those, they discussed basic things Christine got wrong and developed a loose friendship. After about four letters, Christine suggested a meeting. June recommended an interview room since she was a student, and Christine went about finding out if it was possible.

In an act of indiscretion, she set up an appointment to see the infamous June, someone she had recently found out to be Aunt Rose's ex-lover. This interview, her time in the room with a prisoner who held a life sentence, was dedicated to asking questions to elucidate events from decades ago, that her aunt Rose never discussed.

Christine attempted to gauge if June was telling the truth. She needed to know if the legal decision was warranted. She was sure if she listened very carefully, she could figure out if June actually did love Aunt Rose and if the correct decision had been made in the courtroom in 1968. All this, Christine attempted to assess with a conversation. She would have an answer by the end of the conversation. It was her only objective.

June wasn't the same person she had been years ago—when June had loved Aunt Rose and Aunt Rose had presumably loved her. That fact stuck out. Christine's initial assessment was any flame June still held for Aunt Rose was one-sided.

June only half faced her, sitting sideways on the chair, the corner of which stuck out between her legs. June glanced over her shoulder. She held a waning seventy years in her limbs, but she still glowed with energy. Christine didn't mind she threw a sneer down across her nose. Christine pried and chipped at information at first, but the conversation soon flowed more smoothly.

Christine had first heard about June from her great-aunt, who kicked up old memories and dropped them right away. Christine let her get away with her excuses—she didn't remember. June was her aunt's ex-lover. She mentioned she was in prison. That was everything her aunt would tell her. Christine had found out June was labeled a criminal by the media. She was a prisoner with a life sentence. Aunt Rose had fired the gun, but they'd given the slot in prison to June. Christine imagined her day, filled with bitter resentment for her free ex-lover. The lover who didn't contact her. There had to be bad blood. Christine eyed her goal at this point—information. She needed to know what had happened. Christine was interrogating her, asking her to relive it for a law school report, what she thought about the case so many years later. Unfairly picking at issues June wasn't ready to answer, she continued the questions.

June went on, describing everything in bits and pieces. She would pause and continue, restart with irrelevant comments, diverting the conversation. "It was different all that time ago. All the hoopla over something agreed to be truth. If someone thought you were a lesbian and if they caught you, arms were up in the air—sirens roared. It was a travesty, and something was done about it." June continued on about the past, how people thought of her and talked about her.

She spoke about the past as if events weren't real, as if life were a story she was reading to children, the grim side of a fairy tale. Off and on, June would shift, indicating her tongue had taken her too far. She shouldn't have let the full story go. Her knowledge was an out-of-body reflection, too real. The trauma showed through.

Christine's life of rumors, her life, seemed trivial. Three close friends gossiped about Christine and the woman she'd slept with last summer, Amy. Her friends told her to move on, but she wouldn't let the friendship go. They said, "She'll mess you up." It was still the same shameful behavior: whispered gossip, stern talks, and scandalous goings-on. Her reality was different from June's in that Christine didn't have the same amount to lose. Nothing was a malicious, life-ruining assault.

"We were taking risks. Real risks. Higher stakes than today. I didn't want to change the world or loosen people's opinions. I wanted love. She gave me that. So, what else was I supposed to do?" June said. She grabbed at short tufts of hair at the base of her head.

"What people were doing was so important. I don't want to say it wasn't. We had love, and we wanted to keep it. We fought that battle every day from our apartment, from our place of work. In a way, very quietly, but we fought. We certainly didn't change the minds of the world when the murder happened. We acknowledged how strong our love was before the murder. It was so well bonded that I still love her now, after all these years." Her words softened and rounded as she spoke again about her love. She dipped her head as if the frown that extended cheek to cheek were pulling it down.

Wrinkles emerged in the corners of June's eyes as Christine tapped her pencil. Christine stopped to cease any errant irritation. When Christine tried to bring June back and force her to be present, talk about the case, June's vocal qualities changed.

The soft voice June spoke with when talking about the past and love disappeared into one of an aged woman when she spoke about what was going on in her life now. "You see. They all believe me in here now. I love her. My friends in prison. It's okay to be gay, even though it definitely wasn't when they locked me up."

Christine sat stiffly as a board in the chair listening to June, catching every word. As she performed the gesture, she committed to brushing off immature and unserious actions, those not indicative of a law student. She was already in a precarious balance with June, a relaxed new friend facing a studious law student—both skeptical of masked lies, strangers in an unfamiliar room. Christine's great-aunt

Rose was dying. Who was this woman she kept speaking of?

Aunt Rose was younger than June. Yet, even ten years ago, her limbs, as Christine remembered them, hadn't been as vivacious, and her energy hadn't sprouted from her eyes quite as much as June's. June had a staccato bite to her words. She quickened the pace every time she answered Christine. Offended, at times, she looked off into the distance. Christine relied on the fact she must have relished talking to someone.

Christine had hit a deeper nerve. Now, she scrambled to put all the pieces together. She went after the question of love before putting together the details. "Tell me what happened. I need as many details as possible for my law class project," Christine said. She put the tape recorder on the desk and flipped the switch. It had been fifteen minutes of the hour-long interview time slot.

"They say I killed that man with psychological powers." She waved her hands in the air. "They said I made Rose do it, held an invisible gun to her head. Well, I didn't, unless it's a matter of love. Then, I did."

June wasn't going to introduce any more facts. In her letters, Christine had mentioned a few details about the case she had read in newspaper articles, asked to tape-record, and offered anything she could do in return. June denied any money or gifts with short, choppy responses and was willing, as she commented, only for the reason she treasured a change in scenery—"No matter how stale." She squeaked out she was too proud for money. June was up for early release again, but her case, in all the years, had never gone through.

With a sigh, June spoke. "Oh, I loved her hair. It shined so much. Fistfuls thick and gorgeous. I wonder if it still is?"

She switched right into talking about how much she loved Aunt Rose. June veered off course from any conversation Christine prompted. It was as if she was toying with Christine, keeping what she wanted to know at bay. Was there deception in her evasive language, her imploring attempts at sympathy?

The pushback she was getting from June had to be the result of her lying. Christine only gathered she deserved this much, a liar herself. As much as Christine tapped her pencil and asked for the facts, June would drift off or talk about things that happened in prison, the social climate in the sixties, or what seclusion was like. She was uninterested in going over the details, telling her side of the story. Christine needed a basis for events. She had to put together the details, the hazy parts; after that, she would listen to everything else. It was as if Christine's opinion didn't matter. The one point Christine got was June loved Rose.

"When I first got here—so many years ago now—they put me with the most violent woman in the place. They tried to break me 'cause they assumed I wasn't tough. When you have love in your heart, pushing the feelings out for toughness's sake is difficult," June said.

Weakening, Christine said, "It must have been difficult at first." She hoped she wasn't leading her down the wrong path. It was no use fighting June's tense emotions. June appeared to not hear her.

Christine hoped to find out more about this person—Dr. June Ashmore. Christine was sure there was some reason to it all. The story had truth. Aunt Rose had mentioned her several times before, but they never got into all the minute details. This woman, June, was still something to Aunt Rose. The case confounded and perplexed her. She would pound her fist later. She had to know more.

Christine tried to keep curiosity and empathy at bay. She lifted her pencil and slanted her clipboard with the fresh legal pad held tight in the clip. Bowing her left eye into the paper, she attempted to scribble some notes. *They loved each other after all*, she told herself. Her mind wandered as she considered whether she should doodle. She filled her mouth with a grin and drew a mini heart. This was a project in a way—a project for Aunt Rose.

"So, for my assignment," Christine said, situating her clipboard over her lap and crossing her arms. "Let's talk about Dr. O'Malley. You didn't kill him, but you're in prison for his murder. Can we talk about your relationship with him, first and foremost?"

"Look at your suit. To a T. Except for a few wrinkles, you pass for a real lawyer," June said.

What Christine wanted to know wasn't worth her breath. Christine leaned away and let out two grumbling coughs with lips closed tightly. She would get what information June would give her. She would listen.

"First, I'll tell you why I loved Rose. You can see my case log if you want to know what happened. The report details the charges, what the cops decided, so it must be true," June said, wetness forming in her eyes. "You put this in your project—genuine love in human nature weighs more than the power of any law. It supersedes it."

Christine didn't know for sure, but she imagined this statement wouldn't get her an A. Nonetheless, she reflected on the perspective, the power in June's voice. They repeated this argument over and over again. Christine understood a bit about love. As serious as possible, June buckled her up, and Christine had better listen.

June reached into her bra and produced a small triangle. The creased and folded item resembled those footballs kids made with paper in elementary school. The note was beginning to yellow from age and oils and from hands and repeated opening and closing. She unfolded the scrap carefully, crease by crease. She flattened the paper again by making broad sweeps with the back of her hand. The lines were deep and wide from folding and refolding. She read it aloud.

Dearest Rose,

I'm trying you again. It's the two-hundred-fiftieth time. They say I'm up for release again. I've been recommended for release over fifteen times. It probably won't happen, but I wanted you to know. Maybe you'll move out of town. Ha. Maybe you'll remember me and want to see me. Just know I want to see you and talk.

I could save this all for when we meet, but I might as well say it here in case we never do. I knew I loved you when you first came to me and told me you needed a place to stay. I knew I loved you before, of course. When they released you, the tears rolled down your face. You were so happy you were finally free—maybe, maybe, the world didn't hate you on the grounds you were a lesbian. You had this light inside you that went on. Our beacon. You might have been on the same footing as everyone else. No one would be able to limit you. And of course, you were a beacon. Everyone talked; you didn't care who knew you were the person you were. It mattered, though. It mattered to the people who hated you and the people who loved you. I always loved you for your virtue; you were a fighter. We made teeny efforts, didn't we? We made sexuality normal. We fought homophobia. We stood up for our friends. All this in micro steps. Making simple comments to other doctors was one way. We lent Mary money when she lost her job. Remember? I pushed the belief homosexuality was normal, carefully, in my work as a psychiatrist. Even though I could've been barred from practicing psychiatry, it was more important to show other people our love. It was ours, and no one could take that away. No one could limit it—we wouldn't let them.

I hope I helped you be yourself. When I was your doctor, I tried to tell you what everyone else said was wrong. I wanted to build you up and let you be a person. Remember this always: I prevented the electroshock treatments and recommended your release. I risked my job. I did it for you. It was when we were finally together—when you finally moved in, I swore we would always be together. That was me showing my love—my testament.

I still think about you—all the time. You're with me in this wretched place. I eat my meals alone and read books, but it's you I think about and write to so often. If I do get out this time, I might call. Maybe we can get coffee? After all these years, we can get coffee. Please, you can't still hate me.

Love Always,

June

Tears formed in June's eyes. As her low voice subsided, she drew in muffled, jerking breaths, her head held down. She sniffed in sharply as though tears had never come, and they weren't still there.

"I sent a few of them...in the beginning. They were love letters, of course. Rose never responded. Now, I write them and keep them piled up near my bed. The guards threw most of them away last year in a cleaning spree," June remarked. "I should burn them all. All that is left. They don't let prisoners have fire. It's a shame for that very reason." The corners of her mouth rose. "I don't know why I leave the conversation with Rose open-ended. They shut this case a very long time ago."

She played with wisps of her hair, still holding her head down, eyes looking above Christine. June crossed a line. She overshared. The emotions were too much for any rational person to give. Yet Christine listened, absorbing all the details. June had to say what she felt, form words. Had to let love out. That's what Christine figured. Someone would have to remember to care.

"It's 'cause I love her. I'm in prison 'cause of love." June said.

June told Christine about their long drives. The couple would take off and go for miles, almost bottoming out over bumps on rolling country roads. With the windows rolled down on the car, they barely heard each other through the whistle, but it was pleasant. They had planned to retire to one of the towns they passed by.

"We always said we'd stop at hole-in-the-wall spots, but once we got there, we didn't want to stop," she said. "We were scared the town wouldn't quite be as we wanted it to be. So we drove through and imagined a bookstore and a café. The places we might own and work at. It didn't matter, to tell the truth. We had so many more years until retirement. And dreaming was so much more fun."

Christine scribbled notes with a telling smirk that grew in the corners of her mouth. This wasn't law school material. Her research interview amounted to a pile of garbage, useless and unfounded.

With June working as a psychiatrist, they would have had a comfortable life with the money she'd made. She talked about the time they had spent together on vacation up the coast. The time off had given them both fresh sea air. Finally, they'd held hands and sat together, thighs touching on the park bench.

Christine turned to mush and melted in her words. June wanted her words to turn hearts of stone to warm, vibrant, beating souls. That's what she asked Rose's heart to do. Christine had hope for her relationship, which needed more help by the minute.

"I know you're a lesbian. No one else would care. That's why I'm telling you, 'cause you are," June quipped. "Not that I care. I've taken much worse risks. What else could they do to me in here?"

"I am," Christine cooed. "I'm in love, actually. Well, we're going to move in together full-time next month. She's so particular. I hope we don't fight over what to watch on TV on weekday nights or organization of the refrigerator." Christine fidgeted with her pencil and picked at the eraser.

June lifted her head and laughed. "Yeah, sounds like you're in love."

"Well, it's strange, considering there's Amy, my ex. I guess I love her too. They're not the best of friends, I guess. But I'm working at it with them both." She played with her thumbs. She'd relayed too much. Any indication she was a professional, a serious student, was now lost, muddled.

"You'll have to write me some more letters and tell me about them. I'm kind of good at helping to sort out love. Analyzing is my specialty. I like to get letters. Will you send some? I've told you about my love, what love means to me. I've told you it all—freely. Tell me about your experience with love, and I'll meet with you again."

"Of course." Christine submitted to the lonely woman in prison.

They would be friends. If anything, this woman was willing to listen. She was a psychiatrist, after all, and everyone needed a pint of therapy. She would do trivial things for her, write her letters, even if the effort was wrapped in a lie, until she revealed the secret she couldn't yet tell.

"June, if I come back, can we go over the details of the case: what happened, how you saw it? You know the points you felt swayed the jury?" Christine asked.

"Oh my, of course. But we went over the details. We did today. That's what we've been talking about, right? Oh, but of course, of course. We'll go over the details some more," June chimed.

June's final words stayed with Christine. She was up for early release. She might have a shot.

"I'd as soon die in here. It's a different world. I wouldn't know where to begin," June said. As she spoke the words, she wrung her hands. Her veins twisted with her skin.

If she tested the limits much more, they'd have a mess to clean up. The interview would be a crime scene.

Christine stewed on what to say to June about her potential release. Whatever Christine issued, June's anxiety wouldn't have lowered. Her cherished free thoughts were in some kind of hell.

Christine left as swiftly as she came, trying not to draw attention, head down the entire time. Her excursion to the prison was over, but she didn't quite have as many answers as she wanted. And now she had a strange soft spot forming in her heart for this woman in prison for life.

This newfound affection must've been sprouting from her personal life, she conjectured. On the outside, Christine was in love with two women. Amy, whom she had since broken up with, and her current girlfriend, Terrie. She understood that she loved each in their own way but could not decide on her place in both of their lives.

Christine was finishing her master's in information technology. She wasn't in law school, as the application for the interview time detailed. She expressed the same thing in the handful of letters she sent to June. Each one had a unique and colorful stamp.

The bold-faced lie she used to get into the prison was that she was a law student, and her project involved retracing a closed case, June's case, which had gone the wrong way. This meeting was her opportunity to study what happened, rulings, and extraneous factors. That was what June would hear. The information she gathered from the interviews would make her imaginary project so much stronger.

The rock-solid prison grew smaller out of the rear window. June's figure faded from Christine's mind. More questions formed. Still, so many were unanswered. June hadn't responded to any of her queries about facts, and she hadn't cared. Christine was not in charge. She was not an interviewer. Apparently, their meeting was of no consequence to June, locked in that place. Christine understood her commands didn't carry weight. June could do whatever she wanted, no repercussion. It couldn't get worse. Christine scanned the entrance one more time in her rearview mirror. June had only ever seen the front door once.

CHAPTER TWO

BEFORE — 1968

ROSE AND JUNE had fought several nights before about Dr. O'Malley and if they should be together. This night, they fought for the sake of fighting. They both felt unwanted, unloved. Rose didn't think June still loved her. It made June feel emotionally abandoned. The incident, the blood bath of words, was an emotion-filled boilover. There was yelling and tears, conflicted feelings. They slapped June in the face. She let all the words bubble and shake the lid.

Of course, they would be together. It didn't matter what others discussed on their own time. June loved her. She solidly claimed all the words she sometimes held bottled up.

That night, June's words were powerful: "Don't think about us not being together" and "Maybe, we should take a break. I should go out. You can't keep screaming like this." She was trying to shake reason into Rose. If simply saying "I love you" didn't work, like the words hadn't worked the night before, she would trick her into knowing her intent.

She sobbed low and broken from all the fighting. June stood in the living room of the modest apartment and stared down on the couch at Rose sitting. She had the money for a much better place. With her job, June had broader options. But the apartment lobby's coffered ceiling kept her there, and the large living room window wouldn't let her go. And Rose had lost her job. Living was going to get a bit more expensive. The absence of extra spending cash would be noticeable.

THE SINGLE SHOT clapped, and June rushed over and stood motionless at the door. She didn't dare turn the knob as all the scenarios flooded in, and blood rushed to her head. Rose caused the ruckus; without a doubt, the shooter was her. June realized this as she thought back to the moment Rose left the room. The glint in Rose's eyes as she left, her smirk, in the shared room June was standing in, was embossed onto the plaster walls. June's eyes strained, watching a ghost, focusing on the details, making sure it was true. The outline of the gun in her hand, which she held tightly, awkwardly in her loose pocket as she left, barely concealed, pulsed. The item didn't draw her attention at the time because if it did June would've screamed or thrown herself in front of the door. But as she remembered what happened—Rose saying, "Be right back," and turning to leave, with the outline of the bulge—she gasped. The thing in her pocket could've been a surprise for their weekend drive or a present for one of an uncountable number of anniversaries. No, it was a gun.

The pause at the door, hand on the doorknob, was thirty seconds, forty seconds at best. Darting into the hallway, June banged on the doors. A man in his bathrobe entered the hallway and gawked at June, ranting she belonged up the road in an insane asylum.

"What the hell are you doing?" the man shouted out. "I'm calling the cops. What the hell is happening?" He turned and looked back at his wife inside the apartment.

June swayed as if drunk. She stumbled and, in a garbled voice, muttered, "No." Her lips trembled, barely coherent, not fully awake, spitting nonsensical utterings.

"Did you shoot someone?" He darted at June. "What's your name?"

"Yes," she said. The words were all that was articulated as she continued wavering down the hallway to impending doom.

June meandered farther through the corridor and stopped at the stairwell door. Going down would mean she'd find out what happened. Rose's inconceivable act was irreparable. The truth would surface. She stopped still and rested her head on the door. She filled with grief but decided to descend.

When she got to the apartment, June waited at the entrance for her body to calm down. The scene only triggered more emotion. As soon as she saw Rose, her eyes filled with tears, and she could not control her shaking body.

Rose opened the door before June could enter. She came to meet June but only bowed her head and relaxed onto the floor speechless. Her spine rested against the doorjamb of Dr. O'Malley's apartment, and she sat there a mess of unsettled emotions and collapsed frustrations. Her eyes rose up, and then she stood.

June hugged June. "Oh, my god. What have you done?" The blood transferred onto June's body. "You didn't really? How could you? It's impossible." She rocked with gentle sways even though Rose's body resisted.

"He reached for the gun. I brought it with me to scare him." She wiped tears from June's face. "I went to talk to him to scare him. But he got the gun. He pointed the gun at me, but he got shot. He pointed it at me, but he's dead." Her sobs heaved.

June drew back her head with realization and understanding. "How could you?"

Rose's sobs didn't faze June. The evening, the murderous event, ruined everything for the rest of their lives.

"You're so stupid. Why did you do it?"

"I told you. He almost shot me." Rose stopped crying. "He deserved it."

"Our life is ruined—in one fell swoop. You don't even know." Standing over Rose, June slowly relayed the impact to their lives. Her anger and accusations bellowed. These words came in heat, tension, confusion, misunderstanding, and panic. Rose's bullet had left someone dead. Neither of them thought about running. June distanced herself more and more from Rose, stepping away in even steps.

"Why? How could you?" June asked.

In the heat of the moment, Rose spat, "I did it for you." Her bitterness bubbled to the surface.

It was something June had never wanted, never conceived. June understood it for what it was, a lie breaking the silence in a moment of passion. Her feeling and meaning came out as a distorted utterance. The words injured. June was the only witness. Their lives separated forever.

"How could you be so stupid? How could you do this?" June's choppy words were deafening.

Rose winced and jerked her head, sneering at her.

The police arrived, and there were four people in the hallway. "Hands up," an officer in a crisply ironed uniform shouted.

June and Rose both raised their arms.

No one else had emerged from their apartments. Rose and June scanned the cleared area. The officer on the scene pushed June away from Rose, shuttered their voices.

June was first. She was the most subdued, an easy arrest. June even turned as one of them moved toward her. She didn't want a struggle. What they did to lesbians in lockup was horrible. They taught them a lesson. But this, murder, was on different terms. And, even though June wasn't the murderer, she turned for the officer. Fear drove her to it.

"What happened here?" He scolded them and sized up June for restraint before slapping cuffs on her. He waited for her to run. He didn't wait for an explanation.

June and Rose were innocent, or they were part of an accident. They were two women, weak, standing still, confused, until Rose spoke.

"I don't know. One thing after another happened. She told me to do it, officer. She told me to. I had to," Rose said, covered in blood, crying. She moved her head from side to side as she struggled with slight jerks but didn't look in June's direction.

They cuffed Rose second. Rose cursed at the air, at June, as they put handcuffs on her. The cold countenance of a killer crossed her face and stayed there. June watched Rose move with an officer down the hallway. She didn't turn around or catch one last glance as they separated. Rose wanted nothing more of her. The distance grew by miles as she left out the door.

In the parking lot, Rose was shoved into a car. How could Rose say the murder was her fault? How could she not be responsible for what she had done? Trapped in the same chain of events as Rose, June bobbed her head and rocked, ashamed and nervous. In a minute, she'd be ducked into a car, too, no matter how many times she turned and stuttered out she hadn't done anything. She wasn't even in the room. They hadn't even asked. Despite her anger at Rose's words, Rose's implication of her, she pitied Rose. More than anything, June wanted her to be okay when she got downtown.

CHAPTER THREE

TERRIE

CHRISTINE STRODE ACROSS the university's central courtyard on the way to the student center to sign the Class of 2015 banner. She tended to walk with purpose, blind to anyone directly in front of her. Friends would stop to talk to her in class or at a restaurant or coffee shop. They would tell her she blew right past them as if on a mission. They went unnoticed, despite their waves or casual hellos.

Christine thought a lot. Although usually social, at times, she found herself in a mist of foggy contemplation and emotions, going down what-if corridors and I-wish-I-wouldn't-have hallways in her mind. She overthought her partner all the time. She called her a "girlfriend," but she wished she were ten years older so "partner" or "lover" sounded easy. Their classification sounded immature. When a couple says "partner," they are taken more seriously. Saying "girlfriend" puts you on the same level as high school students.

Christine and Terrie had exchanged "I love you." The short phrase had come out a few months ago. To Christine, the words meant she was settling down. More so, when she said "love," it reminded her of the investment as she said it. The more she tried to say "I love you" and move on with life, the more she evaluated her sensibilities.

Terrie failed to see the point of marriage though. They went their own way most days, in her opinion, even though they had been dating for about eight months. Terrie and Christine had become more serious two months before when the semester changed. Yet Terrie didn't carry all her furniture up those stairs. She still paid for her old apartment, and Christine covered the cost for her place, but Terrie spent the night, every other night. Some noticed the convenience.

Yesterday at about the same time, they'd had coffee but off-campus. The library coffee shop was too typical for a coffee date. They tried to find time to date in general, time to bond, keep the romance alive, more than stare at each other. Minigolf, movies, and restaurants let them feel like they weren't shifting into Netflix-movie-night romance status. It was the posed face-to-face encounters Christine craved.

Terrie was more of a surpriser. That's how she showed

her affection. She would bring flowers and arrange them in the apartment. Christine insisted she loathed flowers. Terrie brought them anyway. Someone looking in on their relationship might say Christine wasn't femme enough or was somehow averse to receiving flowers. Somewhere, deep down, Terrie liked that they were there, arranged in the corner, sometimes with an unopened, unmentioned card addressed to Christine. That was how Terrie showed her love, silently, in a way open to interpretation.

Terrie sipped from her large mug, held with both hands. Christine didn't question her strength. Terrie, wiry overall, still held characteristics that made people aware of her power. Her muscles bulged slightly on her lean frame. She carried books or furniture or whatever up to their third-story apartment. Her friends often took advantage of this talent.

The ridges and divots of Terrie's face, caring wrinkles around the eyes, and soft smiles warmed the room when they were together. Angles jutted across her face, creating an overall masculine mask. Gentle feminine dips and smooth skin were present as well. Christine searched for softness and curves along her chin. She gave everything to Terrie. She wanted more emotion in return.

Terrie's ragged short hair says "I've got fire and spunk." Her eyes, though laser blue, would only penetrate one when pushed to the brink. She snapped sometimes, and that caused a rift in their relationship. A few times, Terrie had yelled at Christine until she cried. They always got over it, at least the less frequent occurrences, but at a certain point, Terrie took anger over the edge and did unforgettable things. Her crimson face and her anger stuck in Christine's memory more than the words. When she remembered those moments, while having a firm discussion, she still tiptoed around the rest of the conversation. She didn't want Terrie to yell, and she wanted to go slowly in the relationship.

She had striking features, a subdued electric presence, but her real attractiveness came from the fact that she listened more than spoke. She waited, paused to respectfully let Christine relay what she wanted to say, always calm. Terrie never issued immediacy or referenced escape routes. Her sense of place in the moments she shared with other people, Christine included, made them feel like the only one on the planet, while other universes listened too.

Sitting on a bench in the courtyard across from the library, Christine darted from person to person, looking for someone, forcing herself to focus on the people passing by. She wanted to chat with someone and casually let out the lie she had yet to tell anyone. The suspicious secret washed over her. She'd made up a class project. She felt guilty for what she had done and the deception. She'd met with a criminal for Christ's sake, and she hadn't even told anyone.

A few students emerged from the library with coffees or lattes. Everyone had midterm parties and were gearing up for final papers and exams. The school was a reasonable size. Her graduate school department only included about thirty students. But a sea of underclassmen rushed out of the buildings when class periods changed. As Christine scanned with wonder into groups of twentysomethings, lost souls, she realized she had never even seen the bulk of them. They were unrecognizable.

Christine's feet shifted. She tilted her head as she focused on the sky and the eternal school year. Her gaze was unfocused as she stared off into space. She wanted the year to be over, so she might find a job or think about doing something entirely different. Her mom listened to her vague plans, her wandering thoughts about her life, and told her to grow up. She couldn't clear her head and decide which path to take until she finished the semester finals. Thoughts didn't come. Only the goal stood out.

Christine pulled her computer science book out of her backpack and paged through the bulky mess of technical words. Did this count as studying? One particular review section went over complex CSS stylesheets, a language used to create how a webpage will be presented. She had already learned the key concepts in undergrad. She didn't want to spend time studying for the final. She didn't need to put in the effort. The website project was going to be the majority of the grade. She would breeze through the effort. She had to make a website and commerce site for a client. If she buckled down, pulled a few more late nights, and finished the assignment, she would get an A. The hard parts were done. Her thesis revolved around templates for business cases and justifications for procurement of specialized equipment in nonprofit arts grant applications.

She would go into nursing. Nobody wanted to get stuck behind a computer for the rest of their lives. Quasi-ownership of an office desk and tasks involving playing with network jacks into her sixties held the same excitement in her mind as being a professional cadaver. She wouldn't get one of the good jobs. She'd have to wear grey work suits from department stores, and she shuddered at the thought. She might start over with nursing. They were the people who, with honest intention, helped the world. She'd taken an anatomy class in undergrad to learn more about bones, what was under the skin.

The whole issue of law school sent chills of nervousness through her spine to her fingers. This wild-goose-chase project would lead her right into taking more classes after she graduated. Lawyers made decent money, but she wasn't sure if the pressure would be too much. The damp and musty, mold intoxication-inducing air in the prison conjured a hazy picture of her future. The air was thin, like too many people had breathed. Her mental state would deteriorate.

She wished she had someone to talk about long-term choices with. Aunt Rose was always there for her and would offer sound advice. She would listen, like Terrie, and help as best as possible. She encouraged Christine to dream and carry herself away with wherever she expended effort.

She'd visit Aunt Rose tomorrow, maybe bring her some flowers. She wrote a note in pen on her hand to call Uncle Mark when she got home. Aunt Rose's prognosis was unclear to her.

In some sense, after Aunt Rose's stroke, Christine didn't want to know about anything. Even now, it was best if the family didn't talk about it and what it meant. They all, with silent reservations, agreed. Christine was never in the room when the medical staff discussed details. Her live-in nurse did not want to say anything for sure. Aunt Rose had physical therapy. Christine knew that much. Treatment meant

Aunt Rose still had hope.

Off in the distance, Terrie crossed past Smith Hall Dorms. She coasted across the grass, not following the stone pathway. Terrie never followed the rules. The tall brick wall held window after window. Air conditioners could be seen in summer and early fall.

Terrie's jean shorts with trailing fabric strings showed off her butt, and her long pale legs reminded Christine they were going to the shore as soon as July hit. She wore a smart navy-blue polo shirt Christine had given her around Christmas time. The old thing was Amy's, Christine's ex. Neither of them had a problem with the switch. If Amy ever wanted it, Terrie would give it to her, no problem. The slightly ragged shirt, washed too many times, made Terrie look a bit preppy. The shirt was a contradiction.

Strong, butch, and intellectual at the same time, Terrie showcased complexity. For some reason, she wore glasses despite having twenty-twenty vision. She insisted she needed to wear them. Christine preferred them on the floor. She came home from the eye doctor, who issued her a clean bill of health six months before. She proclaimed herself, after wearing the glasses two weeks, free from the migraine headaches she had been developing. Christine called it a ruse.

She imagined herself calling across the courtyard after Terrie. Maybe, she would finally tell her about this concocted scheme to get more information about Aunt Rose's arrest. She should tell her first anyway. Terrie was gone though—out of sight. After a few moments, the opportunity to chase after her was gone as well.

Strange events unfolded. Terrie was supposed to be at the lab, and here she was looking like she wanted to scale Smith Hall. Awkward and unapproachable, Christine couldn't ask her how come. Scared of the reason, she stepped to the side.

A FEW NIGHTS ago, they had talked, gotten intense and deep on their relationship. Any relationship Christine had ever had with anyone dug for emotion. She wanted Terrie to rip out her most profound feelings and intertwine them with hers. Christine wanted to feel as loved as possible. Love never sprouted the way she wanted it to.

"I do love you," Christine cried. She drove the dagger in with intent. That same intent relayed: "I never want to have to repeat this. I want you to believe and let it be." Christine swore to this much.

"But we never have quality time anymore. When you lived with Julie, you were always over. We always had plans. Now you're off studying, even though you never studied before." Christine wanted to know where she was most days.

Most likely off writing, journaling. Christine would text, but Terrie had always been an absent texter. That was for sure. She'd leave hours between checking and wait hours to respond. She was the only person Christine knew who left their phone in the car when they went somewhere. She didn't want to stuff her pockets with junk.

A few hundred feet past their window, which didn't have an air conditioner, clustered bodies dwelt on the town streets. College students drifted in even parallel lines in the evening light. They looked so young. Christine was in her early twenties. She'd gone right to graduate school after college. Despite her best judgment, she hadn't taken a year off to work. Her parents were ready to help with the money, so she'd decided to add two more years of education to her resume.

Most students were in pairs or groups. The safest travel plans included pairs and groups on this campus. Around the corner, the neighborhood turned sour, filled with dirty streets and dark, dirtier alleys. Terrie usually commuted solo, flying off and out at any whim. The attitude came with the package.

It was not only that Christine wanted Terrie to be there, but she had to be present. She had to turn on the "listening Terrie." Christine cried, "You're drifting again. What are you thinking about?"

"I'm here with you now, more than ever. We love each other to death. But I need time alone, okay? I'm your James Dean in glasses, remember?"

Christine stepped into the window with her. Terrie's arm stretched across her shoulders. They were women, together, in love, and free to do as they wished.

"I love you," Terrie begged, forcing the words to be poignant.

Would it ever be easy to say? "I love you, I guess," Christine said, her eyes pointed downward. Christine made it clear—everyone, Terrie, Christine's ex, and Terrie's ex, even, tensed when Christine genuinely cared with everything she had. She goaded Terrie and invited her to bring something more substantial to reassure her of the love they shared. Christine wanted Terrie to love her more. It was questionable whether she did.

"What about your dumb project?" Terrie said. "That's taking up all your time. It's not only me. You spent hours at the library last week, and you missed Taco Wednesday after class. It's your favorite. You have a subscription to LexisNexis. I don't even know what that is. You won't tell me anything about the project, and it's not even computer science. You're the absent one." Terrie turned and put her arms at Christine's waist, giving her what she wanted. She stared deep into her eyes. "You're the one I can't trust." Terrie's words rang, covering the gist of their argument. Neither wanted to open the relationship. Neither wanted to go beyond the healthy couple, the dedicated, loving couple image they had built up to their friends.

Christine wondered what would become of the project. Absent questioning led to the unfair solicitation of deep love from someone who might not be ready to give the emotion of their own accord.

Often found quietly working in the early morning hours, Aunt Rose's alone, stable, and strong image mirrored Terrie's. They both shared a reserved, reliable image wrought with integrity. Christine liked the stoic, independent type. She admired and adored them. Even still, she tried to break through and make them love. "I'm not going to merge with you," Christine's ex had pleaded. But Christine craved the closeness.

Aunt Rose's words from two months ago had stayed with her. She admitted she was indebted to June.

"An action, however wrong, can have more love than a lifelong friendship," she said.

Trying to grow her love in the wrong way, she made these words without actions, albeit all of them good, trying to show she cared. Terrie gave freely and often. That was her role as the surpriser. Christine should give more love than a thank-you, but what was her purpose? How should she say, "I love you"?

Aunt Rose had mentioned many of these cryptic things before the stroke—always referencing June. She expected Christine to know all about June, and at the same time, Aunt Rose didn't want Christine to know about her at all.

Secretive and guarded at times, Christine tried to be the best friend possible to her. Aging as minutes passed, seemingly all alone, she rummaged for meaning everywhere. Christine's curiosity burned anyway. She wanted her role model to be the exact person she imagined—a bright light.

She'd found an article a week before the stroke. The blurb made so much sense, and yet she racked her brain, wondering why she hadn't asked questions sooner. Here she was with this great-aunt, who had seen the era of Stonewall and before. She'd protested and fought for rights, and yet she might not share that with Christine. She would never listen to Aunt Rose's troubles, accomplishments, or loves now. If only they had bonded sooner, if only she had been a better great-niece and helped out more—Aunt Rose would have loved Christine. She would have opened up.

Even though there was so much to learn, Christine was clutching to an article, regretful. Christine would make her life make sense one way or another. Her past and her history were important to Christine, regardless if she could speak. She would find the truth and Aunt Rose's honor.

CHAPTER FOUR

TERRIE

THE HOUSE WAS set back at least four hundred feet from the road. That's the only thing that made the neighborhood not cookie-cutter suburban. The area was spacious, and the houses weren't tight against one another. The trees were more massive, and the lots weren't the same size. Her house held more aged character than those from the nineties housing boom neighborhoods close by. The builders had skipped the vinyl siding and veneer. For these two reasons, Christine was proud of where she had grown up.

They moved across the driveway, stretching each step

into several seconds, using as many steps as justifiable. Christine's shoes scraped, dragging on the gravel as she lingered. Terrie held the wine she'd scooped off the kitchen counter before they left. Grabbing whatever was close and pretty, Terrie chose wine mostly based on her personal feelings toward the label.

She'd say, "I like this bird. Let's get this one." The picture gave her countless dinnertime stories. It was always something she chatted about. It didn't matter if the bottle was five dollars or thirty.

Terrie had bought the wine several days ago and almost forgotten it. Neither of them forgot dinner. Christine clenched her jaw and released, ran her tongue across her teeth, and bit her lips together. Terrie stretched and flexed her arms nervously. Christine's family skipped pleasantries and moved to tough topics at the door. They "had no problem" with Christine's life, but they wished she would give men another shot. When she had first dated women, she'd told her parents she was bisexual. Even though she had corrected herself a few months later, her parents held on to the fact Christine recognized something in herself that liked men.

Christine's dad never talked to her about his long-held feelings on abortion anymore, but he still talked about the issue with other people. Her mom went to church on Sundays, and some of her opinions and values were uncompromisable. Hushed subtext filtered into any room they occupied together. All their unspoken resentment lay under a dust cover. Christine's parents never vocalized aloud that she or her girlfriends were not welcome, or their thoughts and opinions weren't valid. They never verbalized their reservations.

"Hi, sweetie. Oh, and Terrie, welcome. Come in," Christine's mom chimed.

The home was the same one Christine had grown up in when she was young. Her parents kept the house even after Christine and her brother had moved out. The siding needed to be power washed. Her father abhorred grime and dirt. When he cleaned, he aimed for that brand-new sparkle on all surfaces. He liked everything that way if possible. Her parents kept up the lawn and made sure tidiness spread through the home. The sprinkler system had been installed a year or two ago to mitigate the dead grass in the front yard. Her dad had wanted to pay for lawn care, but instead they'd talked him into installing the system.

"Hi, Erin. Thanks. It's good to see you," Terrie answered. She stumbled with her words.

Christine's mom insisted on Terrie calling her by her first name, but Terrie still spoke with nervous apprehension. Maybe her attitude was from her upbringing with strict parents. She naturally addressed Erin by her last name. She had not yet broken the barrier to being friends with Christine's mom, and Christine held onto only an ounce of hope a peace treaty would happen anytime soon.

"Sit down, girls," her mother broke in. She strode in sauntering, casual steps across the kitchen. Her husband watched TV in his usual chair in the family room. "It's so good to see you both. How are your classes? School's finally going to be over soon."

"Great, Mom. You know, everything is going the way it's

supposed to. Grades are fine..." Christine relayed, moving toward the mashed potatoes. She removed a fork from a drawer and tasted.

"Christine, sweetie. We're eating in a minute." She darted a hard glare at Christine and straight to Terrie. Her fingers adjusted the placemat, squaring it off. "Well...I take a class at the gym on Tuesdays, Thursdays, and Saturdays. You're both welcome to join."

"Mom, you're like an hour and a half away. Anyway, I never exercise. It's not in my blood."

"I mean, maybe you want to try," her mom said. She gave suggestive glances at Christine's waist and continued adjusting the placemat.

It wasn't enough Christine's mom couldn't give Terrie a full, firm hug. She also created distance with things like picking on Christine about her grades and her weight. Christine didn't feel fat. She was able to pinch a hunk at her sides, but she was fine with it. So pushed out by her family sometimes Christine wouldn't even approach the root cause. Christine wouldn't reprimand her mom for insinuating she was getting fat. She wouldn't waste those words.

"Terrie," Erin said, changing the subject with abrupt, blunt force before anyone contested her behavior. "How are your classes?"

"Good. Great. I can get a lot of work done at the store because it's not so busy," Terrie remarked.

Standoffish toward Christine's family, Terrie mirrored the feelings she received. Christine could also tell she was avoiding more discussion of school since Terrie had gotten a few Cs last semester. Terrie didn't know what she was going to do with a communications degree anyway. She finally took her last two general education classes. For several years, she had been taking two classes a semester toward a degree.

"Gary's retiring. They might have a management slot open. I'd order merchandise, stuff like that," Terrie inserted.

The hardware store she worked at wasn't the career she'd planned for in high school, but Terrie's work made her feel important. Christine liked the extra cash from the odd home improvement jobs she picked up in the summer thanks to her working there. Christine would get goodies following the bonus. Christine also enjoyed the way Terrie flirted in carpenter jeans.

"Oh. That's great," Erin chimed, wringing her hand and gritting her teeth.

Christine imagined her waking up in the morning with a sore face from the insincere displays of emotions. Terrie's future included getting permanent status at her job, though she cherished her current freedom while working. The pause and silence made everyone monitor their breathing. No one wanted to be the next one heard.

Terrie wasn't financially motivated. She tried to enjoy what she was doing, and she had already found happiness at the store. It didn't bother Christine. They would make do. She didn't need to be wealthy, as her mom wished for her.

A bleak hope had filled her body when she'd come out to her mother several years ago. They'd sat at the kitchen table. Red from holding her breath, Christine had moved the salt. Only when her mother, rapid-fire, asked what was wrong did she spit the news out.

"I'm dating a woman," Christine muttered, trying to catch her breath with puffs every second. "It's serious, and I can't imagine having feelings for anyone else." She reinforced the permanency of her sexuality as much as she was able and braced for the response.

"Oh, but, Christine," her mother sighed. A long pause ensued, and her mother adjusted random things on the table. She even reached across the table to adjust the centerpiece, a bowl with fruit. The handmade ceramic piece had held bananas and apples for as long as Christine remembered. "Don't you think you'll see yourself with a man?"

She offered suggestions about the boy Christine had dated in high school several years before. She neither kicked Christine out and disowned her, nor gave her a giant hug of acceptance. Christine would still speak to her mother, she just wouldn't accompany her to PFLAG meetings. A sour mood had washed over Christine and stayed with her. The ill intents resurfaced when she was around her mom. They both tiptoed around "the mood," unable to sever the eternal cycle of reciprocal trading unique to families.

Christine wasn't supposed to tell her father. Her mother would breach the topic with him, and they'd all discuss it. For another three weeks, Christine had called her mom, who only reported there hadn't been a good time to bring her issue up. Her dad had been staying late at the office or stressed out about something or other. He loved her, her mom underscored. The topic, unapproachable, eventually ruptured.

After days of constant pressing, Christine's mom told Christine she'd discussed the topic with her father.

Everything was all right. They were still a family. Christine and her mother planned a family dinner a few weeks later.

When Christine came home unannounced a week later to do her laundry, she didn't expect her father to be there.

"So, you're okay with it?" Christine asked.

"Okay, with what, sweetie?" her dad demanded, morphing from relaxed and easygoing to braced with biting tension in seconds.

"You know. Mom told you? About me being a lesbian," Christine forwarded, with a sudden snap into a defensive posture at her dad's reaction to the word "lesbian."

Christine's dad, put off, left the room and mumbled he had work to do. He promised they'd talk about this new idea later. As usual, he put up barriers when he bucked out of his comfort zone. Christine wasn't strong enough, their relationship wasn't strong enough, for her to follow him and confront him.

They had the family dinner a few weeks later, and he'd asked a few questions about Christine's new girlfriend. Christine offered some of her feelings. But generally, conversations flowed naturally over the schism. Christine imagined no one wanted to make the other wince.

As they finished up dinner, Christine's mom asked about Aunt Rose, the aunt she had grown up with who was significantly older than she was. "I know you care so much about her, Christine. It's really so dear."

"I do care about her. The stroke though."

"I know, honey. It's bad. I talked to your uncle Mark. He said she's just not recovering just yet." Her mom's blunt words made Christine lean back.

"Mom. What was the murder about?"

"Oh, honey. Really on her death bed. We couldn't."

Christine had been trying to get more and more details lately. She'd never crossed the bridge when Aunt Rose was lucid, but now it seemed imperative, especially because of Christine's research and her friendship with June. It was such a hushed matter, and even now, her parents continued to brush off the topic.

"Honey, just... It's not important. Would you want someone to know about your mental history?"

"Mom, but it is important. Family, at the very least, should know."

"You're still my child, Christine. We'll talk about it when I'm ready, but not now. Not when Aunt Rose is barely awake."

On their way out, Christine made sure to put her arm around Terrie and kiss her on the neck. Christine eyed her parents carefully to see if they'd wince, but they both appeared glazed over. They'd had several glasses of wine each, and this was possibly the best time to reinforce lesbian sexuality for them.

Christine's mom had rushed to the car with leftover peach pie as they were ready to pull out. She handed it through the window to Terrie and, smiling at them both, made them promise to return soon, the next day if they wanted. Her father stood at the doorway waving, even though he had struggled with motivation to make it to the dinner table an hour earlier.

Christine's childhood window on the second floor, dimly lit by a nightlight, let off a glow. She hadn't been up there in a while. Her mom had moved most of her stuff out and into boxes, changing the old bedroom into her reading room. The light violet color she had painted her space when she had reached age twelve was now deep emerald green. The room belonged to someone else. The color didn't really suit her mom. It didn't complement her features, and it wasn't one she normally chose for clothes. Christine would have to ask about her reasoning on another occasion.

THEY SAT IN the car afraid to speak, to be the first person to yell, as Christine made her way toward the freeway.

"It's not fair, you know. Your parents," Terrie muttered. She leaned her elbow on the window ledge and her head on her fist. Terrie stared off, speaking but not trying to engage conflict. "I feel so much farther from you after we see your parents. We're not in the same room." Her eyes made it to the corners of Christine's.

"What do you mean? It's not my fault," Christine said. She had been thinking about how to get out of the family vacation this year, leave a commitment. She had to wrangle their relationship into more or less the space they were in together. "How can you even say I'm less of a person to you because of someone else?" Christine howled. They were fighting.

"It's not that. It's not your fault. I feel, and don't confuse what I'm saying, your parents are part of who you are. But they don't love me, and they never will. It's hard for me to see all of you when part of you is blocked," Terrie retorted.

"They tolerate you, Terrie—" Christine said.

"I don't want to be tolerated," Terrie cried.

Her jaw stiffened as it had when they'd walked toward the house. She'd ground her teeth at the dinner table when her mom asked her if she had a dress to wear to a party a high school friend's parents were having.

"What about Vic and James and Amy?" Christine said. "They're more my family than anyone. Fran and Andrea? Michelle?" Christine fumed because Terrie, as usual, focused on the negative. She ballooned any "feelings" she got from anyone. "It's not their fault. They're trying. You have to help them get past things, be more open. Help me."

"They're Republicans, Christine. It seems impossible. I want to help you, but I don't have the patience." Her fingers were on her temple, and she darted glances to Christine and out the window. She had yet to raise her voice, but the words were boiling as they came out of her mouth.

The seas were tumultuous. This week the issue was Christine's family. Last week it had been her relationship with Amy, her ex. Terrie acknowledged how precious Amy was to Christine, and Christine made clear her intentions, leaving no room for doubt she would be friends with her ex. That was the end of the conversation. Every time Terrie attempted to open it up for discussion, every time she checked if Christine was cheating, they fought. That fight ended with resolve. When Christine inserted if there was no Amy, there was no Christine and Terrie, she said she understood. The way she loomed over Christine when Amy was in the room was like a controlling shadow. Terrie always avoided them both, scared to hear what the conversation was about since it would make her more jealous no doubt. As much as Terrie relayed she was okay with the relationship, being friends with your ex was reasonable, the less Terrie seemed okay with her choice. Terrie lied.

The chain of events was inevitable. Terrie would go to the diner and journal when they got home. She always wanted to go there lately. She journaled at her apartment when they were apart. But there was a switch. She journaled at the café or the library. Late night, she worked at the diner. Terrie might have been spending more time at her apartment or not. At some point, after whatever conversation or date, she went out to journal, to get away, and that's the only place she ever did it. They didn't even discuss her behaviors. Christine watched her from the window as she disregarded the pathways and moved across the grass in the shortest distance between two points. She stomped, a madwoman, likely unaware of her anger. Christine heard her motions through the third-story window.

Christine almost didn't think anything of it. The diner was the other way. Terrie had gone in the wrong direction away from the lights of downtown. In a flurry of concern before accusations, she scanned for Terrie's mace. The petty weapon was below the counter where it had been for a few days. She'd gotten the spray at the hardware store as an attempt to be safer. At first, she'd come home with a large pocketknife which served multiple purposes. As with everything lately, debate lingered.

Christine cared about Terrie. She wanted to make it work, but Terrie put up roadblocks wherever possible. She hadn't even cared about Christine's feelings on the ride home. Her interactions with her parents in the last few years were a muddled mess. They were incapable of loving her the way they had, and she wasn't sure if their relationship would ever be the same.

Terrie distanced herself, pushed away attempts at connection. Christine hoped to bring her back. Standing in the kitchen, she decided to continue to pursue her, continue to make love work. Those mysterious, sexy eyes were worth hen fighting. She cradled her cell phone, thinking of someone to call and feel weak with for a moment. She didn't have anyone to confide the whole lot of juicy details in. Even Amy and she had barriers. Straightening up, she realized if she let herself be vulnerable, it would be real. She and Terrie were drifting.

CHAPTER FIVE

ROSE

DURING THE INTERVIEW, June had prefaced everything. The lack of facts in the first hour-long session was awkward. With evasive eyes, she rolled over Christine's face and spewed words without aim. Regardless, Christine anxiously anticipated returning later. She liked June, genuinely felt kindness, a willingness to listen to her despite June's over-the-shoulder, chilling glances. June had her self-respect, but if someone uttered, "Head down, inmate" or "Hands behind back, inmate," the self-respect would melt off. At that moment, though, she wouldn't let anyone tell her she was wrong—definitely not Aunt Rose.

Christine had stopped by Aunt Rose's house the next day. She wanted to see her uncle about Aunt Rose's treatment. She rattled the knob on the front door. Christine's dad had lived in the house when he was a kid. Christine's grandparents had left the place to Aunt Rose in the will. Uncle Mark, Aunt Rose, and Christine's dad had grown up in the house. Aunt Rose, older and wiser, claimed the spot as her grandmother's sister's daughter. All the mustiness was theirs. Aunt Rose moved in after her mother's death. Christine wasn't sure how Uncle Mark felt about the exchange.

Uncle Mark always appeared tired when he visited Aunt Rose. Even on holidays, when people are supposed to dress up a little bit, he would only rumple his hair in the front as he entered the doorway. He'd worked with fire insurance before he retired. Christine's grandparents had had Uncle Mark much earlier than Christine's father. He still dressed the same as if he'd gotten home from work. An insurance salesman stereotype, he lacked the individuality that flowed from Christine. White, short-sleeved button-up, slightly greyed. He owned his boring and drab style. The only thing he was missing was a pocket protector. When he talked about his job in long trailing sentences, he evaded specifics. He mused off into space as he spoke, not lying but superficially plain, uninteresting. Christine perceived no one wanted to listen; everyone guessed his life wasn't full of adventure.

"Hi, Uncle Mark! Thanks for being here," Christine sang and plopped down on the couch. She hoped Uncle Mark would cheer up.

"Hey. How's it going? Aren't midterms soon?" Uncle Mark asked.

"We had them. You know—it'll be good to finish with all the school stuff. I'll have more time to come over and visit Aunt Rose when I'm done. I mean, I still want to come by as much as possible. I want to help."

"We appreciate it, Christine. I know Rose knows you're here. It brightens her day."

Christine moved into the kitchen to make some iced tea from a mix. Uncle Mark enjoyed iced tea. They conjured up a loose tradition or common ground around sugary powder or the sun. Pulling the mix from the bottom cabinet, Christine took a breath. The goodness of the house, the history, and the comfort of helping a queer relative came out and spilled all over her.

"How is she today? Uncle Mark, will she get better? I wanted to talk to her. I have to update her on my love life, you know—"

"Will she get better? I don't know. The doctors say she has to do her rehab. There's still a chance she'll speak again."

"She was telling me about June before the stroke. She never mentioned her before, but I found this article about a murder case. She said she loved June. I always talked so much about myself—" Christine muttered.

Uncle Mark had barriers with Aunt Rose in several regards. She didn't need help. Uncle Mark would call to check in, but he kept his distance, waited for her to ask for help. She didn't have a sexuality. He never acknowledged Aunt Rose was a lesbian, never brought her sexuality up. If Christine broached the topic, he veered away with preemptive thinking. Christine guessed his age, guessed about being alive at another time.

Christine hadn't even known Aunt Rose was a lesbian until she came out a few years ago. Somehow, she had bought into the old maid story. No one had ever talked about why she didn't have a husband. She never spoke about it herself. A silent shroud of mystery surrounded her.

Aunt Rose, peculiar and introverted, didn't care about negative sentiments. She wasn't quite what anyone would expect. Aunt Rose lived in her sweats and hardly went out. She sang to herself when she didn't think visitors heard her. Her oddities extended to burning sage to ward off bad energy and feeding birds and squirrels on her porch, tempting them to come close. Despite her age, she had gusto and independence.

Before she was out, Christine had heard her discussing a lesbian friend on the phone. She'd confirmed the insinuations; Aunt Rose was also a lesbian. Christine wanted it to be more than rumors. She didn't want to continue on like everyone else—assuming things about her.

She'd asked her, and they'd talked. Christine had come out to her before she'd gone to her parents. She'd told Aunt Rose about a girl she'd kissed and relished in the details. Christine had found someone and became involved. She'd overflowed with giddiness. Aunt Rose had given the most loving sighs and light coughing laughs. She'd listened and told stories every so often, and they'd become inseparable.

"Yeah. Rose would kill me if I told you. She never liked to talk about herself. In the late sixties to early seventies, Christine, Rose did some jail time," Mark relayed.

"The article said June went to prison—Aunt Rose shot someone." Christine didn't mention to Uncle Mark that she had gone to see June in prison. She wasn't ready to make that public yet.

"Rose was troubled, mostly due to the gay thing. Once, she yelled into the phone, chastising the investigators for following her. Probably why she doesn't tell anyone anything. Checked into a mental hospital for a while. She didn't talk to our parents at that time. She lived on her own, made her own way. She met this psychiatrist, June, Dr. June Ashmore. They moved in together—after Aunt Rose got out of the hospital. The psychiatrist convinced Rose to shoot one of Dr. Ashmore's colleagues. They were vying for a promotion. She used psychology to make Rose shoot someone for her. She got away with murder. She manipulated Rose," Uncle Mark said.

"I don't get it. They lived together. They were together."

"That's right. They did... Aunt Rose did some time too. I think Dr. Ashmore is still in prison. That was a long time ago, Christine—long enough."

Christine finished making the tea and brought Uncle Mark a glass. She looked him in the eyes, pulling her chin in. To him, strife littered the past, an old incident of trauma forgotten. The verdict came through, and justice resolved everything. Why had Aunt Rose never moved on? He only loved her because she was reserved. She didn't broadcast her sexuality. She had this house, worked odd jobs, got a third of Christine's grandfather's pension. Her uncle guessed at her happiness—blissfulness even. Christine, aware of her age and wisdom, understood the torment and unsettling, unacceptance of herself.

With long, purposeful strides, she moved toward the bedroom. She lifted her head. She put a straw in the glass and sidled up next to Aunt Rose. The nurse was leaving for a while, and Christine was going to watch her.

"You loved June, didn't you?" Christine said. She pushed the straw to Rose's lips. Rose's head bobbed, and she mumbled something as she accepted the straw.

The cat crossed the room and lay across Aunt Rose's feet. She purred a soothing noise, but Christine's anxiety rose. She had finally found the one person she could talk to about anything. The one family member who'd kept the secret about who she was, what she went through, was gone without saying goodbye, without a moment to clutch onto, without an answer to her most perplexing questions.

Christine went into the closet and took out the shoebox. The flimsy container was inside a panel in the bottom of the closet, placed there so many years before. It might have been glued on at one point, with the intent to never be broken into, but when Christine pushed on the board, it popped right out. The cigar box would have held at least thirty cigars. It still smelled musky and sweet. The newspaper article sat right next to a few LGBT pins. One said, "Lavender," and another said, "Gay is Good." A short three-inch-by-two-inch square article, thin and yellowed, lay unattended.

> Woman Held without Bail in Doctor Shooting. DA Considers Bringing Charges Against Lover.

> Miss Rose Carol Winster held without bail on charges of murder by Municipal Court Judge Martin Mudds in the shooting Sunday of Dr. Jonathan O'Malley, a psychiatrist at Mayburg Hospital and also employed by the county police.

Christine had researched the case after she'd first found the article. She'd been looking for a lost shoe. The box was inside the cubby hole. The cigar box caught her attention, but she didn't dare snoop further until her aunt was out of sight. Days later, her aunt was at the grocery store when she arrived for tea and chatting. Christine full-on snooped then. Now, she grabbed the article, put it in her pocket, and examined the pins.

Each pin showed rust, or the backing had severe tarnish. The metal jiggled as Christine moved the pins from hand to hand. The rust wasn't enough to remove any feelings she got from them. How much longer did the pins need to hibernate?

She had to broach the topic. The pins should go to an LGBTQ historical organization. Aunt Rose would, without any reservations, vocalize her anger about Christine's expedition in her closet. Christine had always shared with Aunt Rose, told her about her girlfriends, coming out several years ago, and the protests she had been involved in on occasion. Christine had needed Aunt Rose to share more too. The pins and their aged sheen made Christine closer to Aunt Rose—they'd had the same experiences, at different times. Aunt Rose would eventually know she had snooped.

After the stroke, Christine had to put off all serious discussions. Frustrated keeping everything to herself, she let out a few key facts to her aunt, but Rose didn't respond. In the subsequent days, Christine found herself hip deep in the muck of case law. Articles gave different perspectives, with a flair for polar opposites, on the supposed crimes Rose and June had committed. Confusing stories of blame and cause differed from paper to paper. It was so evident to Christine and so appalling at the same time the newspapers spoke about their "lesbian relationship" with the worst regard. They were a menace to society because of their passion for each other. Nothing justified murder, but the reporters painted pictures of monsters.

Aunt Rose's photo from the crime scene was, at face value, that of a young butch lesbian. Her eyes were full of fear and confusion as if she eyed for a place to run. Christine knew she wished she could. Under the haze of imminent permanent incarceration, Aunt Rose's countenance exploded.

Christine pooled through articles at the state library, running microfilm through readers for hours until she found an article. She sat like a tiny ant in the vast, open, and empty library. A five-story ceiling lofted above her. Her chair rattled and echoed as she got up, and the front security guard shuffled. Everyone heard both things. She had been there for over an hour and would be there several more.

A homeless man sat next to her. Twenty other vacant seats were pushed in, empty. She didn't move. He leaned over and snooped himself, stared high at the ceiling, and over to her. He did this several times in ten minutes. He'd fidget with his computer a bit, look up, and crane his neck. He was reading what Christine read, or small bits, and then typed them into his keyboard. Christine shifted the chair, so her back and shoulder got in the way. She was reading about mental illness, specifically her aunt. That's what the newspapers wrote. She tolerated the peculiar man over her shoulder. Another person people might think didn't quite get life.

Every reporter and paper had a different opinion. One would say June was not guilty. She didn't issue the shot. The heinous act was not possible. Others relied heavily on the power of psychology or placed blame on the mentally ill. Everyone agreed Dr. O'Malley, a police psychiatrist, had died, and his death required justice.

Time, steadily ticking, passed with Christine's head down, working. Studiously, she dug deeply and thoroughly into the records. The homeless man pretended to type without even logging in. He screeched the feet of the sturdy wooden chair against the hard tile floor. Everyone adjusted. He got the current newspapers off the rack and settled down to read or look like he was reading.

Christine got a subscription to a case-law website and examined the proceedings. In the actual case summary, Rose testified against June. This part of the case was what intrigued Christine the most. She would pass a psych exam as far as Christine was concerned. But how had this woman "convinced" her to commit murder?

Christine supposed she could be a lawyer. This effort to determine who was guilty would help guide her into the right career. She would be enthralled in the system of law or so turned off she'd never want to be near a courtroom again.

Nestling into the same corner in the bottom left of the closet, Christine drew her knees to her chest as much as they would go. Rose was in bed, watching or not watching TV, smiling at odd intervals. Thankfully, the box lay hidden in the same place. Creased folds showed where the container had been collapsed and reopened. The folds were worn and fragile, making the box unstable. The slightest traceable odor of must lifted from the box. She could be right there with Aunt Rose, on her knees, reaching into the closet. Stooping down, under draped clothes, she hid the box with her sordid past. Someone would've, if not Christine, found the controversial contents in due time.

Christine wasn't sure if the items belonged to her now. If Aunt Rose passed away, she would keep it all. Who else would? Movers would put the rubbish out with the trash. Someone needed to pass down her family heirlooms. Those were the only things Christine could tell Aunt Rose would want someone to care for when she was gone. She would frame the pins or loan them for a historical exhibit. Aunt Rose's treasures would be safe.

CHAPTER SIX

PRISON II — 2015

THE GUARD TRIED to gossip about June as they walked down the hall two weeks ago. He jabbed, "The batty old shit is in a good mood today." As they went, his eyes looking straightforward, he said, "You know she likes women."

Christine was queer, but she didn't speak up. Confrontation in her current predicament, with a man in uniform, with all her lies, scared her. She lingered outside of the guard's line of vision. June cohabitated with guards who taunted inmates with backhanded comments and pushy behavior. Hell, June lived here, in state prison, for murder because she was gay.

Christine ran over June's emotions during the last visit, her words bit by bit. She tested her statements about love, eye in a magnifying glass, for weakness. After all that over-compensation, all the talk about love, maybe, Christine had a second thought. June could have lied to get parole and convinced Christine of her honesty. June was in prison. She believed the charade. June's eyes had welled full last time, when she read the letter, saturated. Her face melted with clouds of sadness.

June leaned in on Christine, tried to gain her trust. She bent at the waist and moved closer, wanting to whisper as much as possible. She was confiding. June let out the most personal thoughts and feelings in this visit too. "We were great together," she would say, or "There was nothing like the two of us."

June said "love" tumultuously. She leered into Christine's eyes, jerking her head to the side, wanting her to know her emotions struck chords. Did the game end when June had convinced Aunt Rose to shoot June's colleague? The actions somehow proved acceptable since they were in love? June hadn't pulled the trigger, but she knew Aunt Rose inside and out. Christine bit at her fist with anger. She must've seen something in Aunt Rose that made her apt to do the deed. Why didn't she stop her? She could have locked her up, told her the worst thing ever—"I hate you. It's over." She could have said anything to calm her down.

"I loved her, honey. That's all I think about." Her mouth hung open. She still talked about the events. She stalled. She dwelt on the periods in her sentences, jaw open. She bled from a stab wound, while Christine fed her quiz questions.

As the interview went on, she began to let out tidbits. It was almost as if she were remembering, saying, “Oh yeah. Also, this happened.” Christine took notes on the morsels that emerged, and that was enough. Twisted in her words of love were images of Aunt Rose, a patient at the hospital June had visited once a week as a backup. June got to know her and encouraged her.

“Her hair, her glow, and she called me ‘Doctor.’ Ha, could you believe it? So formal.”

Aunt Rose was a young lesbian, scared, and she needed support. Other doctors would have given her electroshock or therapy questionable by today’s opinions.

Christine scribbled notes on every bit of information, hidden in verbalized feelings, June offered. Aunt Rose had problems with the staff that compounded her issues.

“Rose wasn’t good at being locked up. She fought the guards and resisted them,” June remarked.

She had classic defiant symptoms. Her issues only obstructed progress, release. She got put in locked rooms often and would yell at the guards who restrained her.

“It was all ’cause they didn’t understand her. No one understood what it was like to be locked up for who you were.” June’s face filled with disgust.

Naturally, June wanted to help. This woman needed someone supportive, in tune with who they were, who nurtured and provided comfort. If June had done anything, she’d helped this one person.

June’s life had been chock-full of women who she bumped into casually or met within groups at the bars. “It was Rose I fell in love with, in the end," June said, her head raising. "Rose was receptive to me. We clicked. We kept each other close, and that was all I ever wanted, someone to keep me right by their side."

Christine clenched her fists to feel stronger, glared up at June, a stranger who was so open about her passion for Christine's aunt. Had she spoken about love frivolously? As June spoke of the love's enchantment, Christine questioned her devotions. She had said it, longed after it, and waited for Terrie to say it to her with the same emotion. Terrie drifted when she spoke her feelings, and the verbal half-sentiments hung on her lips like she was trying to think to herself if she did, in fact, love Christine.

Christine loved Terrie only to a certain depth. She didn't have real founding. Terrie didn't stand in front of a bullet for her or save her from drowning in a river. She hadn't given up something important to her or supported her while she followed her dreams. Her love, saying the word "love," had no end, but she guessed Terrie also hadn't found something that bound the term like cement. Christine wasn't indebted.

Christine wrote to June about it. June wanted to know what Christine knew about relationships. For some reason, she naively told June she was having trouble. She pitied June, all alone in prison. June expressed she would see her again if Christine detailed her life in a letter—like June did for her. She described Terrie and Amy and their current drama. It wasn't a weighing of souls but more of the varied character of caring and love. She was with Terrie, Christine begged to love that woman, but Amy was still so important, so much a part of her.

Aunt Rose had other issues, too, June related—this time trying to force information on Christine. She opened up a little, at least. "She was paranoid and had delusions at times people wanted to hurt her." She voiced there was a cause behind it. "She had to hide her life as a lesbian, and the world was in many ways against her. Rose didn't manage her issues well. She appeared fidgety and frightened a lot, which made others question her state," June verbalized.

That was what made her care so much about Aunt Rose, June cried. Rose showed her vulnerabilities, and June, a self-described giver, hid hers. June mumbled no one had ever used her thoughts and feelings like a reflection, a segue into insight about their life. June, the psychiatrist, was usually the listener, and the relationship ended there. They were sharing experiences, "a life of being gay and almost out and more often than not in."

Regardless, when caught by her landlord in the apartment with a woman she was dating, Aunt Rose's life took a dramatic turn.

"She wielded a kitchen knife at him, afraid he'd get her and her lover in trouble. Ha. Could you imagine?" June asked.

The landlord recounted the incident to authorities with new twists and turns, and she ended up spending time in the hospital. They didn't bring that fact to the surface in any of the case transcripts Christine had read.

And that was why June had partnered with her. Aunt Rose had needed help, help no one else offered. June was her psychiatrist, yes, but everyone else had rejected her. June relayed that it was worth it, at the time, to offer help.

Would she have done it again if she had the chance to live it over—with Rose? Absolutely. But she wouldn't ever partner again with another unstable person. "Everyone is unstable to a degree," June mumbled.

"The world hadn't turned on Rose; she had always been turned to the world. It was a matter of perspective and understanding," June remarked.

Aunt Rose needed guidance from someone who had lived life. June helped to get Aunt Rose released from the mental hospital, saying she'd diagnosed her cured and not a danger. She had reprioritized and would no longer be with women. Instead, she was going to get a job and be a productive member of society. She was sent to a home to get herself on her feet. Her family cut communication with her, and she had no way to begin anew.

"It wasn't solely to keep gays and lesbians locked up," June commented. "That was my firm belief, even if I couldn't always express it," she said. "The idea was so controversial. I never spoke up. Even so, whenever I had a homosexual patient, I ensured they were released as soon as there was a prudent opportunity."

Christine respected June more as the interview went on. She believed in her and what June convinced her she did—it was righteous. Good-hearted June misled no one. Still, due to the fact she loved Aunt Rose so much, because she was biased, she could not let it go. June got locked up.

"Ha. Here I am," June said as she slumped her shoulders and accepted her fate. Despite their love, she was still in prison. She said. "Perhaps that is best."

As soon as Christine heard this, June's story of her

selflessness touched her. When Aunt Rose was thrown out of the halfway house due to her questionable behavior, June stepped in. The women chastised her because of her past and questioned everything she said and did. They were homophobic, and Aunt Rose couldn't survive there.

Christine had notes on June's memories of the smell of Aunt Rose's hair and the twinkle in her eyes when they met. She had notes on how June had fallen in love ten times over. She knew when their eyes met, and they exchanged nods of acknowledgment about their sexualities in a safe space. They knew when they kissed in June's office the first time as a recognition their sexualities were okay, confirmation of both their beliefs. She knew when Aunt Rose called her from the street, saying she didn't have a place to live or anywhere to go.

Aunt Rose moved in with June, and they built a micro family. They had two cats they rescued from the alley behind their apartment and were happy.

"Rose watered the plants, and I cooked dinner every night, even when I came home late," June said.

Aunt Rose would wait for her cooking in the tight apartment big enough for the two of them. Everything was fine between them. Other people weren't okay with them.

"Rose got a job as an orderly at the main hospital where I worked." June described how she appeared in her uniform, responsible and dedicated, determined to do the best job. "I helped her get that job."

She was doing well, and June, in her words, cultivated Aunt Rose's mental health. June made sure Aunt Rose was well. She tried to be as supportive as possible and encouraged her to live a healthy life. They went on trips during the weekend and visited new towns they wanted to live in when they retired. Their bliss carried through years.

Christine listened to June as she spoke. She was a good listener, quiet, and resolved. She asked questions when someone had more to say. June stumped her, though. She couldn't direct June to what she wanted to know. Even with a mind and a determination to tell her story, the bright words came out as a question. June had to ask.

They loved each other with a simple passion, in June's words. A picturesque couple, the two birds had nowhere to go. What Christine expressed about love in the present day was so much different. Love was sopping wet with drama and girlfriends' ex-girlfriends you eventually dated. Her issues were about lies and cheating or questioning how out someone was. It was much different from June and Aunt Rose's experience, true love, love between two people, as June told the story, even though no one else accepted it. No one claimed infighting and childishness. They were the twinned pair pitted against the rest of the world.

The simple life took all their time, and they might've gone day in and day out the same. They didn't need to show off their love or make a fuss or demand special treatment. They were quiet and careful and kept to themselves. They didn't want anything and could have gone on for years. June recalled her complete happiness for the life they had made for themselves.

Aunt Rose did well at her job. The position was her only option, but she made the best of her charge. She was on the other side. She wasn't locked up. The doctors and guards rarely bothered her. Her fear of hospitals subsided. Aunt Rose's work progress reviews were great. June relayed she didn't do well on the personality section, mostly since Aunt Rose heaved large things around and swaggered when she walked, butch things. Her records detailed she acted insufficiently ladylike, but no one wanted to lock her up for scratching her armpits and spitting in the trashcan.

June's language got as cryptic as Aunt Rose's at this point. She stammered and tried to spit out something. "We loved each other, and this man, of all people a *man*, ruined everything. He thrust a knife through our relationship." June said they were in love with each other, so bound and unified, and yet no one let that be. They had to stop love. "It made no sense to either of us."

June ended the interview before the time ran out. She stood up and interjected she would see Christine again. "I have time," she entered, "lots of it."

The whole meeting, they both watched the clock. Every five minutes or so, someone glanced up. Christine checked obsessively because she wanted the information, her questions answered, before time ran out and since she was a bit scared.

June spoke about strength from Aunt Rose. Aunt Rose said she helped her be mindful. June improved people and made them more ready for the world. She relayed she was a psychiatrist, and her daunting career, as a woman no less, was personal and professional validation and fulfilment.

The words June used about love and dedication, fulfilling her career, and making someone else a better person were what Christine wished she could say. When Christine said "love," the language wasn't the same as when June said it. She wanted to hear the word "love," or hear herself talk out loud, like someone who absorbed it, firm in their convictions, who loved with something that could never be lost.

Christine tried to test the lie, the sincerity of June's statements, but she couldn't settle on the conveyance being a lie. She cared for Aunt Rose at the very least, Christine told herself, and if this woman had pitted her against her colleague, she must've committed the crime. Despite Christine's relationship to her aunt Rose, Christine and her untrained, naïve-to-law eyes couldn't believe June had been locked up for the rest of her life, a criminal by proxy. Illogical sentences dashed hopeful dreams. Even though Christine loved Aunt Rose so much, she confirmed this as fact. Aunt Rose had shot someone. She'd killed someone. And this woman associated with her, her lover no less, was in state prison.

Christine had scrunched her face at June, stared directly at her eyes, and did not blink. She didn't understand the love she spoke about, but she bit her lip, bitter because they loved, held love, more than anyone else. June talked to the side of the room and moved her head around. She was speaking to the masses. No one was there. At the same time, June was talking directly to her, saying, "You don't know what love is." Her eyes reached out, and she said, "You don't know how I am suffering still." June must have been bitter Christine didn't appear to believe her.

Her eyes had darted toward the two-way mirror. Paranoid by nature after so many years of prison, June blinked at the wall, never eyeing the mirror for longer than a second.

No one peered in from behind the mirror. Christine snuck a look in an open door on the way down the hall. Rose never showed up to meet her pining hope. She didn't suddenly appear from behind the mirror. Instead, Christine was here. Her stalwart presence was almost enough. Christine wasn't sure how long a person could go without having reciprocal love, or at what point it was insane to pursue someone. At the absolute least, the flame June burned had kept her awake through the decades of loneliness in prison.

CHAPTER SEVEN

BEFORE — 1973

JUNE CRIED IN her cell with oppressive grief. As much as she tried, she didn't blame Rose. The thought of what happened struck disbelief into her every time June tried to rationalize. She lay in her bed as much as possible. Being horizontal helped her stabilize her sadness. She subsumed the weight of the depression. She hurt, and gravity, reality, tugged her body down. She tried to shake the sensibility, so she let the strength against her body consume her, and somehow relief followed.

The regimented nature of prison was dull. June woke

up, ate, mulled in her cell, ate, had rec time, ate, and went to bed. Everything followed a tightly regulated course of events. Her mundane, scheduled life was set in front of her. Every day until the day she died flashed in front of her. Nothing would change. No one improved the consistency, allocation of time and activity, or quality of life. It would be the same. No one, including the guards, had the power, initiative, or care to change the feeling of the place. A cold, hard slat with a one-inch cushion would be her deathbed.

June hadn't visited Rose in jail, so why could she expect more? Of course, June didn't deserve a pity visit. For whatever June had done, she didn't warrant visits. When Rose had needed her, she'd shirked all responsibility. When Rose had needed her most, she'd brushed life aside. June thought about how she must've been so scared and worried. Her life was in front of her. Slamming her head against the mattress and feeling the slat, June tried to bruise the hurt Rose must've had into her head.

The police were snooping around. Officers came to June's work. They asked everyone questions, even after Rose was in jail. They'd resolved the issue, hadn't they? June wanted to go to prison to visit. She was going to go when the air all calmed down. The police were asking how close June and Rose were. They were trying to build a case of assistance. June had helped Rose. They decided June had planned it. She hadn't. She was sure.

After the cops stopped tailing her, she was going to go. She would spend her days with Rose as often as she could until the day she died. The idea of being in prison with her sounded ridiculous. Or was it? Weeks after Rose was in jail,

June conceded. Being in there with Rose might not be bad. They would be together. That was all that mattered. Why hadn't she seen it? She wallowed, without Rose at all.

When the cops asked, she remarked they weren't close. They were roommates. The papers had stated otherwise. Distancing herself from Rose and their accusations as much as possible, she tried to relax. She had to dispel the appearance of attachment. She lied on so many accounts, but bold-faced untruths were necessary. They had to squash the case they were building. A man with a camera watched her. He followed her schedule and was where June was supposed to be at every minute of the day. She made dates with her friend Shirley. They went out together. When someone followed them, they kissed. After the act, they decided an overt display of affection wasn't the best idea. Their brazen actions defined them both as lesbians. They tried for magic, solidification of innocence, on a whim, discussing the point in muted, coded tones before they committed. June's arm was around Shirley. She brushed her hair and leaned in. Risking arrest, she did the unthinkable. She tried to show the police she wasn't with Rose. What they zeroed in on was she was definitively a lesbian, an untouchable.

When they came for her, they were blazing with anger. They burst in with large, loud commands. They were allowed to be incensed because they had so much evidence. They were so confident in their opinions and proof. June cried for Rose, absent of vocalizations, when they came for her. Her emotions screamed. She needed to be with her, but no words came out. Her love stunted, their bond got put on pause. Nothing satiated her fear and nervousness, her gallop toward an unknown future, except Rose's embrace. If Rose were there to hold her, everything would be fine.

The first night in prison, her emotions had overcome her, and they had yet to leave. The sinking pit of her stomach held her to the ground or her bed like a heavy anchor. She thought she might never move ever again. She wept the first night, and the women heard. She tried to muffle the moans, screwing her face into the pillow as much as possible. But when she lifted her head, rising up out of the water to gasp for air and returning, they noticed. No one asked if she was okay. She hoped no one would ever ask.

Marty became her friend in prison. Rubbed with sandpaper, weathered like leather, Marty celebrated scheduled milestones in her day with a snap of the neck. The dried-out skin on her face crackled with lines. She'd worked construction in the cold, hard air. She told June that's what had aged her face and made her look tough. No one ever messed with her, and June hoped the distance would be the same for her because they were associated.

Marty was a lesbian—their first bond. "I run the place" was what she liked to say. Women were scared of her, and that's all June wanted anyway.

She told June to settle and stop being depressed. "Sad will get you nowhere in prison," Marty muttered.

Marty told June a lot of things, and June listened. She was a veteran, a woman with years in a stone-cold prison. June sought advice from her. She told June to forget about Rose. If she hadn't come to visit, she never would. When June talked about the trial, Marty couldn't even look June in the eyes. She turned sideways. "You let that bitch walk all over you? You're a sucker. Don't ever tell me about loving her." Struggling with a sober face, she pushed her fingers into her forehead with a grunt. She couldn't believe June talked about loving someone who had turned her in, who had put her in the can for life. Marty said she was doomed thanks to this woman she had never met.

Marty would never know everything, and June shied away. Marty sought out weak women in prison for romance. Sidling up to them, she told them she cared about them and would watch over them. When Marty got what she wanted or when they got bored, she dropped them. She was all business with women in prison.

June wore a red jacket most days in the yard and cuffed her pants when the rain overflowed and gathered in puddles on the ground. Marty came over to wherever she was sitting in the yard and joined her for the short duration. This occurred four or five days a week even if they didn't have much to say. She said she could tell June wasn't naïve, so sleeping with her wouldn't be fun. She wouldn't be able to seduce her. June wouldn't have fallen prey to Marty's romantic wiles if she tried. Marty clenched a toothpick in between her teeth and hit on women in the shower. She turned on the lights in so many women, but June shook her head. She wasn't attracted to this woman who was working her way through the prison.

Marty offered plenty of friendly advice. June should take her approach and go for short-term, sexual relationships with as many women as possible. June should undercommit for a while and try that out.

"She's never going to come back to you, you know that,

right? You're dead as far as she's concerned. She got you good." Marty spoke as she rolled up the short sleeves on her prison uniform. "She's not ever going to be in your life again, and you have to get used to that. You'll get used to that in here."

"I'll never stop thinking about her. I can't do it. She was my love. I'll have that until the day I die," June said. She didn't want to go outside that day, or any day as far as she was concerned at that moment.

"You better buck up, J. That attitude will kill you. I know people on the outside—people with big sticks. I can help if you need assistance. Call in a favor, you know," Marty promised.

June could see Marty didn't understand what she was saying. Marty didn't know. Never would. Marty would never want a single woman the way June idolized Rose, ever. Prison made you hard.

June tried not to talk about Rose. Seen as weak, June would be a target. She didn't want to contradict Marty's advice or make it look like she didn't respect her and her hardened wisdom. June clung to her like a friend, but she didn't cross over to a romantic relationship. Marty sauntered away, never looking back, each time June softened up or began to talk about Rose. June knew Marty knew better.

After June was able to sit up in bed, when her stabs of depression lightened to let in hopes and reasoning, she wrote. Mostly, she wrote letters to Rose. They were often long and rambling, a pouring out of words. Sometimes, in addition to sentiments and apologies, she wrote short stories about her life in prison. Other times, she wrote poems or rewrote the words of songs they listened to and sang together. Whatever came across her mind, she scratched the words onto the paper. Everything directed to Rose, at Rose, even if it had nothing to do with her.

The letters got longer and longer. A few needed large manila envelopes to hold them since they wouldn't fit in a standard letter envelope. The letters were sealed up and addressed. She didn't want anyone to see them or take them, so she hid them under her mattress. She placed them right where her heart would be. At night, she poured extra love into them.

June never mailed the letters. They were treasures. After a year, she had close to thirty. As much as she couldn't bear it to send them, she resigned to the fact she couldn't. Marty wouldn't let her, for one. She realized Rose had never forgiven her, whatever it was she had done. So, Rose probably wouldn't even open them. A bite of bitterness crept up her throat every time she sealed them. June did so much to save their relationship. She spent so much time writing down things Rose had to hear, even though she never would. All of her efforts were worthless in so many ways. She was going through motions that would never move her and Rose forward.

After that first year, her cell got tossed, and a guard confiscated the letters. He bellowed they were taking up too much space. June wasn't allowed to have them. June wasn't sure what would happen to the notes. Someone would read them. They'd laugh at their relationship, their love. Most of all, she was defeated seeing Rose would never know how much she cared. All the letters, the work, were struck from the record for good.

A few months later, she wrote them again. She couldn't stop. She needed to get her feelings out onto paper. She needed to cultivate her emotions before the cold, hard cell crushed her soul. Free writing was good for her. Writing dried up the tears. The restorative act kept her alive and wanting.

Throughout those first few years, Marty stole letters and threw them away. A bunch of women found them, took them, and read them. June couldn't keep so much stuff, they told her. The guards took them too. She never threw a single one away by herself. She always maintained hope. Yet in some way or another, they found their way into the trash, gone for good. Her soul broke, murdered every time.

CHAPTER EIGHT

ROSE

"HI, UNCLE MARK. How's it going?" Christine said. She hadn't been to see Aunt Rose in several days, caught up in all of the horse shit of college, and sludging through love with Terrie. Talking to someone removed from her daily routine, she adjusted the phone and her voice. "How's Aunt Rose? I'm going to visit. I think Saturday morning."

"Oh, that's great, great, Christine," Uncle Mark remarked. "That's what she'll need. Actually, Saturday really is perfect. I have some things to do during the day, but I wanted to tell you about Aunt Rose," he said, spitting out scattered words trying to get to his point. "Aunt Rose has been saying 'June' a lot. It's like a moan, sobbing, 'June.' She's getting depressed, it seems. And well, we don't know how to talk to her, owing to the stroke. It's hard to tell what she needs—understand her," he inserted. His nervousness gathered like a cloud and hung over them both. Each person on their own side of the phone line had something to reckon with. She wasn't dead, but this was worse, confusing and frustrating.

"I'll be over today," Christine promised. "I know I can help. There has to be something I can do, something I can say. She'll snap out of the funk, I'm sure." Christine adjusted the phone and raised her slouched body only to slouch it again. Christine wasn't sure what was possible.

"Oh, that's great. It will cheer her up, I'm sure. Can you still come Saturday? I asked Aunt Rose's old friend, Sylvia, to come by. They've been friends for a long time," Uncle Mark said. It was hard for him to ask for help.

"Of course, Uncle Mark," Christine said. "Whatever I can do. Should I bring anything?"

When they were done talking over logistics, Christine packed up her textbooks and headed for the car. She would be able to work on her thesis at Aunt Rose's. There was still some literature review and internet research she needed to do for one of the business cases. After she verified a few assumptions, efforts would switch to the analysis.

She would have to cancel dinner plans with Terrie. She had been so adamant Terrie was not showing up, and here she was missing their long-standing date night. Christine dusted off her striped shorts and picked at a spot on her solid blue T-shirt, pausing to load her textbooks in the bag. She was showing up for their relationship, and as many dates as she could. Christine was making the most out of their quality time. Even though her calendar was filling up, she valued being together.

AUNT ROSE'S EMOTIONS bled through her face, opening the room. She invited Christine in with quiet grunts surfacing under her smile. Her cataract-afflicted eyes reached to her, even if they didn't have any focus in them. Christine was worried she wasn't available for Aunt Rose as much as she should be either. Before the stroke, she had come over very frequently to study. It was a quiet place and not far from campus. Before Terrie, Aunt Rose and Christine had spent so much time together and gotten close.

The nurse left for a few hours to get personal errands done. She said she'd return soon and would pick up Aunt Rose's medication. She was so attentive and dedicated to this one person. How much had she missed out on living herself while she was cooped up in this house?

Christine made coffee and sat beside the bed in a large, upholstered armchair. It was the kind with stiff cushioning and thick, tight stitches with cording. The purple flowers and olive green leaves made her cringe, but she was with Aunt Rose. Nothing more was wanted.

She sat reading and looking out the window. Her gaze fell from Aunt Rose due to lack of interaction. The room was a void except for the echo of breath. Christine wondered if

Terrie would want to come over too. Maybe they could make dinner here and have a date night at Aunt Rose's house. But it wouldn't be quite right with Aunt Rose handcuffed to the bed.

The mumble vibrated and shook Christine.

"June," Aunt Rose moaned. And she whimpered again, "June."

Over and over several times until she was angry from saying the same thing, the word she knew best, furious it wouldn't come out the right way. Christine didn't get what Aunt Rose was saying, and it frustrated both of them.

Despite Christine's attempts to cheer her up, her words had no effect. "Aw, it's all right, Aunt Rose. Don't worry," Christine cried. She, with even, steady timing, rubbed back and forth on her arms. Her hand was well above the skin, touching it only at specific points, so the thin skin would not bruise or tear, and the veins would not erupt. "Aunt Rose? What can I do?"

Tears welled, and her head bowed. She continued to chant, unable to get the words out, while her emotions emerged as a flood. "I killed him," she mumbled. Her mouth hung open, and she continued to try to speak. She issued nothing more.

They sat in quiet for another half hour. Aunt Rose had sunk into herself, exhausted. She breathed heavy sighs, taking air in quickly and trying to let the intensity all out at once. Noise only came out in choppy blurts. She lifted her head one last time and softly vocalized, "Love Juuune."

If Aunt Rose had killed the great Dr. O'Malley because she loved June, was there psychology involved? If June had made Aunt Rose adore her, if she'd had power over her, was she responsible for what she had done? If it was out of love, instead of for love, was there a difference? No one faulted June for loving Aunt Rose. Had June said in passing, "I wish Dr. O'Malley were dead"? Was that the extent of her psychological trickery? Or was it more? If June had indeed plotted, if she had used Aunt Rose's blind love as a weapon, was she a criminal? She was responsible for Aunt Rose's love somehow. Aunt Rose might take ownership of her passion, hold love more dearly than murder. Of her own accord, she had, at least, proven her feelings in a wicked way.

They sat for some time until the sun cast down and darkness crept over. Christine read without inflection, monotone, aloud to Aunt Rose. She couldn't believe the madness. She was reading a book for fun. Somehow, she was finding the time. She found it because Aunt Rose needed blunt kindness. Aunt Rose needed to listen to a voice and her words lifted. This was what Christine gave. She went on, reading her favorite sections of a book about eras before June, with lesbians. The pulp novel was written in the fifties, and Christine tried to imagine the times. Tension broke, released, Aunt Rose's need to explain, and Christine's curiosity to know. The most sound reasonable action was to let the mentions of June go, to not push her, even though questions still burned in Christine's mind.

CHRISTINE HAD CLASSES all day Thursday but made it over for a few hours in the evening. She stopped by early

Friday morning to pop her head in too. On Saturday, Christine planned to spend the bulk of the day there. She picked up a crumb cake at the grocery store and got some fresh half-and-half.

She had to fumble around in the back of the cabinet to get the china cups. Aunt Rose probably wouldn't have gotten them out, but the daring twist on the morning made all the difference. Awkward bits of china made Christine feel like a child pulled up to a tiny table with her mom after Saturday morning cartoons. She was past the years of young adulthood, but not quite to middle age still without place settings. Either way, she didn't yet care about shiny, fancy things. She wasn't sure she ever would. She would seek out her own china, maybe one day. Pick it all up in a bundle. The price would have to be reasonable. It wasn't on her radar right now. She brushed the thought aside.

Sylvia came early. The nurse was still giving Aunt Rose her sponge bath, so they set up for coffee first. Aunt Rose wouldn't be having any, regardless. Christine poured two cups and sliced the cake.

Sylvia prodded for information. "So, how is she? Is it bad? Is she responding to therapy?" Sylvia asked. Her cup rattled in the saucer. This sturdy woman with tightly trimmed hair held a dainty cup.

Christine gawked, overly confused anyone would enjoy the jittery things.

"She's good. She speaks a little, kind of emotional lately. She keeps referencing this woman, June. I think she's a past lover," Christine mentioned, playing dumb.

"Oh, June, dear, she's still got a lot on her head. She'll

have it until the day she dies," Sylvia said. Her peach lipstick appeared painted on her powdered face, which was pale and despite the wrinkles, washed with plainness, a free canvas. Her earrings, with dangling, crisscrossing metalwork, jiggled as she shook her head slightly, much as the cup jiggled.

"Do you know June?" Christine asked. The idea hadn't even crossed Christine's mind. One of her old friends would know parts of the story too. She was anxious to pry any information she could get out of the woman. She kept everything in check, a hostess and mere child almost sixty years younger than her guest.

"Dear, I worked with Rose at the hospital all those years ago. I knew of June," Sylvia remarked. She didn't appear like she wanted to get into a discussion and peered toward the bedroom.

"It's just that, well, Aunt Rose shot someone so many years ago, and her lover went to prison. I'm sure you've heard parts of the story." Christine spat out, "I don't get why June went to prison for longer." Christine tapped her fingers. If she had to, she would pry the information out of her. She cared for Aunt Rose; she could know.

"Look, dear. That was a long time ago. This is never something to gossip about, but you're part of the family, at least. It was self-defense. Dr. Jonathan O'Malley, deceased, finally, thank god." Sylvia shuddered. She glared sideways at her as if her statement was a bit of a joke or something everybody knew. "They lived in the same building. He was on the first floor. Both June and Aunt Rose passed by his door daily, and every so often, Dr. O'Malley would be in the corridor or getting his mail. After a while, his wife suspected what was going on too. She was probably the one who cued him in.

"Dr. O'Malley took the issue to work. His accusations. He was ranting and raving all the time, so nobody quite took him seriously at first. He confronted Rose about their relationship and how he believed they were lesbians. He picked on her due to the fact she was weaker in his opinion. After he took the issue to a supervisor, he poked around more—prying. He found out Rose was a patient in a hospital and was June's patient at one point. The rumors spread. He harassed them at their home and work."

Sylvia might have sweated. The coffee might have been a bit strong, Christine guessed. She wasn't sure if she should water the liquid down or switch to decaf.

Sylvia wiped her brow and continued. "Dr. O'Malley used slurs and threats. He put their jobs at stake. June's job became unstable first, but Rose needed to work too. He had a particular bone to pick with Rose, seeing she was a butch. The critical turning point was when the doctor threatened to go to June's boss with photos. How had he gotten photos? I'm sure I don't know what he was doing to get photos." Sylvia twisted her head and strained her eyes as if she had traumatic stress from all of it. "He was so malicious, out for blood. Rose said it every day. He was out for blood. Their lives, the apartment, their jobs were all at risk. That's the way it was in those days—

"Listen." Sylvia looked left first as if she was about to whisper a secret. "Just know Rose shot someone. She would've made it right. Oh, it's so complicated. If anyone—If you ask eight of ten people, Rose should've gone to prison, not June."

The nurse emerged, wiping her hands on a towel. "She's ready now, and she's even got a smile. I told her you were here. You can go and see her."

Sylvia and Christine moved to the bedroom, Christine taking her regular chair. Sylvia sat next to the bed on a chair the nurse had been using. It was close. Sylvia whispered hello and held Aunt Rose's hand, flexing and relaxing. She chatted a bit about what she had done that week and what she would do later in the day. Rose wasn't there. It could've been she didn't realize it was Sylvia or she was hazy that day. She beamed in Sylvia's direction, more off into the distance like she was welcoming someone who was emerging from the closet.

Sylvia smirked, talked, kept talking, at times about nothing. She sighed and kept going, leaning in. She was attentive and gave her all her consciousness. Aunt Rose may have been listening and may have understood. Aunt Rose cooed in muffled tones, but she didn't give any other response. She couldn't share Sylvia's day and give her a two-way conversation. As Sylvia hovered close, kissing her several times, Christine knew they were growing distant. Sylvia only got to come over now and then. The family, Christine's family, was taking over Rose's care.

Christine wanted to talk about Aunt Rose and the harassment from the doctor. But this was not the time or place. Everything ended with a stiff shrug. The conversation was over. They would never bring the moot points up again. The sordid event was, after all, in the past, not something people liked to talk about, after all this time.

Sylvia left after an hour. She had errands to run and couldn't keep her friend waiting. She wished Christine the best with school and hoped she got a job right out of college. Christine waved from the door and lingered there. She had missed her opportunity to ask her back over for coffee again and to visit Aunt Rose.

With no rush to get anywhere, Christine gathered the dishes and put away the crumb cake. She handwashed the teacups. She and Terrie would eat the rest of the pastry later.

When a cup chipped, she offered a firm "Goddamn it."

Christine was full of heartache over the story. She was exhausted and still curious. Her books sat in a stack in the living room. In an unamused way, she played with the cover of a textbook. Christine felt empty, and her mind swayed between school and Aunt Rose. What if the doctor had harassed them? The defense speculated on motives, aligned less likely evidence as plausible facts. That's why Aunt Rose had shot the doctor. He'd blackmailed them, and they'd had no way out. It would ruin their lives, even though the doctor would feel he had served justice. It was so unfair.

Christine tried to shake her thoughts. Why couldn't they look back on the events now and say in her predicament, with the attitudes and laws in place at this time, Aunt Rose was justified to shoot the man? Things had changed so much. She'd acted in self-defense dictated by the rules of the time. If she'd had another recourse, she wouldn't have shot the doctor. She would have gone to the cops. Now that society agreed, or most of society, that it's okay to be gay, could they not say she had to do what she did considering the indefensible laws, corrupt police, and an unforgivable society?

She had been protecting herself.

Even today, people get bullied, Christine reminded herself. Physical self-defense is only acceptable when someone attacks you. Recourses are available today, though, for harassment. You can file charges for certain crimes, or report people at work for harassment. What about someone's life, their credibility, their career, and their love lives? Because of the way lesbians were treated, June and Aunt Rose couldn't challenge all the harms done to them: verbal abuse, threats, and intimidation. They couldn't bring hearsay to the police, especially when their implication as lesbians followed. In the police's eyes, more injury occurred when two women loved each other than when one man set out to ruin two lives.

CHAPTER NINE

BEFORE — 1967

THE WALLS OF the hospital were stark white, and a chill flew through the hallway. June shivered in an ice cube tray of sorts, contained and isolated, with Rose. A slight light peeked through the windows early that morning. Dust fluttered up and down in a ray of sunlight. Patients didn't seem to notice this tidbit of hope that came in every morning—the light. Now Rose was on the other side, an employee, not a patient. She told June she cherished the sun so much more. She saw the sun in full light, felt the warmth outside on lunch, after work, and on weekends. The mere rays she saw on the inside were a teaser. She, but not patients, at any time could be close, or closer, to the real bold thing.

June watched Rose from the end of the hallway, moving slowly in Rose's general direction. She looked down and read patient notes.

With her keys jingling in her hands slightly, Rose moved toward the utility room. She was looking for a mop and bucket. A patient had thrown up in the hallway. Randall must not have taken well to his meds. He still paced throughout the hospital, a new patient getting his bearings. He wasn't comatose yet.

June had watched Rose years ago, almost a decade, as she sat in the same chair all day. The sun crept through the large picture window in the main room during the day and set slowly each night when she was ushered to bed. The memory of nurses feeding her pills as she resisted flashed before her eyes, and she stopped and shifted, fiddling with her notes.

The medications had killed part of Rose inside, and from that she was still recovering. Despite it all, now she had a job. She met society and became friends. She tipped her head up, proud at last. She thanked June a million times over. June lifted her and gave her a new life. It was June's doing, she said. She told everyone she owed her the world.

As she arranged the mop, bucket, and the spicket in the closet sputtered, her keys jingled again in the hollow air. Cleanup, however messy and unappetizing, was part of her job, and she was not above a smidge of vomit. The world passed her by in a different way now. June saw that. She was moving with it, however many minutes her steps took. June jotted down some notes, still observing.

Dr. O'Malley cruised down the hallway, staring at Rose. He backed her down with his gaze. Blatant intimidation was easy for this man in his position of power. He was a doctor, after all. He waited for Rose's eyes to meet his to speak and be heard to the fullest extent and exert his debasing power. Rose didn't look up, though; she only absorbed his gaze and continued to work.

He stopped beyond her, too close—anyone would say the awkward distance was too close—but no one was around. He leaned his head to her ear, and his spit wet her ear as he spoke.

"It's not too late. Quit," Dr. O'Malley remarked. He lifted his head away and laughed a bit. It was loud enough for June to hear. June leaned on the brick cement block wall as Dr. O'Malley continued, unaware of June's or anyone else's presence.

She jerked her head and body a step away in anger.

He rested his hand on Rose's shoulder and rubbed with a jerky, kneading grip. "You're mine. Remember it. Oh, and clean up my office when you're done here."

"Jonathan, you try," Rose broke through.

No one dared to call a doctor by his first name, not even the other doctors, but livid, a mess of restrained hatred, she stopped short of spewing a thousand words. Her address was the most she could do at that moment. A kiss two months ago had jump-started a pursuit, and he left threats with them every chance he got.

JUNE SAT IN the cafeteria of the hospital, not mingling with anyone. She kept to herself as much as possible. A professional woman, she intimidated everyone. People, men, would kill for her job, and she knew it. The day wasn't long enough to have time to be catty. She had a job to do and came in every day to do it. She left every night, ready for a paycheck on Friday.

She picked at her peanut butter sandwich. June hadn't made dinner last night, or she might have some leftover chicken or at least a cooked vegetable. June loved to cook. She took so much satisfaction in her loving preparations. Stirring in love was part of the process, adding things when she needed to add them, timing things until she needed to turn them. It always yielded the same results, and that was satisfying.

Most of all, it was for Rose. Her eyes lit up at beef stew or a juicy steak. June had made poached chicken a week ago, and the gently boiling pot on the stove caused Rose to bubble up with a grin and hug. Her mouth watered as she waited for the juices to drip and the bird to cook. Delighted with every stir, impatient and strangled by want as she waited for the food, she peeked around walls into the kitchen, lurking. The fact she did the dishes and cleaned up, set the table, and did light housework made the deal they had sweeter. Each of them took a task, regardless.

Dr. O'Malley walked close by the table. He stopped across from June. She shook her head, muttered to herself about his professionally inappropriate reactions to her attempts at light conversations. He walked on a cloud, way up looking down, scoffing at everything and anyone below him.

It didn't matter if they were complimenting him or doing something for him. He pooh-poohed their every action. The only person he spoke to with respect was his boss. It so happened O'Malley's boss was also June's boss.

Recently, tensions had risen and ebbed between Dr. O'Malley and June. Ever since he'd caught June and Rose kissing in June's office, he'd held something against them. Looking down at them from a fat-salaried, clout-filled perch, he already held power over them. Still, he had no proof. He still needed to prove the underlying act.

Dr. O'Malley leaned his hand on the table and spoke to several staff members sitting at the table. His arm tensed like a pole, stiff at the elbow joint. "So, you're treating a homosexual, Dr. Adams?" Dr. O'Malley boomed to the staff member. He looked at June, a king to a peasant, and coughed.

June put her head down with a quick, short jerk. Intimidation would not work. She would not let him bully her or mess with her head. What she and Rose were—lesbians — was considered wrong by many people, in many contexts. She could lose her job due to his accusations. She was sure. The fact they had been doctor and patient at one point only put them under more scrutiny.

"Well, don't have sexual relationships with them. That's for sure," Dr. O'Malley commented. A hearty, bold laugh from the lungs came out as he leaned into Dr. Adams. He was close enough for someone to think he was going to tell a secret, but his words erupted in a pulsed audible tone. "June knows something about relationships with female patients, don't you, June?"

They all turned to stare at June. The chairs shifted on the floor all at once. No one spoke. They were looking for a response but also realized they wouldn't get the one. Dr. Miller nodded disapproval, and Dr. Meeks squinted his eyes so he could see her facial reactions.

"Who do you think you are, Dr. O'Malley?" June entered. Her commanding reaction was solicitation to stop these childish games. She set her sandwich down with disapproval. "How dare you make an accusation? It's unprofessional."

Dr. O'Malley's face transitioned from surprise to disgust. Someone had questioned him. Insubordination was not allowed. No one challenged his authority. "Dr. Ashmore, I am doing my professional duty. Someone needs to stop these illicit offenses."

"She didn't," Dr. Adams quipped as he lurched forward toward Dr. O'Malley.

"Oh, my. Oh, well. That's—" Dr. Meeks stumbled out words in sporadic tones.

June rose and pushed her sandwich into the brown paper bag with the carrots, untouched. Her stomach turned. Her gut would stay empty and nauseous for the rest of the day.

When she got to her office, she rummaged in the drawer for the letters she and Rose were exchanging. They were simple notes that gushed "I love you" or asked what they were having for dinner. Some had hearts or notions of affection. Nothing remained for chance discovery. She put Rose's broken watch in her pocket, stowing it away until that evening. She couldn't have anything of Rose's in the office.

Before she left to attend to patient duties in the main room, she grabbed a photo of her and Rose in a town about a mile away. They glowed with quivering expectation, their arms around each other. A stranger had taken the muted-tone picture with June's camera. She was a nice older woman, unaware of their relationship, who dripped with compliments they were perfect friends. The woman mentioned she wished she had a friendship as good. She said she missed one thing in life—a partner in crime.

June pocketed the evidence and left out the door. It was her one pleasure to look at the photo throughout the day and think about Rose, the woman she had tried to find for so long. Even better, June had her in the flesh when she went home at night.

THAT EVENING, ROSE relayed the rest of the day's events to June. Dr. O'Malley had told Rose to clean his office. Rose, of course, was only tasked with cleaning up after patients. Housekeeping went by and cleaned the offices. "He wasn't just miffed; he was angry, beet red angry, June. It was almost as if something else was bugging him," Rose said.

Rose paced, visibly upset. "It's not my job to clean his office. I'm not office housekeeping. That's what I told him," Rose said.

Rose said she made it quick and to the point. She didn't want a fuss. Still, she was tired of ignoring his threats and insinuations. Something should be done and management would never act.

When he took a folded piece of paper out of his pocket, slapping the triangular shape up and down on the clip-board—that's when she'd started to worry. "He said, 'I have something.' Very sternly. He fussed with it in his pocket, and I almost laughed until it was very serious." Rose turned her back.

"He had gone through your office. He said he 'cleaned' your office, almost as a joke," Rose said, stopping short. "He had evidence of our relationship, and I could hear it in his voice."

Rose's and June's notes were usually short and sweet. They gave loving words of encouragement and often expressed excitement for weekends or dinner. It was always something to keep their hearts going. Most of them she signed "Rose." She sometimes meekly scrawled "Love, Rose," or "Yours always, Rose." She varied the closing sentiment with the wind.

They never addressed them to each other because, as much as they liked to express their love to their partner, they weren't stupid. They were always careful, cautious. Everyone was. All their friends and the people their friends talked about were cautious. They all discussed their secrecy, the ways to live so many didn't accept.

"He unfolded the paper carefully and deliberately," Rose said. The tiny notes they wrote were always folded in a signature tiny triangle small enough to pop in a drawer or shove in a pocket. Rose had immediately recognized the shape when Dr. O'Malley produced it.

Rose tapped her fingers on the kitchen table, issuing an unheard "I love you," in Morse code to June. They folded all of their notes this way, so they both would identify precisely what they were.

"'Dearest June,' Dr. O'Malley began, and I knew. I couldn't believe I addressed it to you. In fact, I didn't. He said some more baloney I never said. 'I love you naked under my satin sheets—I love you like chocolate touching my lips. Wear it for me tonight. Love and tenderness, Rose.' Something like that. He gave a big smile and rolled his eyes. Totally thinking I'd believe I wrote it. He said it was signed 'Rose.' I know I didn't write that one, June."

Rose held her breath and steamed with anger even now. Her pallor came through red as an apple. "I won't be stepped on like this, no matter what my position is."

"Did he give the note to Mr. Gordon?" June up until now had listened very quietly, as she knew best to do when Rose was upset. But Mr. Gordon was both June and Dr O'Malley's boss, not Rose's.

Rose scratched at her head obsessively. If someone took the forgery for the lie it might well be, she had a shot. They wouldn't write any more notes. June would have to lie her way out of this when Mr. Gordon called her into the office. Mr. Gordon would want to see her. It was a matter of when.

Chapter Ten

Terrie

CHRISTINE'S PHONE RANG and startled her. Usually, she left the ringer off, but this morning she had set the alarm with a new tone and left it on. After wiping her wet hands on a dishtowel, she answered. Water had seeped under the phone case. She took in a deep breath and tried to recall where she and Amy were in their relationship.

"Hi, Amy. No, it's fine. I've got this thing, but what do you need?" Christine asked.

"Terrie's been hanging around outside my place. I ran into her a few times," Amy said. "She was pacing the last time. She quit smoking, right? I'm not sure why she's there. I wanted to tell you."

"Was she waiting for you? I'm not sure what you mean—what did she want?" Christine asked.

"I'm not sure. Terrie doesn't know I can see her from my window, but when I ran into her downstairs, she acted like she was just passing by," Christine, confused by the seriousness of the incident, half listened, eyes veering away. Amy's voice got softer. "Christine, when I said hi, she wanted to talk." Amy's speech was direct.

"Maybe she was passing by and simply stopped." Christine listened to the hush on the other line. Her and Terrie's relationship thrived on frustration. She didn't need to decipher any more code. "I have to go, Amy. Things are weird between us lately, but I don't know how to decipher this...from either of you."

Christine tried to make sense of the subtext. If Terrie was waiting for Rebecca, Amy's roommate, she was out of luck. Rebecca had completed most of her classes and generally worked two jobs and stayed with her parents most days. She was never at the apartment. She was taking one class this semester to finish her degree. It was an effort to put an early dent on her student loans, even though a better job might be waiting for her after graduation. She didn't have time to do anything—let alone run into Terrie and rekindle a friendship.

Amy's thick, long blond hair made her seem like she should be at the beach. Her crisp blue eyes said she should take up modeling. Beneath the Barbie doll exterior, she bled like everyone else. She saddened, acutely so, when someone forgot to call. She'd confided in Christine many times since they broke up a year ago, telling her about painful, distracting, unshakable ideas. She imagined Christine's death, a stalker murdering her, and lived the event over and over again for days. She called her every few hours to make sure her heart still beat.

Weeks ago, Christine was at the diner with Amy when she told her about her sadness. She wasn't your typical blue down-in-the-dumps unhappy. She was unable to move forward with her day. Amy drew long, slurping sips from her coffee cup. Christine assumed she didn't hear how it sounded to her. But her eyes lifted slightly. In almost a whimper, she had asked if Christine would go to therapy with her.

They had discussed the coffee that night. Christine never ordered the shit again. One cup left a hole of unsatisfaction in both their stomachs. She inhaled the burnt and bitter swill, a mud puddle with lots of water, in quick jerking bursts. She assigned the sludge one word, unsatisfying. A thin ring of sloshed, murky clear liquid hung on the side of the mug, showing its washed-out, watercolor character. They both agreed they would never find a cup less flavorful, less weak. They debated whether they should try to for fun.

The next week she went with Amy to therapy, and she divulged more than she had ever let anyone else hear—all while in the presence of her therapist. The therapist didn't do much but listen and hear. She told Christine it was so important she was there, so someone else saw.

Amy became much more open in that therapy session and afterward. Sometimes, what Amy had to say scared her, made her uneasy. But she attended to it; that was her job, to be the quiet listener. Amy became an emotional, healing-through-speech friend. Christine gave a lot to her after that therapy session, possibly too much.

After weeks and months, Amy got better. She picked up the hobby of going to arboretums and flower shows. She met people for lunches. Her depression lifted, and everyone sighed relief. Christine edged herself out and let things move forward for Amy. She became independent.

For several months, Amy called infrequently. Christine finally was able to move on with Terrie—until the past month. Amy would often call with nothing much to say, nothing traumatic. It was as it had been before Christine was her listening ear.

Recently, Amy had found someone new. Amy said she had blue eyes too, but Christine was sure they couldn't give Amy's drop-dead glances. A few times during their recent phone calls, Amy drifted. The lifelessness surfaced. Christine couldn't say she drifted into her depression again, but she was aware. Amy would tell Christine she was upset Jill had said something. She'd stay in the house all day, stuck on whatever menacing words she'd given her. As far as Christine was concerned, she might have commented she didn't like Amy's shirt. Amy got sensitive.

Her mood had gone downhill, and Christine paced, as usual, trying to make the altered situation better. At the same time, they weren't in a relationship. She didn't even want to be Amy's best friend since they broke up. Her new girlfriend should be the one taking over, calming her, listening, and offering advice. Christine shouldn't be crossing

Jill's boundaries.

Christine didn't want to hide her story—the drama with June—from Amy. She wanted to confide in her too. But there was no room for it. Amy's constant panic took up everything in their lives in their friendship intimacy if you could call it that. With all the time spent on Amy's issues, there was no room for back and forth. There was no way to broach so huge of a topic and potentially have it consume Amy. Amy at times, Christine admitted, was fragile.

CHAPTER ELEVEN

PRISON III — 2015

CHRISTINE TOOK A black canvas briefcase with her this time. She found the leftover at Aunt Rose's house but didn't realize it was covered in cat hair and dust until she went to get out of the car. She brushed at it even though it would never be clean. The fur, at best, rolled into a ball and worked itself into the fabric. Her outfit, this time, scratched at her joints less. She wore a deep-red pullover shirt, left untucked over her tan pants. She entered the prison with a comfortable stride on this visit. Her legs, unrestrained, carried her freely through the doors. No one had suits or ties. The staff had button-up shirts and khakis. Why shouldn't she be able to dress like a mirror image?

On the last visit, she had appeared more like a lawyer, and the ploy had somehow supported her firm conviction in the lie she was telling—she was working on a project for a law class. She had bought the suit from a department store. Wasting money, she had picked it from the rack, slid past the dressing room, and ran to the register. She had never been good at watching her pennies. She only hoped she would get a decent job after she graduated and make use of it.

Christine's crapshoot wardrobe ended up including whatever was on the left side of her closet and whatever was on the top pile of pants and jeans. Things often ended in a plain-Jane appearance. She mused over her partner's fashion sense more easily, perhaps as a screen for her own neglect. As Terrie got ready in the morning, Christine would pop her head out from the covers. To Christine, a great dresser put clothes on quickly and left the room without looking back. Terrie always looked back, but Christine didn't hold it against her. In spite of depression, when Amy dressed, she never hesitated to choose the best option, never questioned her decision. She worried about so many other things. Clothes would be too much.

Christine matched her car this time when she emerged from the Subaru. Rising out of a beat-up, awry vehicle in a full suit turned heads. Anyone could see through her lie. A few takeout containers were on the rear seat. Her backpack sat in the passenger's seat with several loose notebooks. The bright-red backpack with silver reflecting stripes functioned so people could see her in the dark. After tossing school IT books into the essentially utilitarian best friend, she secured her day. She had taken off a few novelty pins before she arrived. She left it behind for the neutral briefcase. With extra effort, she smoothed down the fibers on the showpiece. She'd had to stop by the library that morning, so she was running late. Exhibiting a half-rate look, not professional at all, she hurried to make her interview time slot.

The woman at the desk looked her up and down and asked questions about who she was and who she was there to see. She stared, paused, smiled like she didn't believe anything said, even before Christine replayed her inane purpose. Christine had to wait, and the forced delay must be a punishment for being late. She sat in a nearby chair and picked lint off the briefcase.

Rough characters passed by her. All of them could've once been in prison—everyone except the button-down-shirt-and-khaki types and those in uniform. And even for them, questions emerged; her eyes lit up. Christine stood out. She wasn't here to say, "I love you. Miss you." She wasn't here to drop off some books. Yet she wasn't a lawyer going in to discuss a case with her client, either. Her purpose amounted to checking up on someone's status.

Christine's actions, ludicrous and unfounded, unspeakable, and unacceptable, perplexed any number of people. But who cared or guessed? Did she need to know? She went on living, understanding Aunt Rose had had a lover and gone to prison. For some reason, though, it pressed inside her to find out whose fault it was and if they loved each other. So, what if she'd made up a story to get an interview?

She could, blinding everyone, have had to do a web project and needed a meeting. She wasn't doing anything backhanded, simply asking questions with someone who wanted to talk back and getting more time than through a glass on a telephone.

She entered the interview room, sat there, and waited. The same details stuck out; a carbon copy of the other interview room surrounded her. The green table, constructed with applied metal around the edges, glistened with a dull patina. The buffed-hard surface might've been a slate chalkboard. Christine was afraid to run her chewed fingernails over the top. She used her pencil to make a mark.

The guard reentered with June at her side. She uncuffed June's thin, bony wrists. If cuffed to the full extent, her wrists would collapse under the pressure. The metal clinked, and the catches clicked as she adjusted them and pulled them up onto her belt.

While June sat, pleasant and calm with an overflowing grin, the guard waited beside the door. June didn't even remember she existed. The guard, over her shoulder, hiked her belt, holding all sorts of pouches and tools, including a holster for a gun or a taser. Uncomfortable with the belt sagging at her thin hips, she turned her body and adjusted again. This whole person, their muscle, and their commanding voice were needed to escort June, be her shadow.

"You the lawyer?" she asked. She questioned in a direct manner, with command. She snapped something on her belt, which made Christine sit taller.

"Kind of. I was allowed an interview," Christine remarked, speaking to the guard with direct intent.

"I'll wait outside."

"That's what they did last time, I guess," Christine said, then paused, wondering how often prisoners got interview time.

The guard jiggled the handcuffs in her belt and left. This aging woman, still in a way sprite and quick-witted, would never attack her or make a move. Christine remembered their conversation from last time. This woman could never kill anyone. In fact, she hadn't.

What she had done was use her mind, her training in psychology, to convince Rose to shoot her colleague. They decided she'd done the deed in the caselaw. She had resorted to trickery to get the job done. As Christine rehearsed the court decision in her mind, the justification for hating her, it didn't seem quite right. Last time, June had stated love for Rose in a more genuine way. Christine still would not let her guard down.

"Hi, June. How are you? Thanks for seeing me again," Christine began. She called her June with a leering half-cocked stare. She needed to act as if she was a professional. Still, if she said "Ms. Ashmore," the limp words would sound more like she was addressing her as if they were in a child-adult relationship rather than a client-lawyer situation. She had such a connection to Aunt Rose, and she was so much older. Undeniable beneath any lie, June had helped Rose grow up.

"Well. It's nice to see you again. I'm surprised you showed up. We got into the heavy stuff last time." June chuckled and rolled her eyes, seemingly at herself. "Who needs the facts anyway?" June taunted her.

June rang in on how, when you love someone, you become more open to things. In this case, June was more open to new people, namely Christine. Love made you powerful, and June had kept it through all these years, bottled the sin.

"Ms. Ashmore," she said limply. "Can we please go through the facts today? I can't write a paper in total about your feelings." She chuckled, partially out of nervousness. She mostly pried for information to support her false motives.

"I told her to call the police," June said. From the way she spoke, there wasn't much else to it.

"In the case, on the caselaw website, it mentioned Rose shot Dr. O'Malley because you told her to, and you denied it," Christine detailed.

June fiddled with her fingers as Christine rocked the pen side to side higher than the notepad. Lowering her head, June squinted her eyes shut. She was reliving the mistake, making trauma hurt less.

"We had never fully planned anything. Rose said she'd kill him if she got the chance, but we never took it for absolute intent. It's like if you said, 'Ooooo. I could kill him.'" June lifted her fists and tensed her arms into her side. "Well, maybe slightly more serious than that. But you get the point."

Christine put her head down and listened as she wrote. June stretched to look her in the eyes, and the invasion made Christine concentrate even more on her pad of paper.

"It broke my heart when she said I told her to do it. She told the police right away. They barged in the door. She was trying to roll the body up in a rug before I got there. She was so angry and covered in blood. The officer testified. It broke my heart," June said. She stared at the ceiling. Her eyes squinted, tense folds, again as if she wished the tale weren't true. "They said it was some kind of test. They decided the first thing you say in an emotional incident is never a lie. So, she was there in a panic, and that was the first thing she squeaked out—or the first thing they heard. And you have to believe the act, the words, the intent. Who is to say what intent is? That damn res gestae. I'll never forget those words."

The room caved in with June's retelling. Everything darkened. The spotlight on Christine, June shined words to illicit reactions.

"She lied right away 'cause she was angry. She wanted to blame someone or something. It was a knee-jerk flight reaction, all right. But she was lucid and aware of the impact when she said it," June pleaded. "She would have never said I did it if she was in her right mind," she mumbled.

June's understanding of psychological response came across as more well-founded to Christine. Not in a way that relayed June understood psychological mind control or techniques to manipulate someone into committing murder for them, but commonsense understanding.

"But I told the neighbors to call the police. I banged on the wall from the hallway. They never fathomed I could have knocked on the door. The whole damned thing was my fault. She hated me with justified anger. She knew I told them to call. She had every right to hate me," June mumbled, stammering out words.

"After I was charged, I let Rose do minimal time and walk free. It was my apology," June relayed. "She shouldn't have done it, anyway. I would never have wanted it.

"They said I bought the gun. I never bought it," June related. "It was my account at the store, but she bought it. It was for protection anyway," she muttered. "He was trying to ruin our lives. I was about to lose my job. It was hard to say if he wanted more than that."

June went on about the trial. She was giving critical details Christine wanted to know. This interview was less of a tease. Bored, on edge, and angered by the slightest incident or words this time, she was testy, ready to end the discussions.

"It wasn't my gun. The cops said I bought the thing, but I didn't. I didn't even go to the store," June mentioned. "I never took it seriously. Why didn't they believe me? What else do I have to prove?"

Christine sat silent the whole time. Something in June's face, her disgusted eyes and quivering lips, shattered disbelief. Christine knew, in an instant, acknowledging her naivety and still concluding the act was truth. She hadn't known anyone could go so deep in a lie. She turned her head sideways and blinked at the dimpled walls. The story was the same as last time. Her eyes had searched the extent of the room. Like every corner of this place, the walls constricted and suffocated. She sidled up to the table in a cell disguised as a room. They were locked in together, and she couldn't release her opinions and reasons for being there.

Aunt Rose had blamed this woman for murder. She had sent her to state prison; that was an essential truth. And June still loved Aunt Rose. They had their bond. Christine found herself at an unexpected end of the spectrum. She almost didn't forgive Aunt Rose. Christine didn't know what she would even say if Aunt Rose talked back or how she would look at Aunt Rose when she returned home. Aunt Rose would never be able to explain or justify or correct so many things.

Christine wished she had never initiated this crusade of curiosity. This strange imperative she had to find out about Aunt Rose's love life pried at her anyway. How she felt now, she had no right. The confusion and guilt were rooted in her prying and her lies. Her feelings, loaded with guilt and betrayal, bubbled to the top.

Christine's arm fell out across the table. Afraid, she didn't extend it all the way. She, too, now squinted her eyes, attempting to shade her vision from something that couldn't be true.

June reached her hands across and held Christine's fingers, closing her hand. "You're not supposed to get invested," June said. "Don't they teach you that?"

Christine's hazy focus on the details of the case overshadowed June's words about emotional investments.

"Yes, of course. It's only you shouldn't be here. It's so unfair," Christine cried. If June had convinced her, used psychology to sway her, to be on her side, she didn't care. She believed the forgiving words and meek pleas for understanding. This woman wouldn't be in there after all these years if it weren't for her silence. It couldn't be.

"It was 'cause I was a lesbian and 'cause I had a career. It's best anyway." June released her hand, patting it on the table a few times as if it were a baby's cheek. "Is that enough for your report? Enough of my own words?"

June was ending the interview. She had lost patience or didn't see the point. Maybe she didn't want to rehash the events.

"Yes. I think I have enough for the report," Christine commented, tidying her notes on the table, shuffling the papers between her hands. "I feel like no one's helped you. Can I write to you still? Can I see how you're doing? Maybe come and visit?"

"Honey, you don't need to come here. But I like letters. It'd be nice if someone took the time and sent me a letter to me, for a change. Ha. The other girls—they get letters. You know how it is." She straightened in the chair.

"I got your letter about Terrie and Amy. It was touching to see you have two people, two people you obviously love," June replied.

Christine talked about Terrie a bit and how she was in love with her, not Amy. It was distinctly different, she clarified. Amy was her good friend, or they were working on that too. She told June about how she made pros and cons lists for them both, and Terrie always came out on top. She tried to imagine not watching a classic movie with Amy or cooking dinner with Terrie. She drew the line in their friendship as necessary. She wanted Terrie as a lover but couldn't risk her friendship with Amy. She would never be able to decide. If one said she couldn't have the other, she would have to do without them both.

June mentioned something rather strange as their time drew to a close.

She said, "Take care of her. You never know if something will ever happen to her." She laughed and swiftly moved on.

It was almost like she thought Terrie had something to worry about. June went right back to Rose.

Christine left the way she came. The same desk clerk who was so untrustworthy, so suspicious, asked if she would return. Christine acknowledged she didn't think so. She'd gotten what she needed. Christine might talk to June for hours, but this specific time she wouldn't get much more. She had notes, a feeling of love, a story about someone who had once loved Aunt Rose so much.

Christine couldn't shake the feeling she owed June for Aunt Rose's actions. She needed to find some way to say she was sorry for what her family had done. The whole unjust affair was unconceivably considered acceptable. This woman had been locked up for her entire life, and she had never fired a gun. Christine flirted with the idea of becoming June's lawyer or helping in some way. Would she prove her aunt a criminal? Regardless of the debate, she, an invalid, would never go to prison at this point.

Christine tested the locks on her beat-up Subaru before firing the ignition. The parking lot, however secure, marketed as a playground for perpetrators. Locks were real. They kept people out. They kept people safe. Christine turned her head and watched a bulky, square man pass right by her door. She wouldn't look him in the eyes in the real world, somewhere other than this unreliably safe parking lot.

Locks were safe, except if you broke them to get in. Or made a copy of the key. If someone broke a window, they were useless; a pointless effort if someone tricked you into unlocking them. So many locks weren't real. They offered no absolute protection. People break the law despite them, despite saying, "No, you can't go in here." They don't keep people out. They only survive for appearances.

CHAPTER TWELVE

BEFORE – 1968 – MURDER BY PROXY

JUNE ENTERED THE courtroom with her lawyer, a half-rate hack. His tie gripped his neck in an odd knot. The extra length of fabric wouldn't behave. The part usually kept behind was sneaking around the side. He tried to get his bearings and stuttered to find his spot. His face glazed over in a hot red as he and June moved closer to the bench. He was the best option, affordable, recommended by a friend. Given the quality of her relationship with Rose and the contentious evidence, a number of firms were hesitant to take on her case. Too distraught to care, she took her current lawyer without hesitation.

When they settled into their seats for the whole affair, she and her lawyer exchanged a few words. They had prepared, rehearsed, gone over the facts, but June was at a loss for how to retain her freedom. June's trial sought to prove she had used their relationship and her role as Rose's psychiatrist to convince Rose to shoot Dr. O'Malley. The murder, a product of passion, aimed to protect June from losing her job. Rose, already charged and in jail for being the actual shooter, would get a lightened sentence.

June, falling back into herself, glanced over toward Rose as everything got underway. Rose didn't look at her then, but she would off and on throughout the trial. She would fidget and throw confused looks, never hatred, never love. Her prison clothes set her apart from the rest of the people in the courtroom. The fact she was a lesbian set a mile-long distance between them. June was in the same classification and elicited a similar muted look from everyone. A criminal in plain clothes, she pulled herself into the defense table.

June longed after her, wanting the life they had, but didn't beckon Rose to look back. Agitated and confused, she shifted in her seat, unable to see or hear. June understood, and she held comforting looks on her in case she turned. June remembered when they had scheduled Rose's electroconvulsive therapy. June had told her intending to prepare her. Eventually, with her pull as a doctor, June had gotten her off the list and saved her. They both knew it. In the courtroom, Rose had the eyes of a crazy woman, the same eyes that had come out when she'd learned about the treatment. They were the eyes of someone unfit to make a statement. She jolted and careened in her chair. If she made another trip to the hospital at that moment, it would be a death sentence. She'd never get out.

The jury sat in a corral made from the same wood that ran behind her, a fence from all the people who were not potential criminals. An older man, a woman whose blouse choked her neck at the top button, a young well-groomed professional all bucked in the corral, ready for something to happen in the show before them. To June, they all bit their nails dead set against innocence. They were disgusted to have to be a part of it all, uncomfortable. This was what June thought and what was likely correct.

June watched the fanfare with a quiet demeanor. The main event, the rest of her life, unraveled before her eyes. It all meant to June that Rose didn't love her. It was inconceivable to blame it all on Rose, even if she was already in prison. Did Rose want her? Did Rose misunderstand anything June had said? Did Rose construe June's position, a doctor, as psychologically manipulative? Rose would get less time, but it was ludicrous she had to sacrifice her dearest lover for her own sake. Yet she had.

Dr. O'Malley's wife testified about how the two had harassed him. He'd complained about it at home. She spoke with sharp hateful, justified words. Her husband was dead. Mrs. O'Malley pointed at them both, but for the longest time at June. The real perp, she had started the whole thing, instigator, initiator, the strongest harasser. She was a colleague and unprofessional. She deserved to have her license taken. The loss of her right to freedom was unquestionable.

When she stepped down, Rose rubbed at her nose one last time. The wife blinked at June with bullets in her eyes. Rose sat restrained, the woman who had wielded the gun.

A hospital staff member spoke about June and said June targeted the good doctor. She always threw malicious words his way. "I'll get you," they noted June relayed. "Watch your back," was what she mentioned in passing. June articulated some of those words. Those words were always prefaced with "If you don't stop it," or in response to "Watch your back." The staff member didn't even know the half of it. She hadn't even been there to hear it. She only recounted what the "good doctor" had told her.

It must've been the way Mrs. O'Malley told the events, leaning in with emotion, burning the incident in the jury's brain. They leaned and listened. They heard her when she talked about June and Rose's homosexual relationship, their dirty life. They proclaimed it was wrong, and that's all they needed to know to close the book.

A psychologist took the stand to say Rose had a pliable mind. She, an ex-mental patient, responded to authority and coaxing. She was apt to go along with what anyone with some sense of power would say. Pliable and moldable, Rose took action when anyone made a suggestion. And June took advantage for her career. The psychologist testified, "In a moment of stress at the scene of a crime, utterances should be held as truth. In this case, Officer Marks has testified Ms. Winster gave declarations such as: 'She told me to do it, I did what you said, and I had to.'"

The young professional picked his teeth when he decided on the verdict. The old man hung onto two words of guilt, not to be let go. The tight-lipped woman gasped so many times she didn't seem to listen to a word more. June heard her decision before she spoke. When Rose took the stand, it didn't matter anymore. It didn't matter to the case. June slammed her hand hard on the thickly lacquered almond table. Whatever came out of her mouth was moot. She was heartbroken. It was inconsequential what happened from there forward.

June spit tears as soon as Rose walked up the steps into the wood compartment next to the judge. June cried while Rose shook and jerked, a mess of anxious, paranoid motions. She tried to straighten up. She blamed her and the full extent of her actions. Rose turned red with anger when she eyed June. Everything between them was over.

"Did June tell you to do it?" The simple question from her lawyer asked her to be straight to the point. It would encapsulate the whole trial, even though the jury had decided after the second witness. June's opinion counted for something, at least.

"She tricked me. That's what I understand," Rose mumbled as she exchanged glances with the judge. "She told me about how horrible he was and how he was going to ruin our life. She told me I had to show her I loved her." Rose peered over at June and jerked her head away. She couldn't stand the sight of her lover, her companion for life.

The judge nodded and goaded her on, sympathetic and inquisitive with his eyes. He wanted her to gush the guilt all out, cry on his shoulder if she wished. She drew out her sentences to do that, added every detail she could.

June twisted her head to the side and let out an

exasperation of air. She couldn't believe what unfolded. They were the ones telling her to go, encouraging her to tell all. They were more psychologically impactful than June might ever be. Someone should declare a mistrial.

"She bought the gun for me. She gave the weapon to me and told me to shoot Dr. O'Malley," Rose commented.

The opposing lawyer introduced a receipt as evidence. The washed-over slip barely showed letters, fraudulent in every way. June had never bought a gun. Still, the prosecution said Rose could not have purchased a firearm without a legal residence, which she did not have. She was only staying with June. She wasn't on the lease. June had bought the gun so Rose could kill Dr. O'Malley.

"Stop it," June burst out, and the gavel dropped three times.

The courtroom went silent. She couldn't believe the lies, and it was an outright lie. June had never bought a gun and never, ever, verbatim said to shoot Dr. O'Malley, despite what conclusions Rose may or may not have drawn. This trial was a farce, and Rose was implicating June on purpose. She wanted to be free and free without June no less.

Their life, the long drives to small towns, were over. She wouldn't love again. June decided right that second. No one would put her weakened heart through this. She wouldn't let her heart stray. She wouldn't forget those long drives, regardless of if she ever got to do them again. Rose was her lover, and she would never remember her sitting there, surrounded by carved walnut barriers too glamorous for their simple souls. For the rest of her life, she would try to blank out this moment.

When June settled into her spot at the stand, she only mumbled out answers. The bones in her butt jabbed into the chair, and she had to adjust—slouching, resting weight on hip, tail bone, thigh. She was vaguely aware of her surroundings in dazed confusion. Booming lights cast down on her. The countless stares, a certain kind of glare, in the crowd were from bigots with hateful opinions. They all hated her. Here she was, last, and everyone knew but June. She let out last gasps for air while dragged underwater.

It was over, no matter what she said. The young professional rested his head on his hand. The young woman stopped sitting up and listening. The old man nodded his head every so often, awake, dipping the weighted balloon down with his eyes. Even June's lawyer adjusted his tie, afraid to come to terms with the courtroom's decision.

"June, tell us about your relationship with Rose," the opposing lawyer said.

June bumbled through an explanation. They were terrific friends, friends for life. Nothing more could be relayed. She avoided crossing the line into a homosexual relationship as long as possible, but the lawyer dug it out. He slashed her across the body, defaming who she was and who she would be for the rest of her life, as the typist pecked away and took careful notes.

"June, was your job at stake?"

June replied she didn't know, even though she did. It was.

"Rose lost her job due to rumors, correct? Dr. O'Malley did his duty by informing your supervisor of your illicit actions?"

June understood the truth, and she could've killed him for it. It left them helpless, on one income. Rose was unable to function at her best without some structure in her life. She mumbled he was harassing her.

"He deserved it, June, didn't he?"

She mumbled no one deserved death. The lawyer cut her off, proclaiming a solid motive and action. This was what had happened as he related the events. She was guilty. He spoke with impactful words.

"June, did you tell Rose to kill Dr. O'Malley?" June's lawyer countered. It was one of his only questions.

Trailing a long breath, she said, "No, I didn't." She spoke with her library voice. Why would she ever want it? He had harassed them, and he had deserved what was meant for him, she said, but they would never do such a thing. She viewed the jury, questioning, begging.

"I loved that woman as a sister, and it is beyond me to nurture hate in someone you love. I am a doctor of emotions. It's true, and I temper them, not exacerbate them. They don't train you to make weapons in college. They train you to bring out humanity."

June finished. She had conveyed her piece. Brokenhearted, she left the stand, not caring either way. Her love, Rose, had broken her heart in so many places by doing this. She stumbled on her feet when they called for the verdict. She rested her fists on the table in front of her.

They turned in the verdict after less than a half hour. The odds were stacked and stacked again against June as each person testified. She was doomed, and she watched it happen, silenced by a judge in a courtroom.

She had lost her life in the sentence. She had lost her love in the words. No one gave either back. She would die wondering what might have been, and that was the worst thing ever. Her limbs were limp, and she collapsed to the floor, curled up in a ball. Everyone hesitated to help her. When someone did come over to her soft body, only one person did—the bailiff. Everyone else receded away from the criminal, dispersing to their own lives.

CHAPTER THIRTEEN

TRUTH

CHRISTINE OPENED HER laptop and stared at the bright screen in the small office she shared with Terrie. With the curtains closed, she typed. She was making real headway on her thesis. She couldn't believe her unwavering progress. Christine was ahead of the game and would maybe finish before everyone else if she kept up the same pace. Her laptop's organs buzzed louder now. Something churned inside. It didn't quite have the speed she wanted. The hunk grinded gears, ready to bust at any minute, so like a spot-on future IT professional, she backed up her work to an external hard drive. She had hoped it would last a decade. She only imagined where she was going to get money for a new laptop.

She moved around some of the June files on her desktop. She wanted to look deeper, get more information. She needed to go to another library or get firsthand interviews with people who had been at the scene of the crime. But it would take time out of her schedule. Time dedicated to schoolwork and her pathway to graduation. Terrie was also a primary concern. She would need to get her opinion in due course. A conversation, one they'd have to sit down for, was creeping closer and closer even though she tried to keep it at bay.

Terrie was already up. She was in the other room, making breakfast. Christine wanted to cozy into her desk chair and get some work done on one thing or another, but the food smelled so good. Bacon and hash browns. Did Christine smell a quiche? She would get a shower after breakfast and would make an entrance into the kitchen when she got her thoughts together about where she was on her thesis. The coffee maker beeped. Terrie always made the coffee last.

Christine had to poke around at the Amy issue. Gentle words would figure out what was going on with all the lying. Christine cast her eyes toward Terrie's phone when she was texting and tried to overhear conversations. Terrie wasn't cheating. Their lives had misunderstandings but not too many. She didn't want to look like a fool. She locked the computer and inhaled a deep sweet breath of air, air made with love.

"It smells good," Christine whispered, surfacing. "You got any sugar for that coffee?" She bumped Terrie with her hip and laughed. It was impossible to be angry at someone who cooked for her. Christine ascended as royalty.

Terrie helped herself to some food and moved out of Christine's way. "Give me a kiss, you." She stole it in the same breath. It had been a good night last night, and Christine was as satisfied with their lovemaking as their communication skills the last few days. They were beginning to talk, be adults. They overlooked the small stuff and cherished the good.

Yesterday, they had made it to drag bingo at the brewpub with Jesse and Sandy. A double date. Nothing stopped them from looking like a perfect, well-adjusted, wholesome couple. They loved a night on the town, not cooped up in the apartment, searching for a new YouTube web series.

Jesse and Sandy were out and about queers and frequented the gay bar downtown. They were both people who others pointed out in a crowd. People wanted to know if they were in the same place as them. They were both hot. After a matter of time, they were a thing. Sandy mentioned that Jesse had rescued her. They went out, did stuff together, and sex naturally ensued, conveniently, since they were always together. Everybody knew each of them, but people were beginning to know the new them, each as a couple.

As they ate their food and blotted at bingo cards, Jesse asked, "How do you make it work?"

Jesse and Sandy were talking about making deeper commitments, making time for each other. Christine was floored, blushing, almost doubtful they were asking for advice. The couple of the century, yeah, right. Christine and Terrie were trying. For most couples, it took multiple tries.

In a way, it was good to see another couple struggling with getting serious. Christine and Terrie had gotten past that. They were serious. They couldn't cope or adjust or gel with where they were. They were still working the logistics out. Debating ensured a healthy relationship. Christine didn't mention any of this to the people across the table.

Jesse won a free beer, which was perfect considering they were the only one who liked craft beer anyway. Terrie won three sets of beads toward the end of the night. The beads were weird, and she gave them to the people at the table next to them. When they showed interest with an "Aw. I wish I would have at least gotten beads," Christine handed them over. The rest of the games were a bust, but none of them would shy away from another double date at drag bingo.

Here they were—the happy couple who went on double dates. They were becoming known and seen. It solidified their status as an item. They were easing into normal coupled life.

Christine and Terrie sat at the coffee table and took bites out of their food in silence. Certain subjects were not broached. She had no way to begin. Terrie had made this fantastic breakfast. They were going to spend all day with each other. If Christine bellowed accusations at her, she might cave the relationship.

"I talked to Amy the other day." Christine poked at her quiche but didn't want Terrie to think she didn't appreciate it. "She said you were outside her place. How's she doing?" Her tone reeked of suspicion and accusation even though she reserved a lot.

"Oh, Amy. Yeah, she's good. I mean, I was talking to Rebecca, and I guess some things have me worried."

"Oh, Rebecca. How's she doing?" Christine was going to hit the nail straight through even though she didn't know where she was aiming. She took another bite of the eggs and tried to listen, provoke Terrie to speak.

"What? It's not a big deal. I'm worried about Amy. I was checking on her for Rebecca. I was hoping to run into her. Amy's building is around the corner from my morning class. I walk by it. Why not walk by Amy's building on my break if I'm killing time?" Terrie asked. She gulped another bite of quiche and dipped her head, delighted.

Christine was apprehensive, unconvinced. Christine couldn't surmise that Terrie cared for Amy any more than she did. She was skeptical of her actions, almost accusatory. "You're worried about Amy—" Christine questioned, shaking her head in disbelief. Christine couldn't extract any data from Terrie. She poked and prodded, fiddled with the circuits.

"Okay. Okay. Rebecca told me not to tell anyone, but Amy is suicidal. Rebecca thinks she is going to do something drastic. It's her girlfriend. She's toying with her emotions. I know it's her. I know Amy and I aren't the best of friends, but I was legitimately worried. I wanted to check on her. Who is she anyway? No one knows her. She can't hurt Amy," Terrie said.

Terrie stabbed her fork into the eggs, adamant, making a point, spitting out words. "Well, I was snooping. I had to find out what was going on. Rebecca told me Amy went on crying for days."

All at once, understood as never before, Terrie was trying to run into Amy, to gauge or ask questions. The approach might be taken so many ways. It was not out of character for Terrie to be discreet about something, but this, like no other instance, must be understated because it was uncalled for. Or, she was cheating.

"It's just, you can't stalk Amy. She's not suicidal. It looks weird. You know if anything is going on, we will work it out. Tell me." They had talked about an open relationship before, and Christine would break up with Terrie if that were what she wanted. She had seen how it went on and was not interested in the painful process of breaking up.

"She is. I believe Rebecca. According to Rebecca, Amy wouldn't get out of bed, at least. In the last episode, Amy stayed in bed all day for days at a time. That was years ago, but still." Terrie mostly looked down while she talked.

Terrie didn't know more about Amy than her. Terrie had no idea. Christine was very close to her. The thing was Terrie didn't know, and perhaps Christine hid it from Terrie, didn't want Terrie to get jealous or expose Amy. The story belonged to her. But now it was all out before them. Stunted, offended, Christine didn't know what to say.

Christine resigned to leave it as it was, with her in disbelief, and Terrie done saying the last words. Christine grabbed the dishes out of Terrie's hand and made her way to the kitchen. She would do the dishes right away and her project for class later. She would go on the bike ride and picnic with Terrie.

Christine tried to keep the momentum going. The positive date, the great sex, the open talks with no yelling. They were both pausing and listening. Who needed therapy? They were adjusting and learning to be better with each other on their own. Maybe love is grown. It takes time to learn each other's intricacies—go through the worst of it to find the best of it.

Christine made sandwiches: ham and provolone. They hadn't shopped together yet. Each still got whatever groceries they wanted. They often ate what they bought. Today, Christine took Terrie's provolone because the sandwiches wouldn't be right without cheese. She pulled out some Nutter Butters and put some cookies in a plastic bag. They would have fun; they would not argue.

CHAPTER FOURTEEN

TRUTH

CHRISTINE WHISKED TERRIE away this time. She merely facilitated someone else's trip. The full-day couple outing was, of course, a Terrie date, but Christine had planned it and didn't mind coming along. Terrie had begged for this day for ages, and Christine lost more time every day on her June project. She was the giver this time, and Terrie didn't need to thank her. Christine was grateful they hadn't been fighting and hoped to continue this way.

They got their bikes together and packed up two back-packs. Christine put the sandwiches in a lunch bag and grabbed a bottle of wine. Christine brought a small candle to make things perfect. A farce to some, she relished in their cheeky love. Christine brought a thick wool blanket to sit on when they got there. She had made it perfect. She had prepared the meal and everything.

Terrie set up the bike rack and loaded the bikes on Christine's car, getting it ready before Christine even made an appearance. Christine puttered around with her phone, sure Terrie wouldn't care either way, equally, if she wanted to help or didn't. They aimed to go down to the Rails-to-Trails for a refreshing twelve or so miles. That was enough to make Christine sweat and Terrie hungry for more.

They got to the car park, adjusted the brakes, and pumped up the tires. There was no reason they shouldn't take the day off, go on an alone date, and not fight. It was true that sometimes they were open like other healthy couples, and at other times they couldn't let what they were feeling come to the surface. Christine wanted a happy day in the sun. The stress of arguing was not what she needed as graduation came down the pike. Graduation loomed and decisions regarding her girlfriend and her career were not far behind.

The leaf-covered trees provided the most refreshing dampening shade. The muted hot beat of the sun in the open showered them with warmth. Squirrels were on either side, scurrying onto the trail and then off. The paved path supported casual bikers. They gaped left and right, swerved. A slight grade increased in elevation, so it would be easy riding on the return.

Sparkles of light came through the trees, and she

wished she shared the view, the image, with Terrie, held the moment together. Terrie would bike way ahead and wait. She twisted and put her butt to the side as she looked behind her from far away. It drew Christine's patience, but she did have a nice butt. In a way, she wanted to ride side by side. Shouldn't this be a perfect side-by-side lover's ride? Christine tried not to take herself too seriously.

Terrie stopped ahead at some ruins. A foundation, a chimney, and bricks littered the area as if a bomb had gone off. Nails and rust were strewn through the clearing. She contended that the chimney might be an oven made for a summer kitchen.

"It's perfect," Christine drew in, taking control.

"This must've been a house," Terrie articulated. "Probably late nineteenth century. Look, the mortar is flaking off. The gritty gunk was waiting for me to pick at it." She fussed with the bricks, jiggled them in their spot, investigated. "Flemish bond. The brick is in Flemish bond." Terrie understood a lot of random things. "I guess I should leave it. No sense in ruining history."

Terrie was interested in history, mostly early civil rights and industrial history. She never fully justified a switch to a different major from communications, but she read a lot. More times than not, she left a book saying it was all useless.

Christine read lesbian literature from the twentieth century, partially due to Terrie's inspiration. A bit of reading would make her more well-rounded, at least. She needed to take the time to explore, experience a personal growth, and she wished she had earlier. Now scrambling to find out what she wanted to do on the verge of graduation from graduate school, she couldn't say she'd ever really found anything besides what was in the textbooks. She felt an apathy and loss of direction, empty and mechanical. She wanted something different but didn't know what and didn't know what book to look it up in. She put two more tough years in and didn't question it once. Not until she met Terrie, who was so versed in so many things, did she open herself to ideas and other occupations.

"Just think, we could be a pair of young lesbians, taming the land. What do you think?" Terrie held a long blade of grass in the corner of her mouth. They had already conquered the land in the center of the foundation, smashed the foot-tall straw like weeds with their shoes to put down their blanket. "Why don't we move to a lesbian commune, work the land, like those dykes in Canada?" Terrie asked.

"If that's what I told my parents I was going to do with my degree, they would freak," Christine responded. Christine's parents would do more than freak, not that she cared currently—not that she had ever bent to their demands.

Terrie's offhanded comment might not have been serious at all. It was true, though, neither of them had a direct course after graduation, and no one guaranteed they'd be together. With so many possibilities, so many opportunities, staying together was the real question.

"Yeah. You'd build houses, and I'd sew or garden or something," Christine added.

"Or, we could be like the Van Dykes, go vegan, gather up the gay family, and take off across the country—I'm serious." Terrie stretched out wide on the blanket, head to the clouds. They had unfurled the blanket together, even though it didn't take two people to do it. They both laughed at their scene. They discussed how neither of them had ever lived in a rural place, or a vehicle for that matter, for more than a few days. Christine lit up life that day. The sandwiches and goodies were enough for a light lunch. Blush wine was tasty, even out of red party cups. They twisted their forearms around each other and drank. Wine spilled in spurts and dribbled down Christine's chin.

"I know you're suspicious of me. You were asking a lot of questions this morning. Maybe I am holding some things in, but I know you're doing that project. You're keeping the whole thing secretive. You're not telling me anything about it. It's the same thing."

"Uh." Christine was caught. She was so sweet today. She hadn't come clean because it wasn't clear if what she was doing was legal. "I met someone in prison." Christine's snark came through as a smirk grew on the side of her mouth. Now she'd done it. She would have to tell it all.

"It's such a long story, Terrie." Christine regretted every painful minute of coming clean. So much deception came from Terrie. "I fell into it, really. I told you about that woman I was writing to in prison. The one that knew Aunt Rose." Christine gulped wine. "Well, I set up an interview with her to meet her. I told her I was doing a law school project."

"That's got to be illegal. Did you lie to get interview time? Why didn't you talk through the phone thing? You can't do that. You're going to get caught." Terrie shook her head.

"The phone thing was so impersonal. I wanted to gauge the reality of the story. You know, who was truly at fault. So,

I lied." Christine kept it simple and to the point. That's what she had done. Christine shouldn't have lied, held information from Terrie. She shouldn't have lied to keep up her ruse as an interested law student either. She had yet to come clean to June about her relationship to Aunt Rose as well.

"I, I didn't tell her about Aunt Rose yet. I lied. I told her I was a law student." Christine became more and more suspicious. Terrie would never understand.

"Well, was she lying? Whose fault was it?" Terrie didn't even care how deep the crazy story got now. She didn't care Christine was digging herself to the bottom. "You believe this crazy prisoner over Rose?"

"I've done the research. It was neither of their faults," Christine said, punching her fist into the dirt ground. "It was different. That's what she says. And, she says she loves Aunt Rose, still does."

"Do you think she's lying—manipulating?"

"She has all these letters. I don't know. I wanted to see her face-to-face, partly since I wanted to know if she was lying—to see if she was a horrible person. She isn't, as far as I can see. Somehow, it must be a big misunderstanding, but Aunt Rose ratted on June. She admitted it was her fault. Back all those years ago, being a lesbian and out took on a different form. In the public eye, it was much worse." Christine tensed. She felt so bad for not blaming June, not saying Aunt Rose was utterly innocent. But Christine believed June. Her sincerity and heartbreak slipped off her sleeve. Christine's only resolve was she owed June something. She needed to make it right.

"I have to keep writing to her. It's the least I can do.

Eventually, the Aunt Rose thing will come out. She's gotta be so lonely." Christine understood June's emptiness in measures. "She doesn't want to see me anymore. She spit out some details and said that was it. I think I was too pushy. She was frustrated, I guess. At least, she mentioned to me I could still write," Christine declared. She drifted in and out of Terrie's line of sight trying to make eye contact, wanting Terrie to see her investment in this thing and know it was okay to withhold information. "I believed her, that she loved Aunt Rose. Even if I don't see her again—I got what I needed," Christine said. "I need to gain her trust before I tell her about Aunt Rose."

"Seems contentious. Who's to say she'll accept you after you tell her? I don't know, babe. You should tell her now and see what she does," Terrie interjected.

They quipped about appropriate biking outfits and how they weren't avid enough to wear bike shirts. Even Terrie, sporty as she darted down the path, didn't feel quite right in a bike shirt. It said something about her, her investment in biking. Still, uniforms had their merits, and when Terrie told Christine how bike shorts had butt pads, she was sold.

Power walkers passed, working up a sweat. Neither of them was sure about the rules and regulations of speed walking. They mused about getting old, what they would look like at eighty. They teased about where they would live and how they would get along. Terrie would be the uptight, quiet one who snapped at you. Christine would be the old nag, always cleaning up after Terrie.

Well into an hour, they continued to jabber about how close the squirrels on the trail would get to humans.

Unsuccessfully, Terrie attempted to feed one a bit of food two feet from her. It wasn't meant to be. Terrie, the farthest thing from an animal whisperer, didn't even have the ability to make a trained dog sit, after all.

They wrapped up the garbage, and Terrie threw part of her uneaten ham sandwich into the woods, swearing the animals would thank them. A lot of the day was left, but Terrie understood when Christine mentioned she had to get back to her thesis. Terrie had to go to the library this weekend anyway, and it had limited hours on Sundays.

As they pedaled their bikes, each person trying to meet the other's pace, Christine sought comfort.

"It's okay. I understand. It's family stuff. Don't worry about it—be more open. It's fine to talk to me about it when you're ready," Terrie said.

That was the thing. That was the difference between Terrie and Amy. Christine always worried how Amy would react, what would happen if she said certain things. Terrie and Christine yelled at each other, spoke true feeling, but somehow it bred comfort and honesty. They relaxed around each other, free to say what they wanted to say. To speak about June, the one thing Christine had held from Terrie, from everyone, was a relief. She was able to relax and hear an honest perspective. *It could only pull us closer*, Christine thought.

The sun was still high in the sky, and they made their return on the trail, a little short of the planned six miles out. Terrie rushed ahead and waited off and on, and Christine was okay with it.

CHRISTINE GOT HOME and took a hot shower before she set into her work. The warm water, splashing freely, relaxed and rejuvenated. Christine rolled back the day's sweat and exercise. She reached past the shower curtain and opened the door, trying to see around the corner. Terrie might pop in. She hoped, and as she breathed harder in the steamy hot shower air, she heard Terrie call from the living room she was going out.

Christine texted Amy to say hey. They needed a date for the gay family reunion. She sent her the dates she and Terrie were available for the next two weeks, three smiley cat kissy faces, and the words, "Let's get the family and get our gay on."

She turned the laptop on again, disappointed she hadn't spent the day working on her thesis and the night loosening up. Amy would review the grammar in the section she had recently finished. She'd give good feedback. It was only a matter of time until the semester was over, and a new life began.

After Christine had spent a few hours of rereviewing the literature, finalizing the introduction of comments and excerpts from professionals in similar situations, and getting the bare bones of her analysis of the last case study set up, Amy texted. It was like her to wait to text back, even though she had probably only been half studying herself. She wanted to look busy.

"I'll send out the homing beacon to the children and in-laws," the text said.

They needed to find the time more often than twice a semester, even though everyone lost touch and faded into the ether. Terrie would make something spectacular. Christine would make Terrie let her help.

Christine eased into school mode as the evening wore on. If Amy were suicidal, if she were depressed, Christine would be the first to know. She was there for her. Wasn't she? Terrie reached out as much as she wanted, but she'd never know Amy as well as Christine did. She was her best friend and her ex. She loved her and wouldn't hide anything from Christine.

CHAPTER FIFTEEN

NEWSPAPERS

A MUFFLING RAIN slapped the pavement outside, layer over layer. Christine couldn't justify doing anything different than moping around in the house. The lights had flickered, and it was enough to reassess the placements of flashlights in the apartment.

Terrie had left for work hours before, and the apartment felt removed from the thunder outside, but empty. The powerful weather, caving in her building's roof, conjured up feelings of a scary story you'd heard in childhood that still had a lasting effect. Hopes abounded for a night alone on the couch with Terrie. When Christine had enough of her mild dreaming, floating emotions, she went to her desk and pulled out the folders of information about June.

Christine was unsure what drove her to create this crazy chain of events with June, a real person, with real feelings and opinions. With so much out of control, Christine careened through the relationship. June had become so tangible with her personality and direction, which was so distinct from what Christine had imagined.

Christine pooled through her notebook and leafed through the pages of the small case file on June and the occurrence so many decades ago. A photocopy of her first letter fit loosely between a few responses.

Dear June,

Hello, and thank you for giving me your time. I am a concerned student. The details of your case seem absurdly unfair and ill-advised. I am at a loss as to why the jury found you guilty. All of the facts in the case point toward your relative innocence in the murder of Jonathan O'Malley.

As I have stated, I am a law student, and for a class project, we are delving into the details of contentious cases that didn't seem to turn out justice in our eyes. I have chosen your case as my case of interest.

I am hoping we can delve into a dialogue about your case so I can make well-founded decisions regarding the verdict. Please let me know as soon as possible if you would be willing to fill out a questionnaire and be available to respond to questions and have a discussion.

Thank you,

Christine Kurven, student researcher

Christine followed up the letter with a questionnaire asking things like: Do you think justice was served? What is your most compelling argument, at this time, for your innocence? What do you believe was the swaying factor in your case?

She couldn't believe where she had come from as she reviewed the questionnaire. Where did she get off? She suspected June also thought she was off-key, but she did her best and gave some more essay-like responses to some of the questions.

The answers, doodled on as they were, gave Christine a sense of who she was and validated her general feelings about the case.

In several reasonable answers, she pled innocence. These were the first things Christine believed. In the beginning, there was deep underlying anger and accusatory tone to everything Christine did, while she did research and asked herself questions. That was how she had even approached June in the beginning. How could her aunt be guilty? It was not possible—not for someone she loved—to do something wrong. It was unbearable to think your loved one should be in prison while someone else actually suffered her fate.

June answered questions stating the police force plotted against her. Rather than her manipulating Rose, the police had influenced Rose and the case. The jury was a pile of homophobes in her mind. She had no hope it would lean in her direction. These ideas sparked potential legitimacy. Christine was intrigued but far from convinced. The effort would require a lot more to prove June innocent in Christine's mind, yet at every instance, her image of the crime and justice blurred before her eyes.

Christine organized a stack of books, pausing before she continued to arrange June's stuff. To Christine the documentation was a project, albeit not a school project. She hesitated to pack it all up, leave it for bust. She had done neither harm nor good. Christine continued to stall, delaying the inevitable project cleanup.

It crossed her mind she should throw all the junk in the trash, stop harping on something that didn't matter. This investigation was never something she had talked to Rose about. The result wasn't worth getting arrested for who knows what. The only purpose served to satisfy some weird curiosity best kept at bay.

She turned to one of the newspaper articles she had printed from the library. She regrouped the rest of the materials with that one on top. She always reexamined the tabloid truth. The whole thing, life in the sixties, was unfair.

The newspaper article was one of Christine's favorite pieces of evidence, in that it resonated with her. The flimsy piece of paper summed up the tone of the whole affair. She puffed up her cheeks and blew out air in disbelief. It was as if it were an alternate universe, and the newspaper painted a picture of guilt all over someone who couldn't be anything but innocent. It was like everyone doubled the blame, justified the issue. They were so mad they were gay. The article read it was okay to accuse them since they were gay. They were guilty before the facts became clear.

> INSANE LESBIAN KILLER SHOOTS POLICE DOCTOR
>
> Two lesbian lovers, Dr. June Ashmore and Rose Carol Winster, are accused of shooting a police force psychiatrist, Jonathan O'Malley, in cold blood, outside his apartment in Arlington Vista. Authorities are pointing toward the involvement of both women in the incident.
>
> Dr. Ashmore worked at the same hospital as Dr. O'Malley, and coworkers said she went crazy. The shooter, Ms. Winster, is an ex-mental patient and suspect in an investigation into damage of property around the apartment building. Dr. Ashmore is accused of masterminding the plot and using psychiatric training to manipulate Ms. Winster into killing Dr. O'Malley.
>
> Ms. Winster said at the scene, "I did it 'cause I loved her." She is on record as saying, "June told me to do it." Police are saying Dr. Ashmore conned Ms. Winster into shooting Dr.

> O'Malley because she was trying to get a promotion.
>
> The description of the murder accounts for Ms. Winster entering the home of Dr. O'Malley at 7:12 p.m. in the evening. Shots were heard throughout the complex, and Dr. Ashmore was seen in the hallway. The gun was registered to Dr. Ashmore. Dr. Ashmore's involvement is in serious question.
>
> Ms. Winster was previously charged with assault twice and spent time in a mental hospital. She was seen as insane and dangerous by coworkers and neighbors. The neighbor who made the call to the police station is quoted as saying, "They were both crazy, and both deserve to be in prison. They are both guilty of so many things."

Christine wanted to rip up the article, remove the piece of paper from history and her sight. The thing stood for justice gone wrong, and she was fuming. Christine couldn't make things right and move past what society had done to June, her life. She was in prison and wouldn't get out, and so much time had elapsed while she waited for something she could never have.

Media had twisted the facts, influenced a society of people who already had certain feelings about LGBTQ individuals. How could these people not see this was an event, however tragic, the same as the next? A disagreement, an argument gone wrong. A shooting. The news had to twist the story, sensationalize, and garner public concern. The story likely rang in the minds of people otherwise occupied with their own lives.

She fumbled with the recorder and its accompanying wires. What would she do with the recordings? The accoutrements served as a disguise. She didn't need to record it. She only wanted to look credible. Christine doubted she would ever listen to the audio files again. She dumped the folders, documentation, notes, and recorder into a box once used for a shirt she'd given Terrie on her birthday.

Her computer, Hilda, she called it, had a bright spectral light and left Christine's eyes strained and exhausted after full days. Christine fiddled around with folders, moving June's audio files into a folder off the desktop. She wasn't sure she would resurrect everything, but she wouldn't delete them just in case. At the next backup, she'd put them on the external hard drive.

Opening the audio file on the computer one last time, she listened: "She was the love of my life. It was so hard when she told them I did it—to save herself," June mentioned, spitting out what she didn't want to say. It had to be spoken.

Christine wrapped her arms around her body, elbows facing front. This love was ebbing too high and was now crashing over her. Too hard to contain, her words rose as well. She had to get it off her chest. Or maybe it had been a forced fallacy, conjured up to make her seem more relatable, garner sympathy. Christine couldn't believe it. She raised her arms to stretch, feeling the heaviness of her hands way above. Christine extended sympathy to June in both decades.

That was it? Case shut? Christine had found this woman and given her respect. She had listened to her, a simple heartwarming gesture. Aunt Rose had created all this mess, sent her lover to prison no less. Responsible, culpable, she was at fault. How could she ever repair it?

Christine wasn't sure if anyone would ever find her documentation and see the same injustice that bled her eyes when she went deep on the case. It wasn't worthwhile to stumble around, fill in a lawyer, and present her case. Someone had already seen it before. Besides, June had a lawyer, a cheap attorney, albeit, but it was her life. Christine was too naïve, unaware, not good enough a friend to intervene and give her two cents.

June was up for early release. Christine might even make a character witness? How could she help? In her own words, June had remarked it would never happen, it never did, but she deserved any humanity the system of law gave her. Nothing took back all of those years. Nothing made it better, repaired the damage.

Ideas of law school floated in and out of Christine's mind. She might represent her case, pro bono. The sentence would continue years, likely decades, before she was even qualified to help her.

A GoFundMe and solicitation for money might help June get a better lawyer. Perhaps, she would do that. She would float the idea to June maybe after a few more letters, after she came clean about her relationship to Aunt Rose. Who knew how that would go?

June would feel betrayed and used. She would resent Christine for not being honest. It was surely a botched conversation or letter as it may be. She would again need to make it up to June. Christine owed her so much.

"You gonna help her or what?" Terrie said over her shoulder, a plain blank form in a dark hallway. She picked at her arm in a way between a scratch and a pluck.

Christine turned to look at her and voiced, "There's nothing I can do. It's not my place. I barely know her." Christine shrank in her chair and put two more pens into the pen cup holder. "I— What if it was her fault?"

"You don't have to do anything. It's up to her to ask for help if she needs it," Terrie piped up. She ran her hands on the doorjamb. "I'm making lasagna tonight. Better develop an appetite." She patted her belly, or what there was of one, and lifted her shoulders in a shrug.

"You're my everything," Christine lulled, grateful as always to have Terrie making her dinner. They kissed, as the moment called for, as a good couple should.

She closed the laptop and said to herself in a piped-down mumble, "Case shut." She stopped prodding. She wanted to be a friend now. That was the least she could do.

SHE EASED HER hands onto Terrie's hips and rested her chin on Terrie's shoulder. "Smells good." Terrie slipped away.

Christine wanted nothing more than a blissful dinner and movie. They had their pick of plot lines, even. In respect of their elders' struggles with pop culture, they were determined to find a nineties classic.

Christine took all of the dishes to the kitchen, intending to clean them later. She started to relax and unravel. When it was movie time, Christine sat on the floor between Terrie's legs, leaning on her and the side of the couch. "You know. I'm glad we have this time together." Christine pushed herself on Terrie.

Christine was relaxed. Terrie shifted in her seat. Christine shrugged it off as though she was leaning on Terrie wrong and moved over. Terrie stared off into space during the movie. They didn't cuddle.

"Come on, eyes here." Christine drew, trying to get Terrie into their romantic movie night. She was hoping they would both be in the mood but found herself connecting with the reverse side of Terrie's head.

"What—? I'm here." Something was bothering Terrie, and Christine tried to pry it out of her.

She sighed off the shameful conflict. At least they had a presence, time to be together even if they didn't connect. Christine picked at some lasagna that had gotten on her jeans. She swore there had to be a better way to make this relationship work, communicate better. Communication was, after all, a primal human need. For two people to do it well together wasn't a rare occurrence, but most people certainly worked at it.

CHAPTER SIXTEEN

UNSENT LETTERS

CHRISTINE ENTERED THE dampened house, muffled by insulation and sorrow. Christine stood and took in her surroundings: her great-aunt's house and what it said about her as a person. Her furniture smelled of stale must. Christine wrapped her fingers around the carved wooden claws on the arms of the sole dining room chair left from a set. The rickety thing had transplanted itself into this house, as far as she could tell. Thrift store purchase, Christine supposed. Aunt Rose owned next to nothing besides the house. Thrifty and reserved, she had never let on that money was ever scarce.

Christine had watched her leave to make monthly deposits at the bank several times, check in hand. She made do, but she didn't have extravagant new contemporary furniture either. Rose chose slightly dated, often gaudy pieces so she could sit on the arm and not worry about spilling food. She also simply liked embroidering. That's what she had told Christine. The furniture was so strong it almost deserved rough treatment. The couch patterns included small scrolls and florets. The armchairs mostly doubled as dining room chairs, claw arms, and rivets embellishing them. The oversized floral chair off to the side said the room didn't have a theme at all.

Rose often walked barefoot over the rug with floral designs, worn in several spots. Fringes splayed out at the ends. Hardwood floors set directly over strong joists. Christine had always loved hardwood floors. They were classier than carpet in many regards. She imagined a future home to have that aesthetic. With a few rugs over the top, leaving large swaths of bare floor, the room would look fantastic. In the evenings, when Christine visited regularly, she would slide over them in her socks.

The curtains, a thick ornate window cladding, hung rigid until pushed out of the way. The house should be *more* since Aunt Rose was so much more. She was a purple sunrise, ginger tea, a Dianne Arbus photograph, and a hooting owl at night. She held vibrant life, and Christine wanted her energy to resound in this dampening house.

Dissonant art hung on the walls. A latch hook rug decorated the sitting room. It was from the seventies, a relic. A Monet poster print someone might have had framed for her hung close to the corner of the wall near the kitchen nook. She had made fun of impressionism several times that Christine recalled. The poster never moved. Christine remembered that much. Another landscape had large swaths of farmland. Christine didn't know the artist, but she decided she liked it best.

Overall, it didn't seem like Aunt Rose's house. Someone had made choices, but they were lackadaisical choices or inherited decisions. She still hadn't impressed her resounding voice on the place, and for that, Christine felt upset. It should be more. It should echo her feelings and mood. With everything propped up, showpieces, the home took on a hollow quality. No real life existed.

Photos of people lined a small table with drawers near the front door. Her friends were in them. Sylvia and some other people Christine didn't know. They were not her lovers. Christine could tell. The frames were teal blue with gold swirls and plain silver metal with an art deco feel. Christine had never studied them and their dated clothes. She hadn't reflected on the expressions of the people in the photos. Now she did. She wondered about their lives and if they'd come to a funeral. Aunt Rose did a lot of listening. She had a lot of advice, but she never let Christine in. She never told her about her loves and escapades. Possibly reserved due to the age difference, Aunt Rose held stuff in. Christine wished she had that time to do over.

"She's sitting up," she said absently. Christine coughed to snap herself into the moment.

Aunt Rose had such great color. She looked vibrant and excited. Her lips gathered. Sun pooled in a hazy yellow square in front of the window, diffused by the curtains. The magical light kept Aunt Rose awake and alive.

Christine had come in the front door with her key, feeling guilty for not having come to visit Aunt Rose in the past few days. She threw the set on a key ring, and the metal jingled and tinkled on the "Welcome" key chain.

"She sure is. We're reading the paper." Some applesauce or other mush and a drink with a straw sat next to Aunt Rose. Uncle Mark adjusted the fully open paper. He held the news up in front of him and shook the thin, inked paper to shake out the kinks.

Uncle Mark slowly turned pages, pausing, as he sat and read with Aunt Rose. The room, warmed from the sunlight, created a cozy and relaxing place.

"Uncle Mark, what was Aunt Rose like when she was younger?" Christine asked. Ideas of what Aunt Rose might've been like in the sixties ran through her head. She wondered what it was like, how she had survived.

"Well, when she was young, she had short hair like it is now, I guess. She was tougher. Christine, life was different. It was illegal." Uncle Mark was edging away from the conversation. Christine was interested in Aunt Rose's life as a lesbian.

"I know. It's just Aunt Rose would never talk about things. She bit her lip so often," Christine mentioned.

"They beat up lesbians. It was illegal...to be with someone of the same sex," Uncle Mark relayed. "She still went to the bars. She still was seen with those women." Uncle Mark folded the newspaper in his lap, gathered the rustling paper up. He spoke as he folded, concentrating on the paper. "Your great-aunt was a liberated woman. She stirred things up. She had the spark of life, and no one got her down. Never for a moment did she think what she was doing was wrong."

Uncle Mark talked about Aunt Rose, and Christine listened. They proclaimed her estranged to the neighbors. The family got involved after the arrest. She needed someone too, so thankfully they provided assistance through the trial.

"She was a firecracker." Uncle Mark spoke about her outbursts in the courtroom. She itched for closure. It was June's fault, and yet it wasn't somehow. Her moods and emotions stuck out. Everybody understood or didn't understand, he guessed. Uncle Mark said prison would do it to you. She broke out in a fever when she spoke. Stress abounded, ringing throughout the room. At one point, she made eyes at June, crazed, staring with bugged out eyes. Uncle Mark said she was bitter but confused. When she left the stand, she didn't look over once. After she went home, she cried for months. "So, I guess she loved that woman if that's what you want to know. She cried for months."

Uncle Mark told Christine he was happy his parents helped. While Aunt Rose did her time, they were worried for her, he alluded. June and Aunt Rose were in the same prison at one point, but they got put in different sections. June was in max, and Aunt Rose had more freedom. Christine's grandparents gave Aunt Rose money to get small things in prison, and they developed a new relationship.

She wrote to them and told them about how they had never loved her. "We did, but she had gotten out of hand. She ran away," Uncle Mark stated simply. Uncle Mark pulled at his hands like he was concerned.

"When Aunt Rose got out of prison, we were there for her. She was part of the family again. She promised never to embarrass us again and to make us proud. It was amazing. The craziness disappeared from her. She was a new person—got a job. Stable and bright, she woke up on time, went to work, and came home and rested. Maybe prison did do her some good."

Christine winced as she listened. As if blind to Aunt Rose's sexuality, he remarked only about her subdued compliance, her ability to play the game. The family hid her in a closet because she was a lesbian. Embarrassed by the murder, her family's pressure continued, suffocated her true person.

Aunt Rose moved in with the family she was born into so long ago. She made that decision. She must've narrowed her view in the mirage of safety. She must've forgotten June, forgotten about their love. All that same time, while June was in prison, she didn't forget Aunt Rose. She still burned in her memory, from what she had told Christine.

Christine came into the picture late. She would've helped her be who she was. She was sure of it. If she had come out to Aunt Rose sooner, they would've shared so many more of her memories. Aunt Rose was closeted to that day, in a world with so many more freedoms for LGBTQ people than decades ago. She rarely made her friends known, and never spoke about other lovers. She kept so much from Christine that Christine had to pry tidbits out. Her fear ran through her core.

It wasn't so much she couldn't be out in public. Everyone had reserve and prudence with their sexuality to a degree. But she found it difficult to be out around her family, people who Christine imagined would never get her in trouble or chastise her.

Even Christine, when she openly stepped forward, continued as a shadow of her family, unable to be a real person. Aunt Rose might've been scared of Christine just the same with no reason to trust her, the same as the next.

"Sylvia was by yesterday. I told her you thoroughly enjoyed chatting and she should visit again," Uncle Mark said, interjecting.

"Sylvia? I didn't think she'd be back again so soon. It's good to see Aunt Rose's friends sticking by her," Christine said. "She is such a nice lady."

Aunt Rose did have friends who cared. She wasn't all alone. Her gesture to look after someone in her community brought warmth. Sylvia was no doubt a lesbian, another aging lesbian trying to relate to the world and all the queer kids who ran around without any care in the world. Christine wanted nothing more than to be her friend, too, and share her experiences and wisdom with her.

"She was asking about Aunt Rose's papers. She wanted to check for something. She's kinda funny, that one. She's always eyeing things up." Christine's mouth gaped open as she responded to Uncle Mark. Christine didn't have any idea about the reason for the intrusion. Either Sylvia was worried about evidence of something, or she was unbecomingly nosy. It was overstepping bounds to want to reminisce with someone incapacitated by a stroke by going through their stuff.

"I'll talk to her about it when I see her again. She's

bound to be looking for something specific. I'm sure I can find it and get it to her," Christine said. Christine didn't even know how to broach the subject with Sylvia. She would have to pick at the topic carefully. She would invite Sylvia over for tea again; that was a must. "Maybe she wanted to remember the good things about Aunt Rose."

Sylvia had a seat at Aunt Rose's funeral when she left them. She would tell her other friends, the ones Uncle Mark only heard odd tidbits about, the ones hidden from sight to keep things smoothed over with her family. Sylvia would see to the affairs and take everyone out afterward. Christine imagined her role. Their celebration of life would be separate yet more intimate than the ceremonious farewell Christine and her blood relatives would sit through.

Aunt Rose had one good friend in her old age. Christine only hoped someone would have her back when illness descended on her, when someone wanted to throw away her journal or her small collection of stickers or her first gay pride flag. Where did all the stuff go if you didn't have any children to clean up after you?

After Uncle Mark left, Christine went to the bedroom. Someone rolled Aunt Rose to her side, and her head slumped squarely on the pillow. Christine never revisited the cubbyhole in the closet. She wasn't sure if the secret box was left for anyone to find. The contentious contents might've been meant to be hidden forever. Or incriminating evidence could have been left as a testament so someone would know. She could, without vocalization, get her crime and past love off her chest, without ever telling a soul. Christine couldn't ever imagine Aunt Rose meant for the box of guilt to be a memento, but that's how Christine thought of it.

A strong feeling struck her as she waved goodbye to her uncle. She had never run her hand around the edges, all the nooks and crannies. The box had been haphazardly thrown into the hole and off-kilter.

Removing the panel, she peered in with the light of her phone. No spiders or creepy crawlies were in sight. She brushed the wood slats on the ground inside the hole. Between her index and middle finger, she caught hold of a folded piece of paper. After taking a second to curse herself for not looking closely earlier, she lifted the paper out into the open and the light.

This triangular letter, unpeeled brittle corner by brittle corner, was from Rose. The two sheets stuck together, and they crinkled as she pulled them apart.

Dear Beloved June,

I love you with all of my heart, and I will never stop loving you. Wind drifted into the window yesterday. The curtains only rustled. I thought it was you like I think it's you every time a car passes, or leaves fall. I'm blowing air out from my lips now, hoping eventually it will get to you, and you'll know it's me.

Do you remember when we couldn't find your keys? You accused me of hiding them, and I said you really didn't want to go out that night. We both went at it back and forth. I remember the look on your face, the red, not anger but sadness pouring out. It wasn't because you thought I hid them but because I said you were lying to me. You didn't want to go out.

The police tricked me. They made me say you did it. When we got in the fight when I came to prison, you were angry. I had "turned you in." It was the police who twisted my words. The night it happened, I was speaking from shock, and they twisted my words. But what you said—you hated me. You had so much hate in your voice. It was true the things you said about me being selfish and stupid. It was my fault—I took us both down—I did it in the first place.

The police said you were going to go to them with details of other crimes, other things we had done, people we had killed. And it all wasn't the truth. I believed them until the day in court when you looked at me with tears rolling down your cheeks—you wanted me to say I was sorry. Surely, you could never wish harm upon me.

Do you remember we still went out? We even, after all the tears and the sunken anger, made it out that night. There were yells. A few. I remember. But we hugged. It was a firm embrace. It always was. I've never had it since. In the hug, we dropped the anger. In the kiss, we moved past the sadness. Then, it was over. We were back to the day we first met; the love we held would last forever.

We went out and had a great time, and when we returned, we made a key hook. We made it together. I would've never done it alone, but you told me where to put the nail. I hammered, and we promised never to lie again and never to accuse. Here I did it again, and I lost so much.

You have to know I love you with all of my heart. They threatened me. They told me they have details of crimes we didn't commit. They said if I take back my statements, I will be charged with more offenses. They have our fingerprints at the scenes of crimes. They said the case would never be shut even though they're giving me my freedom.

I love you so much, and I can't risk more harm to both of us. I feel it is so selfish. It's not fair I'm not in prison too. I'm so sorry and guilty all at once. They said your best hope is at parole. I'm lighting this letter on fire. I can never send this.

Kiss back into the wind,

Rose

The letter trailed off at the end. The words "letter on fire," scrawled diagonally and lackadaisically, amounted to a scribble. The words spilled to the edge of the page.

Christine lifted her hand and lengthened her finger. Stiff when she pulled the tear from the corner of her eye, she pushed out a sighing breath. Aunt Rose, now over her shoulder, lay napping. Something had to make sense to her still in her incapacitated state. Her moans and grunts were trying to form words. No one could make sense of what she was saying or realize she could even think at all. There was so much frustration.

Here Christine was in plain sight deceiving Rose. She would be furious, yet Christine still felt the compulsion. The need to know more heaved inside her. No matter how back-handed, how big of a lie, she had to find the truth, and now she knew their predicaments. She had to make history right.

The clock ticked on the wall in the living room. The old box with sharp edges would tick, maddening Christine and likely any person under thirty. But the annoying thing some-one might call a piece of art belonged to the person who owned the house. A dampened clap would sound on the hour. It wasn't a tolerable single ring. Some might call it obnoxious.

She went over to the wall and removed the clock to shut it off. She flipped a switch on the back, and the last tick sounded. She felt apprehensive about it, but she removed the relic of a different generation, one that was too slow. Aunt Rose adjusted it every week or so. Christine had watched her do it, but never fixed it on her own. Since Aunt Rose's stroke, it had been hours off. Christine took down a piece of Aunt Rose, and she knew this house was like hers, too, but would never loose Aunt Rose's spirit.

Christine made herself at home. She grabbed some iced tea from the fridge and took her worrisome mind to the couch. She had a place in Rose's house. She made her feel like more of the person she was. Christine was sure of that.

While stretching out her back, she leaned over the coffee table, Christine got a pen and a fresh sheet of paper ready. At an almost ninety-degree angle, pen to paper, she wrote:

Dear June,

It was for good reasons, the whole thing, but I've lied to you. It was wrong. I'm sor—

Her story, her need to find the truth came with lies. She had to make June understand. She owed her so much at this point.

CHAPTER SEVENTEEN

AMY

THOUGH GENERALLY PLACABLE if she woke up at a decent hour, Christine was not a morning person. When she was up too early, this early, she went over the edge. Her bright and shiny morning would be a muddled mess of emotions.

This morning was one of those horrid days. Hammering resounded in the living room, and Christine was up. Her blood pressure rose, and she felt her body pulse harder as the anger grew. It was 7:00 a.m. on a weekday. She just wanted to sleep. Christine, irked and irritable, rose to confront the inevitable.

"What the hell?" Christine let out a deep yawn despite being awake from baby toe to matted hair.

"They fucking forgot a bolt. How could they package this up and sell it and forget pieces—pieces integral to putting it together? I'm going to have to go back to Ikea." Ikea was affordable. They chose Ikea. With Terrie's experiences and woodworking skills, making shelves by hand should've been a breeze, but it took time. It would be heavy. In reality, Ikea simply proved more affordable.

"I'd go to the hardware store and pick it up, but these bolts are only used by Ikea. No one else uses them because it's fucking idiotic not to have a standard bolt." Terrie hammered hard into the brand-new television stand until the pulp center split. "Decision made. Fuck Ikea."

"Um, you're scaring me, and it's 7:00 a.m." Christine was struggling to get Terrie to calm down.

It wasn't the first time Terrie had gone bat-shit mad. It was getting out of hand. Any tiny reaction would set her off.

"Look. It's over. I broke the crappy thing. No worries."

"I'm starting my morning, getting a shower and a coffee. Then, I'm going to Amy's. I have to help her friend with her computer. Damn thing froze, and we think it's because of updates not going through."

Terrie cut in. "Figures." She visibly moped. She dropped the hammer and threw small pegs and metal screwlike things at a bag about four feet away. "Why do you like her so much, anyway? What does she do for you?"

"Uh, she's my friend for one thing. Why do you care?"

Terrie never got it. She was stuck on what happened

and what didn't happen, which was nothing. Healthy relationships were important. The friendship Christine had with Amy helped her get through things. Christine didn't want to share every shred of intimacy she had with Amy with Terrie. Terrie got jealous of every conversation Christine and Amy had without her: the decisions they made on political issues, the people they talked about behind their backs, and the good movie they watched together. Christine just couldn't give her exactly what she needed. Her relationship with Amy was somehow a big chunk of Christine, something she needed, but something she needed to keep at bay. A whole different Christine was left for Terrie, but she was unsure if it was enough for her.

"Because I love you. That's why."

"Nothing will ever happen between Amy and me. We're over. Just trust me on this. There's certain things about her I just can't fall in love with." Christine was serious. They were getting into a fight about someone else, someone who never heard the argument. The unbridled yelling wasn't about Christine and Terrie, but Christine and Amy. She didn't need to feel guilty for having a best friend.

"It's—I love you. That stuff." Terrie lifted her head up and blinked. She pushed out her bottom lip and gave sad, imploring eyes. "Please love me," she pouted.

"I do. I do." Christine got on the floor across from Terrie and stretched out her hand to meet hers. "You have to let it go. We're friends." She grabbed her index finger and shook it side to side a loving metronome. When she leaned over to kiss her, Terrie's arms relaxed followed by her body. Christine begrudgingly had come down to her level and humored her. She was never going to learn like this.

When Christine left to meet Amy, the broken Ikea furniture was still in the living room. Somehow, it was the spoils of a battle. She picked up the hammer herself for an instant and banged down. Even if she wanted to muster anger, Terrie's emotions were greater.

AMY HUNG ON the open door and shifted the smooth surface in and out fanning as Christine came closer. They exchanged a big hug, heads moving past the other person's shoulder. Amy was ready for a day out. A friend's day out. Friends only, they joked. They both lived for these days, even if part of it was going to be spent helping someone fix their computer.

Amy had begun dating Jill a few weeks before. She was a chemistry major in her third year of classes, so she never had much time for Amy. Her course load was intense, and she had almost failed organic chemistry last year.

Christine felt a certain way about Jill. She was busy all right. In a way, she hoped their tryst wouldn't work out. Amy would be available for her. Selfish, she understood, jealous nonetheless.

"She's great," Amy commented. "We get along really great. She's quiet but fun, with a warped sense of humor. It's perfect for me. She makes me laugh." Amy relaxed and waited for Christine's response. She picked at her jeans pockets and eyed her untied shoelaces. Amy wasn't giving her much to work with at all.

Christine didn't want to hear about her. She understood enough. It probably wouldn't work out. Amy dwelled on fine details, editing her opinions all the time. She was more interested in their bonding. The semester was ending, and Amy was one friend Christine wanted to hold on to after school was out. Their friendship was ready for the long haul. If they moved away, they would still visit each other.

"Wow. You slept together yet?"

"Yes. Amazing. We wouldn't be together if the sex wasn't." Amy's face reddened.

A barrier still existed between them. They weren't together, and certain things were taboo. Christine didn't want to get too into their sex life. Someone was bound to get jealous or judgmental, self-conscious, and offended. "But not like you and me." She winked, flirting more than Christine ever wanted.

They both realized they should change the topic. "So, Ryan needs help with his computer. We could swing by and fix it, see a movie after. Interested?"

Christine replied, "Right. Okay. That's what we planned."

RYAN'S HAIR SHOT out every which way, frazzled by the morning. "I had a large USB drive, but the only time I ever put all my files on it was once right after I got my new laptop. My photos are likely gone, right? I had things like transcripts and tax forms too. Paystubs." He scrunched up his cheek. He didn't seem overly optimistic about getting his files back.

Christine knew that his photos would be hard to get back if it was even a possibility. The documents would be easier to resuscitate.

"A version of my thesis from three weeks ago is on a different USB drive." He flailed his arms for the first time. "But I've done so much work since."

Christine did a hard reboot, used the CHKDSK command, and let it run. She wasn't able to save any of the information, but she gave him the phone number of a guy who recovered files and photos off computers. He had the right software. Christine was positive he'd get the data and pictures for Ryan, but desperate action would cost money. The tradeoff would be worth it, Christine told him. He was hot and available. This piqued Ryan's interest, and his ears perked up. Christine grinned because he had a boyfriend, and they were very much together.

Amy joked with Ryan about his lack of computer skills. He needed to make a name in the world. He needed to learn Word. Ryan laughed, "Ha ha." He reminded her he'd helped her with a PowerPoint last year. She couldn't figure out how to make the transitions do what she wanted them to do, and Ryan used his "skills."

"Didn't you get an A on the presentation?" Ryan asked, sheepishly inquiring.

"Yeah, for speaking quality and delivery," Amy retorted. "All right. I do owe you."

She tidied up the kitchen in an expression of motherliness while they waited for the hard reboot. She, too, was getting sentimental about the end of the year. She and Christine talked about worrying, and the few people who would stick around in the relationships they had developed. Everything was wrapping up. As much as Ryan and Christine told her to sit and chat, Amy cleaned.

They drove to a diner to get some lunch before the movie. The local independent theater was going to show a classic film matinee of *The Rocky Horror Picture Show*. It was worth their time. At the diner, Amy turned serious. She had something bottled up she needed to talk to Christine about. It was imperative she, someone, should know, Amy said.

Amy tapped her soup bowl, anything but lifting the spoon. She was off in space. She agreed to things with grunts of acknowledgment. Amy began to repeat everything Christine said, mimicking her but barely paying attention. Christine didn't have anything to work with.

"Christine," Amy started. "I need to tell you something, tell someone." Amy swirled her spoon around in the bowl, evening the oil at the surface into the rest of the soup. "Someone wrote 'dyke' on my mailbox at my place. And it said, 'jealousy is for the birds.' Whatever that means. What does that mean?"

Christine clinked the edges of the bowl with her spoon. She swirled the tepid broth out of frustration and anxiety. "Wait a second. Someone wrote what? On your mailbox slot? In the lobby of your apartment?"

"They wrote: 'Dyke, jealousy is for the birds.' I have no clue what it means. Is it a hate crime, and am I supposed to be scared? I don't know what to do."

"Did you report it to campus police? They need to

know."

"Yeah. I reported it yesterday and took photos. I cleaned it off this morning. What does it mean? Who could possibly be jealous? Is that what it means? The only jealous person I can think of is Terrie." Amy continued to swirl the soup. "Of course, it couldn't be her." She raised her head from the bowl for acknowledgment, confirmation.

"Wow. Yeah, Terrie gets jealous, all right. You should have seen her this morning. But it wasn't her. No way." Defensive, Christine spit out choppy words. Of course, it wasn't Terrie. How could it be? Not one of their friends accused her. Amy made an offhanded comment. That was all. She was stabbing at air.

"No, of course not. I don't know who would have done it. Who could it be?"

When someone is restless and a victim, they try to place blame, Christine thought. It was easiest for her to name an abuser in an attempt to put a face with an act.

"It's fine. It was probably some rando. It's a hate crime. No lesbian I know would write a slur on someone's mailbox. It's definitely some homophobe." Christine, too, wanted to place someone, know the criminal, and put them at the scene of the crime. Not knowing was the scariest thing about all of it, not knowing when an assault might happen again.

"Yeah. I guess you're right. Do you think there are hate crimes on campus? Does that happen? I've never heard of anything happening, but I guess it does."

Amy had never heard of a hate crime in the time she had been on campus. Neither had Christine. They were at a loss for how to even react. No one had outlined a protocol for them for this at orientation. They discussed if they should shrug it off, like a catcall, but Christine was adamant.

"We have to be safe. Let our friends know. Don't keep it a secret."

They would both ask around if something was happening on campus. If someone was making real threats, they should all be aware, mindful of their surroundings.

"Okay. I will, for sure."

They went to the movie, but it wasn't as engaging as they had hoped it would be. No one was in costume. The tension in the air shook the theatre. The two had some odd laughs together, but no one was on the floor dying. Their smirks at the screen still had a bit of fear, and they were apprehensive. No one in the theater looked awry. Even if someone did, what would she do? Leave? The stress was exhausting.

Christine and Amy ran up to Andrea after the show. She had come alone. Her girlfriend, Fran, was busy. Christine physically pushed Amy forward to urge her to tell Andrea what had happened. She stuttered out an explanation, the whole time saying it was nothing. Who knew who she was covering for? Christine would have been mad. She was already livid. Someone had come into their world and displaced it. The defamation of property, let alone the psychological impact, was a crime, and someone needed to be held accountable. Her self-esteem, the part of her that told her it was okay to be who she was, shouted into the world this was not okay. Most people agree what happened was not okay.

The campus police couldn't do much. The cops took a report and said they would patrol the campus apartments more closely. They would station someone in the area at night. No one had come to them with other information. The only other similar incident was when someone had spray-painted swastikas in a commons area last year. No one else had reported being hurt. That didn't mean it wasn't going to happen. Everyone would have to be alert. No one launched a formal investigation. The police treated the report as a hate incident, but they couldn't do much. That's what they said. Amy reminded them she was a target. She was in danger, but campus police couldn't do anything more.

Christine reminded Amy she was a person. She, they, deserved the highest level of investigation. She told Amy and Andrea they shouldn't overlook them. Christine and the small group tried to think of ways to bring attention to the issue, make the community aware. They would tell all their friends, even before the gay family dinner. They ended up with the most effective solution, relying on the police. Christine would go with Amy. They would go in and push them to work on the complaint.

They parted in the late afternoon aware of their surroundings more than ever before. Christine wanted to walk Amy up the stairs of her apartment. She wanted to stay with her and hold a weapon. With Christine's acknowledgment of the severity of the situation, she became more withdrawn and fearful. Both of them guessed what was around the next corner.

Fretting with concern, Christine immediately went to the hardware store after she dropped Amy off. She bought some mace and drove right over to Amy's apartment. Christine felt strangely protective over the incident. Someone needed to look out for Amy, and with the best intentions, Christine thought she was the right person.

Amy thanked her and sent her away. She would deal with it, she relayed. The world was already too crazy to walk around paranoid and afraid. No one needed to shelter her, but she took the mace and waved goodbye.

CHAPTER EIGHTEEN

TERRIE

CHRISTINE SIPPED A beer and basked in the sunlight. She had finished a crucial part of her thesis. She'd made a breakthrough, even. Issues with the awkward end results were ironing out. So, she'd pulled a beer out of the fridge and drank.

Pushing away the curtain, wrapping herself up in the drapery, Christine looked down and glanced at Terrie. Terrie was three stories below. She didn't see Christine peer out the side of the window behind the curtain.

Cross-legged with her head down in a book, it was

unlikely she'd look up. People passed by her and didn't look twice. She took up enough space in the open area of a grassy patch of lawn beside the apartment that no one ran over her. All the passersby bobbed indifferently out of the way when needed. Out of the entire student body, Christine was probably the only one left curious about why she was sitting there.

Why didn't Terrie look up toward her and strum a guitar or recite a love poem professing her love? All of that might be childish, but her young heart asked for it now. Maybe Terrie would surprise her when she left. Sweep her up as she was leaving and take her on an adventure or to a romantic restaurant. She would be waiting with flowers in the car.

She did look up then, right at the window. Head on fist, book down, she looked up, scanning. But her eyes moved downward, and she returned to reading.

When Christine left the apartment, out of curiosity, she had to move around the corner of the apartment building until Terrie was in view. Her car was on the other side of the building, barely out of Christine's line of sight.

Avoiding awkwardness, Christine said, "Whatcha doing?" Terrie was on the ground, still cross-legged. Christine towered above her and swung her arms behind her.

"Reading," Terrie sputtered out, startled.

Still, Christine pushed for an explanation. A grassy knoll wasn't the most ideal place to read.

"I'm taking in the day. It's gorgeous outside."

"Well, we can go to the park and read, if you want?" Christine asked.

"No. It's just as well. I'm going to run upstairs and get something, and I'll be off. Are you going out?" Terrie questioned.

"Ah, yeah," Christine said, not disclosing she had spotted Terrie from the window, and came down to pry into the oddity of Terrie sitting on the lawn.

"Well, I'll see you tonight, right? I have so much to tell you about the drama with those two girls. You know the ones Mindy knows." Terrie got up, dusted off her butt, and kissed Christine on the cheek. "We'll have quality time, right? We'll make up stories about what people we hardly know are doing. Like we used to."

"Yes, Terrie. We'll have a great time together. What you said. What you want." Christine responded, aiming for her car across the way. Christine caught Terrie looking at her as she went. Christine's words trailed behind her, imploring and seductive.

Things added up in a vague way she couldn't quite confirm. Christine sat in her car until Terrie came out and left. Unembarrassed, she made her way up the stairs to their apartment. The same rickety steps creaked in the same usual places. At the top of the steps, she forced down her distrust. As she turned the key and entered the apartment where she and Terrie lived, she fully realized she also had secrets she didn't share.

Terrie's cubbyhole of a closet always hung half-open. A simple, two-foot-deep closet with seven equidistant-spaced shelves gave new meaning to the word disarray. It was a linen closet, but it was too shallow, and it was halfway down the hall. Meant to hold towels, the shelves were too close together and not quite right. Its mystery purpose didn't scream out. Terrie would leave the door ajar, rifle through papers, and read things for twenty minutes on end, all as she stood there. Christine never went in.

An uncovered bulb hung from the top of the closet, and a single string with a little metal end sprung up after she turned on the light. Papers occupied every nook. Years of mail, coupon flyers, and junk were at home. The closet said Terrie had already moved in. It didn't have a filter. A file tray sat askew on one shelf, while odd books with pages tamped down in different directions were high up on another. A wedged-in skillet stuck out at Christine's knees. She lodged a foot-high stack of used gift bags in the corner. The tragic mess was nevertheless her space. They had discussed it and decided Christine wouldn't go in so she wouldn't get upset at the mess.

Christine went right for the easy-to-dislodge packet of folders attached with a rubber band. Effortlessly, she picked out the freshly used items. All those things that would fall out and all over the floor.

The folders held several things. Photos of Amy spilled out. They were the kind Terrie had probably printed at the pharmacy. Terrie had taken them from her phone. Some were from a distance, and a few were up-close shots. One appeared to be a photo Christine had taken with her phone. Pictures of someone else stuck through the cracks. Christine didn't know her. These were also photos from afar. The candid shots showed her carrying on without looking at the camera. Christine found some notes that didn't make sense: a phone number, a few strings of numbers, an address, and a lot of doodles. A receipt from Birdie's, a restaurant off campus, for a burger and shake was wedged in the pocket. A receipt for a gun was also tucked inside.

Christine pushed the papers together, organized the photos into the folder, and put the rubber band on the way she had found it. She shut the door because she'd found what she was looking for. She didn't need to pry anymore.

None of it made sense to Christine. She acknowledged two things: she had betrayed Terrie's trust, and something terrible had happened. She couldn't bring the issue up as if it were nothing. She was snooping in things that weren't hers. Still, she couldn't go to the police over a receipt for a gun. She bit at her nails. Nothing, no action came in clear.

Christine wondered if you were allowed to call the police and put a watch on someone. The awkward conversation would be like, "This person is suspicious. Can you put out your feelers?" Christine was pretty sure this wasn't a standard procedure. It must be her job, not the police's, to look out for Terrie and confront her if she did anything irrational. It would be such a waiting game, and Terrie would never tell the full truth. She hadn't yet, at least. Christine didn't want anyone to get shot.

Christine picked up the phone and dialed Amy's familiar number. Their relationship was distanced to say the least, but she wasn't above a quick check-up call.

"Hi, Amy." Christine got it out. Right after, she needed a pause. Tables turned. Christine bared her manic, paranoid side. "How are you? I wanted to know if you had seen Terrie."

"Not since I talked to you about it. I assumed you talked

to her about it." Amy was not having the drama today. "You don't know where she is? You should call her."

"Uh, no. I know I could call her. I...I wanted to know if she was still being weird."

"Well, it's none of my business, Christine, but she's your girlfriend. You should get to the bottom of the pot with her," Amy said with an abrupt stop. No one spoke.

"Well, we're doing the family dinner next Saturday, right?" Christine asked.

"Yes. I'm excited. It's not going to be weird, right? I mean Terrie's Terrie, but we're good, right? I'm bringing my girlfriend, Jill." Amy had yet to talk about using that word. It would be interesting to see what she looked like and if she deserved Amy.

"Yeah. It'll be fine. Sometimes I'm not sure what's going on in Terrie's head. Do you think she's—I mean, is she off?" Christine hesitated, not wanting to make the interaction weirder between Amy and Terrie. She didn't want to accuse people of murder. Christine wished Terrie were the person around her all the time, so she didn't hear crazy gossip and think crazy things.

"No, she's weird and needs to calm down and act like a person. The world's full of people."

Christine left the conversation even more struck with doubt. Amy wouldn't speculate, and she didn't want to elaborate without more concrete evidence.

Over two months ago, Terrie and Christine had talked about getting guns. They went to the range, and Terrie shot one. Scared of the earth falling apart, Christine decided to wait until the next time they went. There never was a next time, and Terrie never brought it up again. Christine didn't want to be involved. It was easily explained.

The only thing they had been looking for was a thrill. The built-up anxiety of mass shootings and the need for self-defense had made them seek out an experiment. Perhaps, they could understand why people used guns. Guns only amounted to a bad idea. Nothing good ever came of people shooting guns. They had left the range at night; words were left behind. Christine was immune to Terrie spouting "come on" and scaredy-cat taunts. They'd glanced at each other when they got to the car and put on their seat belts to drive home. Neither of them had stated it was a good idea to buy a gun.

Christine bit harder into her nails at the cuticle. She couldn't blame Terrie, the lies and the secrets, since Christine was just the same. It had never come out to Terrie that Christine had slept with Amy when they were together. They were only together a little while, but they went at it. She'd always kept the close encounter a secret. Amy kept it a secret like Christine, and Christine trusted Amy to keep it quiet.

It was the end of summer, and they went to the beach, the backdrop Christine loved best for Amy. They were on a friend vacation. Terrie thought it was okay beyond all expectations, even though they broke up a short while before. Christine, while staring in the mirror, repeated several times "I am over Amy" before she left. They went on this friend date, an extended mini-vacation, and Terrie didn't care. She articulated if Christine cheated, their relationship would be over. She had better find out now before their relationship got too deep.

Christine hid every moment of the tempting kiss and soft cuddling on the patio. Friend cuddling, and they giggled as they did it. She also hid the night they'd spent in bed having great sex. Drifting into the night with Amy had her guilt-ridden, but it left a glow on her face. If they ever did it again, which they both could, it would be good. Christine had left that at the door too. When Christine peered into Terrie's eyes, she never remembered those moments with Amy. The love she had for Terrie was separate. Love grew all the months after she slept with Amy. She had been in the same room with both of them only a handful of times, and she had to look away because she held so many loaded emotions.

If she asked Terrie about the receipt, it would be like an interrogation. She wasn't entirely honest either. She and Terrie hadn't discussed an open relationship. Terrie would certainly break up with her if all the lies in their lives surfaced. Christine could do without intense conversations at the moment.

When Christine got to her car, surprised, ashamed, and indescribably teary, she broke. Her car was spotless. The exterior freshly washed, a wax coating freshening up the old paint. The interior gleamed. A pencil-thin vacuum or picky fingers had gathered up all the bits of pretzels, all the unnamed gunk, and every bit of fuzz and dust. The steering wheel shimmered, lightly coated in a glaze of freshness.

CHAPTER NINETEEN

ROSE

THE EMPTY HOUSE echoed for Christine. A strong wind rolled through and took everything away. Christine half expected to find tumbleweeds in the corner. In actuality, dust and grime were the only things left, casualties of housekeeping neglect from over the months. She took a Clorox wipe out of the bathroom closet and worked at the inside of the toilet before she grabbed the brush. People would come over later. She would need to make sure the dining room table had space for casseroles and snacks. Hopefully, relatives and friends would bring them. Sucked in by sadness, Christine didn't have time.

She didn't hear anyone in the house and confidently proclaimed no one was there. A distinct absence of sound gave the room a certain mystique. The hollow cave was without even a death rattle. The opening and closing of the front door would shake the whole house. A crisp chill prompted Christine to adjust the thermostat. They would come like a tornado and change every inch of the house. Every inch of the house soaked in the essence of Aunt Rose would wash away.

Aunt Rose had died the night before in her sweats, in the bed where she had been for several months. She slid into a more translucent version of herself, coated in a mist that wouldn't let light in much at all. Aunt Rose was only up to mumble every so often. The rest of the time, her body lay flat, quiet, hardly awake. She slipped into a cradle with a rustle in her lungs.

Christine stayed over last night with the nurse without Terrie. Christine took this time. Uncle Mark was there for a long time too. He left at night, almost angry when he complained he couldn't sleep on the spare bed because of his back. Uncle Mark's wife visited and brought some meatloaf no one would eat. Christine stayed into the night. She chose the couch over the spare room. When the nurse checked on her at 5:00 a.m., she was gone, expired.

The nurse rocked Christine's shoulder as she awoke. Her eyes opened without a struggle because of her unrest. After she yawned, she was fully awake. She had lost her friend, her confidant. The nurse made eggs she knew no one would eat, and Uncle Mark arrived at 7:30 a.m. as the ambulance was taking her away. Christine had wanted to wait for Uncle Mark, but he told her to call the ambulance. It was over.

Uncle Mark's big hug was the kind that comforted Christine more. It was a giving hug, not a sharing one. His embrace relayed Christine's pain was greater than his, and he gave his love to replace the vacant hole. The embrace gave Christine's feelings legitimacy. Her sadness was visible. Bulbous tears dripped one by one from the corners of her eyes, limp hands, and burdened shoulders. There was so much more to know. So many questions Aunt Rose didn't answer. It scared her to think she might answer them herself. If she were wrong, their relationship would be a lie.

ARRIVING LATE AND quietly, people came prepared for a funeral. The plot was off a path and over a ridge, and several individuals, most in odd pairs, had trouble getting up the slope. Some men in black suits with white shirts and ties helped the women up and over. Terrie held Christine's arm as they went up, even though she didn't need the help. Christine wasn't sure if the men in suits were from the funeral parlor where they had been or the cemetery. They were big, stronger than you might picture a funeral worker. But she didn't think they were family because of the uniform-like quality they had. They held clasped hands at their waist with a broad stance, looking out at no one.

The hole in the ground, which was what it was, was small and unassuming. Bright-green turf covered the ground–the staff in suits lined up several bouquets, some taken from the wake. Christine had the most tears. She was sure she made the biggest puddle at their feet as she wiped her eyes with her sleeve and sucked in the mucous gathering at her nose. The church hosted the funeral, but they kept things light. The pastor said she would've wanted a quick service. It was the most comfortable way in an uncomfortable situation with a family, one now deceased.

Not a lot of people were there. Aunt Rose lived a long life, or everyone else had a hard life. At any rate, they must've been all gone. Family came in from different places. Some drove from other states. From what Christine gathered, no one flew. A handful of friends, meek in the way they teetered around with a cane or walker, rested on any corner or heaved to stand straight. Christine wanted to know them and talk about their lives and Aunt Rose in her younger years, but she couldn't muster the strength to kick off the conversation.

Christine's parents were hovering but didn't engage with her other than a quick hello and superficial talk of graduation. Christine and her parents knew that Christine's relationship with Aunt Rose was something that didn't compare to her father's exchanges with her. He and her mother barely searched for Rose in the room at family functions. Christine, on the other hand, developed a bond her parents couldn't begin to understand. Their sense of family was deteriorating, and no one was making a move for change. Her father and mother gave her that day with Aunt Rose and everyone else who cared about her. They steered far away.

Sylvia was talking to an older man in a light tweed suit.

He was slim and aging, like most of the people at the gravesite. Sylvia leaned in and whispered something in his ear. He drew to the side, and they both laughed. Sylvia's black pantsuit and the gentleman's pocket-handkerchief were a touch too much for the funeral. They were about the only two who, while sad overall with tears in their eyes, held their chins up.

When the urn arrived, carried by Uncle Mark, the outside air dropped heavy and lonely. The feeling of Aunt Rose's house after the death, the tumbleweeds, entered the outdoor space, carrying her to her burial. They buried the urn and ashes next to her parents. Christine had no say in the location. No one asked her. She didn't offer, even though she knew how Aunt Rose would feel. Christine would exhume the urn once they had all died and would bury the forgotten ashes in a better place, never mind Christine didn't know where that would be, who Rose needed to be near in death, or where her remains should go.

WHEN EVERYONE WENT to Aunt Rose's house after the funeral, a lot needed to be done. Terrie stood by Christine's side when she beckoned her. The long day consumed hours while cherishing years. As Christine attended to family and friends, Terrie washed dishes or took out the trash. Although Christine loved that Terrie was there and was a part of this with her, they were both more helpful making other people more comfortable.

Terrie and Christine gazed at each other from across the

room several times only to continue what they were doing. Terrie might've been a bigger help by not being beside her every minute. And at the same time, Christine wanted to lay her eyes, and the bridge of her nose, on Terrie's shoulder and gasp into her shirt. It was the missing connection that made the next several days so much harder.

Sylvia had more warm thoughts to give at Aunt Rose's house. She hung tight to the same man. Her arm curled around his at the elbow, and her body leaned into him for stability. With her eyelids, at last, dabbing her eyes dry, Christine wanted to talk to the two on a rational level. Despite her newfound cap on emotions, she took deep breaths as she approached them.

"Hi, dear. I'm so sorry for your loss. Rose was such a great woman," Sylvia said, loosening the grip on the man next to her.

"Hi, Sylvia. Thanks for coming. I know it would mean a lot—and for coming all those other times when Aunt Rose was sick. I know she knew you were there," Christine replied.

They exchanged the long-drawn-out words of the depressed and wounded. After they stood looking at each other, trying to find the right height for their put-on smiles, Sylvia spoke. "Oh, gee. Excuse me. This is Leonard. He's an old friend of ours." She patted down her hair; the cropped bob might've gotten some hairspray early in the morning. "We were all kind of good friends, as you may know."

Christine abruptly responded, stiffening her spine. They were all gay, but they had no clue about her. It frustrated her they hinted around at things so much and couldn't be open and straightforward. "Oh, yes, Leonard. Aunt Rose talked about you too. A little. She never relayed too much, only you all were very close." Christine gulped, being it was hard to be open around frustrated, reserved people. "Aunt Rose mentioned you both were involved in the AIDS memorial quilt in the eighties. It was the work you did in the past that is so inspiring to my generation in the fight for marriage equality. I mean. I'm glad for all you have done." Christine was out of breath.

"Honey," Leonard said. "We know." He stopped short and shifted his weight, relying on a cane. "We're so happy you're with us." He relaxed and tilted his head as he stretched his neck, not looking at Christine in a new light. He already knew who she was, and he reflected on what they had both articulated. "It was great you were there for her." He held his hand out and onto Christine's hand where it sat still, resting on her thigh.

Twenty or so people drifted in and out. Everyone brought something to share. Christine needed to meet people at the door since a casserole dish by itself was awkward and unbalanced enough in certain hands, but a doorknob to contend with threw everything over the edge. She had picked up a meat and cheese tray and a veggie platter at the grocery store that morning. They were the least eaten things.

Everyone mingled in groups of two or three and kept their voices hush. People moved throughout the house and noticed everything Aunt Rose had left, things that would get packed up and distributed to Goodwill, an attic, or the trash. It would likely only be one of those choices.

When Christine returned to visit with Sylvia and

Leonard again, they weren't within sight. She had hoped to catch up with them again and feed off their energy. They were a recharging station. They were so kind and gentle.

As she passed through the hallway toward the bathroom, she checked in Aunt Rose's room. The retreat, a place to sit down. She walked past and leaned into the crook of the door to take in where Aunt Rose spent most of her days the last several months. Christine didn't think anything of it when her gaze moved to Leonard and Sylvia in the room on the hospital bed. When Sylvia shoved a set of papers in a drawer in the nightstand, she found herself put off.

"Hi again..." She trailed off, unable to scold them for going through things.

"Oh, gee. It's you, Christine," Sylvia whispered. She lifted the papers again. "We wanted to save the memories, the evidence." She smiled, taking in a belabored breath from the scare of Christine entering the room. "So much will get thrown away. We do this at all the funerals."

"No worries, Sylvia." Christine sighed. She would have given them the contents of the house if they had asked in the moment. "There's a bunch of stuff I want to keep. I'm sure Uncle Mark will let me. After I go through things, you both should come over and take some memories home."

"Oh, dear. Thank you. We didn't mean to snoop," Sylvia said, though she probably did mean to snoop, and she would have taken things. "It's— We'll find some things about June. Rose said she left some things about June."

Not thinking anything more of it, Christine responded with words before thoughts, "I've found some stuff already. Yes, there are some things about June. The whole thing was so sad."

From down the hall, Uncle Mark checked rooms and called her name. Someone wanted their dish back but wanted to leave the food. Would Uncle Mark transfer the food? Uncle Mark needed help. She left Sylvia and Leonard as they gathered themselves up, asking Christine to please call them to come over and visit.

"What was that all about?" Terrie asked as they intersected.

"Oh. I have to introduce you to Sylvia and Leonard. They're great...but weird, I think. I don't know. They were looking through Aunt Rose's stuff. You don't think they were stealing, do you?" Christine asked.

"No. I'm sure it's nothing." Terrie shook her head and continued eating the food she'd been able to stop and get finally. "People steal things, though. Maybe people steal things at funerals? I don't know... It's probably nothing."

"Yeah. You're probably right. What were they looking for?" Christine asked.

"I don't know. You lose inhibitions when you're old," Terrie inserted, taking bites. "I'm going to eat this, and then Uncle Mark says Mrs. Hardigan needs a ride to her house. I don't know how she got here."

"You're the best," Christine chided with a big grin. "They're coming to take the hospital bed tomorrow, so I have to be here for that."

She drifted off to the kitchen. Someone had dropped their whole dish, and it had shattered. They left when Christine showed up to clean up the mess.

Amy stood off against the wall, waiting for some

seconds with Christine. She came over as Christine fumbled, bending over with paper towels.

"Hey, let me help," Amy said.

"Oh, you don't have to. I've got it." Christine wiped up food and ceramic, dropped it in the trash, and repeated five or six times. When she rose from the final wipe, more of a smearing, in a sense, she greeted Amy with a stuck laugh.

"Thanks for coming. It's so sad. I know." Christine had introduced Amy to Aunt Rose once.

They shook hands and generally got along. She had touched Amy with her kindness and openness toward her when Christine's parents were still unsure. She hugged Amy with the biggest hug she could muster and let it drop from her shoulders in a sudden shrug.

"She was such a great lady. So sweet and kind. She treated you so well," Amy said, offering kind words. She leaned on the wall with her arms crossed and looked at Christine, asking her to be okay with her eyes.

"I know it's so much. It's been a crazy day. I'm glad you came."

As Christine moved past Amy, Terrie looked right at them. She sat with her butt against the wall, hands deep in pockets. She wouldn't come over. Christine was afraid to wave her in. She stared with the lightest grin, a lukewarm smirk, and a questioning face.

THE NEXT MORNING, Terrie asked why Amy had come. It was a place for anyone who had memories. Her jealousy was palpable. She didn't need to compete; Amy was over, had been over. Terrie's foggy eyes imagined the past and projected it onto the present.

UNCLE MARK PICKED Christine up at her front door to take her to meet with the lawyer and get lunch. At lunch, they talked about Christine's schoolwork and what she was going to do after graduation. Christine mentioned the rockiness of her relationship with her parents, but Uncle Mark changed the topic, not wanting to engage. Following this, Christine ate her burger in reserved bites. A conversation about her girlfriend would be unwanted as well. If she were to bring it up, she imagined herself speaking loudly, bluntly, and awkwardly to someone unreceptive and stunted, who wished she would quiet down.

Uncle Mark's eyes wandered around the room. Perturbed, he held his lips tight the whole time. He was trying to regulate from Aunt Rose's death, and perhaps he was becoming aware of his mortality.

When they arrived at the office, they both took seats opposite the lawyer with a large wood desk between them. Christine hadn't fully expected to be in the will. She had desperately imagined when she went to see Aunt Rose something would be left. Realistically, she assumed everything would go to Uncle Mark, a successful retired businessman who footed the bill for her in-home care nurse.

Christine, dumbfounded, was in a room with a lawyer, and a document extended from his hands. She had inherited

Aunt Rose's house and some money to cover taxes and insurance for a few years. The tear in the corner of Christine's eye was part leftover sadness, and part regret she hadn't done more. Humbled by the news, she slouched into her seat.

Aunt Rose left a sum of money to Uncle Mark and an amount to Christine's father. She also gave Uncle Mark the car. Uncle Mark held a tight smile, and Christine could see he wished Aunt Rose had left him the house. He didn't contest her decision though and held his hand to Christine's back as they went, saying they would find someone to help sort everything out. He didn't seem sure Christine was adult enough to handle a house, especially with parents she was currently feuding with more than ever.

Christine wanted to live in the house. The peaceful and convenient location would allow for easy trips to familiar places. The yard was great, and it had a garage. In her mind, she was mowing the lawn on weekday nights and throwing parties on the weekend.

She was glad she had enough extra cash to make that happen. She wouldn't need to sell. It left her in the same state, the same area even after graduation, and she was okay with it. She had grown to like the city and the sense of community she had developed with friends. She would tend her new roots in her aunt's home.

CHAPTER TWENTY

BEFORE — 1974

My Love June,

It's so good to talk to you again, lovely. I'm having such a hard time. I never go out, and everything is so scary. The world is so big and bold. It's too much for me without you. I screamed for a full half hour wanting you by my side. I know it's crazy. Any person would. I know it won't do any good. I won't remember the things that separated us. I can't. I can only think about our lives and how they'll be. I think of you often. You're by my side, and you hear the things I hear. When I talk, I talk with you in mind and think of what you'd say. It's always something good. I want to share the world with you. I want you to come with me when I go out into the world. I'm trying every day to get up the courage to go out.

I think my aunt and uncle will freak if I go anywhere alone. They're not used to it. They're suspicious. It will be hard to pull the wool over their eyes. They're bound to know if I run into anyone. Maybe, that's why I'm so scared to go out. I know they'll kick me out, and I'll be on the street. I'll die out there. It's winter, even. I'm not sure if I'll go. I have to think it over some more, but I wanted you to know I'm thinking about it.

Do you remember when we first met? 1957. I remember all the moments, all the feelings, regardless of place. The way you looked at me. I was lost and afraid. Nothing was wrong with me. You knew. My head was down, and I walked around lost. There was no way to fight so much hate, so much accusation. You watched me and waited from afar. Our eyes didn't meet until I was in your space, summoned. When I looked up, when we were alone, your love was so much, so much. You were the one who had love before me. You told me. You told me it was okay to love.

I remember my broken watch. You were going to

have it fixed for me. I never could've afforded it without you. You were my savior so many times. What I would give for that watch now, something you touched, something to hold close. I'm not sure if they took it when they searched your apartment or even where any of it went. I relied so much on you, and now I am alone. Don't worry, my relatives take care of me, but I am missing you so much.

Lovely June, what if I meet someone? Could there possibly be another person out there to spend my time with? I'll never be able to duplicate you, but maybe I will try to find someone to talk to so I can stave off the loneliness. I want to speak to someone, nothing more. I will never give my love to anyone else. I hope you know.

I need to be discreet though. Nothing less is acceptable. My aunt and uncle can't find out. No one can find out. June, I'm so scared. I don't know if I can do it without you. I am so lost and tired and anxious and cold. I'm nothing without you.

I want you to forgive me, June. In some way, I imagine you have. Our love is still together somewhere out there in the stars. Even though we can't be together physically, our thoughts and feelings still comingle. I'm still attached to you. Nothing can ever break that. I hope for god's sake what I have done to you won't sever it.

Loving you through the loneliness,

Rose

CHAPTER TWENTY-ONE

FAM

SCALLOPED POTATOES WERE on the menu, apple pie with homemade crust too. They weren't sure what everyone else was bringing, but there would be casseroles and cooked sides. That's what the dinners had always been. One lone soul would bring chips and dip, and they would be over for the entire dinner. The person would be chastised. It would be a scene.

Even though they were a pair and, like Christmas presents, they only needed to bring one thing from both of them, Christine still had to participate. She would look lazy or like a freeloader if everyone agreed Terrie did all the cooking. Christine chopped some apples, swished around the kitchen, and cleaned up the mess Terrie was making as she was spilling and splashing. She felt better because she had a role. The couple's activity bonded them. Everyone was happy.

"Why do we even have an apple corer?" Christine asked. "We're hitched up, but we're not married yet." Christine slapped Terrie's butt while she moved past her and over to the trash can. They had, in fact, not yet been together for a year.

"Hmm. The bag and the receipt were on the table last week," Christine chided. She only hoped for the energy to bring up the other receipt she had found.

"That's because we're making apple pie. It'll be damn good too." Terrie bit into a loose apple slice. She wiggled her jaw. The apple crunched as she chewed slowly.

Terrie smiled and shook her head and changed the topic.

This dinner was about warm fuzzy feelings, queer friendship. It was the kind of dinner you relaxed into, even if you hated particular people that particular day. The one thing Christine cherished the whole year through were those days they got thirty-odd gays in a room and made them eat dinner together. The rainbow-tie event was a way to maintain sanity, happiness, and a positive attitude.

Christine didn't initiate the friend dinners, but she had attended them her first semester, then in the fall, then over the summer. The nights were something she hoped for. She took ownership of the event even though some of the undergrads had seen more dinners than she had.

When she and Terrie gathered up their dishes and serving utensils, they eyed each other and kissed. The happiness welled up between them, even if it was only due to the excitement of the dinner, and blew away any resentment, misunderstandings, and confusion. They held hands as soon as they reached the bottom step of the apartment building, switching dishes to a single hand, and they made their way to the car.

"I WANT TO thank you all for coming," Vic announced, head high, glass in hand. She was ready to get drunk herself. "You're all my family, and that's about all. That's all I need to say. Thank you for being here. This is my last semester. Wooo! I want to continue these parties, and everybody who's graduating better come back from wherever you are and attend." People were fading in and out of attention, but several people held arms around the shoulder of their neighbors or at least leaned in close. "Get drunk." Those in the room clapped and whistled. A few people hooted from around the corner, and all was normal.

Amy showed up late after everyone was already eating, dropping off her dish. Christine didn't want to seem too eager, so she and Terrie lurked in corners, and Christine especially avoided eye contact. Eventually, as they were passing to get a seat after grabbing two more drinks, they connected.

"Christine. I'd like you to meet Jill," Amy started.

"Oh, hi. It's so nice to meet you, Jill. I'm Christine." She bowed from anticipating it for so long. She held out her hand, but instead of shaking it gave her a big hug. Christine wasn't usually a hug-at-first-sight girl, but her open and welcoming sentiments couldn't be avoided.

"Hi, Amy. Nice to meet you, Jill," Terrie said.

The focus had been on Christine and Jill, Amy being good friends with Christine. Amy glanced at Terrie, perturbed and unamused. She wanted to be away from the interaction altogether. If Terrie had spooked Amy, she hadn't gotten over it.

"Hi, Terrie," Amy said. Jill followed with hellos, as well.

They all moved to a couch and chair out of the way. Amy sat on the chair, facing Christine at the corner of the couch. They leaned in and talked. Terrie slumped on the large cushion at the back of the loveseat and folded her arms. Jill sat on the floor beside the chair but looked off and into another room. The friends were conversing.

"This girl's been bothering me," Amy confided. "She's butch and very forward." She whispered as if she didn't want Jill to have to deal with it. "She ran into me like every day at the coffee shop and sat down. She wrote notes on napkins as she left. She gave me her number, and in another, asked why I didn't call." Amy had a quiet, perplexed look, similar to her tone when she'd called Christine about Terrie. "Well, somehow she got my number, and she's calling me—"

"I can talk to her if you want," Terrie mentioned. She was leaning over with stark straight eyes. Her right hand cupped her left fist. A bit of snark showed through.

"Ah, no. That's okay," Amy said. "I'll be all right, I'm sure. She's bothering me is all. Well, I guess it's friendly playing. It's unwelcome. I don't know. She'll stop soon, I guess." Amy kept catching herself, trying to excuse everything away.

Terrie looked over again and gave a firm nod. Christine pushed her. Terrie was always so stoic and chivalrous, too much in fact. Did Amy think she was going to beat her up? Terrie was ridiculous once again.

On their way out, Michelle stopped them. "I'd tell your ex to look out for that girl. She seems nice, but let me tell you what I heard," Michelle said.

Christine was responsive, playing into the gossip Michelle was offering. Obviously, no one could be as good of a girlfriend to Amy as Christine. "Oh, boy. Here we go. Whatcha got?" Christine asked.

"Well, her family's in the mob. That's what they say, at least, and they don't like it their daughter is dating this woman." She took a big gulp of air and scanned the room with the corners of her eyes. "Well, maybe not the mob, but they're rich, and they control like all the diners here. It's weird." Michelle went left and hard right. "They all know one another. It's some illegal shit," Michelle whispered.

"Michelle. That's ridiculous. They have money, so what?" Christine said.

Terrie grabbed Christine by the shoulder and tore her rudely away from Michelle. "We have to go. I'm going to pass out." She nuzzled up close, taking her by the arm so Christine followed, and they made their way out the door.

CHAPTER TWENTY-TWO

SYLVIA AND LEONARD

THE BUSY MORNING rush ensued. Christine had no time to get the place set up for Sylvia and Leonard to come over. They were supposed to arrive at 11:00 a.m., a typical time for retired people to get out and about. But it wasn't a decent hour for a college student prepping for finals. She continued to scamper about getting the coffee and wiping down the counters when they arrived. As Christine occupied herself rushing around, they talked amongst themselves and scanned the room for things that were different now. They pointed and discussed.

More changes would come. The pictures that hung on the wall would come down. She'd change the rugs. The furniture had to stay for now, until she got some real money. She finally had those hardwood floors she wanted. Terrie promised to refinish them before she moved in.

This place that Aunt Rose had barely lived as herself in was so strange. The suburban vernacular ranch home, definitively not a Frank Lloyd Wright, was eclectic but much less overstated. It fit her fine. It was, as Rose had been, in the closet in a way. Aunt Rose had virtually left the door open for rearrangement and organization. Christine had plans to use bold colors and find not-so-stuffy furniture. She had to be careful to make it not too much like a college dorm room, but she had great ideas floating around in her head.

Christine had inherited the house, but she was waiting until the semester was over to move in. She wanted to move some of the junk out and get some rooms painted. She had to refinish the hardwood floors. Terrie would have to help her do the work, the labor. They didn't have the time with graduation looming. She was too busy to go through anything but a large stack of junk mail and hundreds of magazines, mostly *Outdoor* and *National Geographic*, piled in the corner of the spare room.

Christine didn't want to think about Terrie moving in yet. Of course, they decided Terrie would move in. Christine constantly rethought whether they actually should. That wasn't to say she wasn't in love, just she had a weeklong headache from finals and was beginning not to value the concept of truth.

When Leonard and Sylvia entered the house, they

walked in and said hello. They wore what Christine imagined was their best going-out clothes. Leonard had a button-down collared shirt similar to what he wore to the funeral, but this oxford was in blue, a more relaxed cotton. He wore jeans, while Sylvia chose slacks with a comfort elastic waistband. Her shirt, a button-down with intertwined floral motifs, hung loosely around her torso. For a second, Christine wondered how these two had gotten here. Who had let them drive? Sylvia still had her license, and by the looks of it, Christine gauged she was well into her eighties and maybe close to her nineties. Leonard had large glasses that hung on his nose. He constantly squinted, looking above and into the glasses.

"Honey, look at that pile of clothes," Leonard interrupted, holding his index finger to his lips as he spoke. His tone was, in fact, quiet, but Christine still heard them talking.

Christine's uncle had gone through the clothing when Aunt Rose was still alive. A charity he was involved with asked for help, so he took liberties and picked out a few bags of things Aunt Rose would never wear again. He had never taken them to the charity, and there they sat through the death, burial, and up to present.

"She'll have to clean house. I'm glad I don't have to do that," Sylvia said as she adjusted herself in her seat. "It's so much. It's a whole house. She'll probably paint it orange or something."

Christine mused older people didn't realize how loud they were since they were going deaf. She forgave them for finding fault in the same instant.

"Hi, you two," Christine said in a condescending tone, although she didn't mean to be. "Here's the coffee and some cake. You liked the crumb cake last time, didn't you, Sylvia? I got the same kind."

"Oh, yes, very much. Thank you," she replied. Christine had forgone china and was using regular kitchen mugs and plates. They were much easier to grasp.

Sylvia and Leonard didn't have much going on, and they said as much. At a certain age, exciting things in life turned from going on spectacular vacations to finding ripe avocados and the right kind of pomegranate juice at the grocery store. They spent little time on answers when Christine asked how they were doing, how their day was going, or if they had any plans later that week.

Christine was dying to hear stories about Aunt Rose. After Aunt Rose's passing, stories were what she missed most. Christine wanted to know about the good times and the hard times. She needed memories of Aunt Rose to hold on to forever. Christine told Sylvia and Leonard about Aunt Rose and their time together, the stories Aunt Rose told. She asked about that time they all went to New York to try to make it there.

Sylvia interjected with a burst of exhilaration. "Oh, dear. We didn't go to live there. We were nothing in the gay world, of course—but in New York, they weren't big shots about everything either. They had their community, yes. They would have accepted us, yes. But we were outsiders either way. We were visiting the bars." Sylvia glanced at Leonard to confirm, even though it didn't seem like he had gone. "It was such a big city. You get lost up there. They were doing something, though—anything they could. It was 1960, and we wanted to see. If we lived there, we'd have gotten eaten up."

Sylvia rambled into a story as both Christine and Leonard sat on the edge of the seat. She loved the attention and her audience. Sylvia was up on stage. Her eyes lurched forward, not at either Christine or Leonard, and they glazed over as she tried to recreate how it happened.

Aunt Rose got in a fight with one of the women at the bar. She wasn't butch or femme, but just Rose, she told her. The woman, all studded up looking tough, without a doubt. Well, Aunt Rose didn't like it. It was true Rose had been more butch when she was with June. After being alone for so long, Rose did what she needed to do. She didn't mind doing things that took grit or using her strength. Not at any point were either June or Rose hard and true anything. They didn't fit into the cookie-cutter roles.

"Rose didn't need to wear a tie or arm wrestle the boys to know who she was. She held to it," Sylvia reminisced, fixing her hair in case someone would judge her performance. "Well, this woman. She looked at Aunt Rose and said if she arm wrestled her and won, she could stay with her femme. If not, or if she didn't want to arm wrestle at all, we both had to leave."

Rose was embarrassed and wanted nothing to do with it. But that was the butch's rules and they were in her bar. So, Rose arm wrestled her, and she won. She was mad. They were in New York, and Rose showed her up at her bar. They weren't even from the city. Sylvia mentioned they felt awful and put out after the whole ordeal anyway. To spite them all, they both ordered two tall beers. They were always weak beers as Sylvia put it. Well, they chugged, standing right in front of the butch, beer dripping down Sylvia's neck. She remembered the day so clearly, she told them. They drank the beers, she said, and then they left.

As Sylvia told the story, the butch wanted to go home with her. That's why the fight ensued, but Rose wouldn't let it happen when she insulted her.

"That Rose, I'll tell you. She was one hell of a lesbian."

Sylvia and Leonard, the odd pair, asked Christine more questions. They prodded in the nicest but bluntest way possible to find out what she was keeping in the house, what she would do after graduation, and if they were allowed to look around the place.

It was slightly weird, but they snooped in plain sight of Christine. Leonard got up and roved around with his oversized wooden cane, tooled at the top, giving it a more elegant look. Sylvia lifted things, papers, and possessions, and opened drawers and cabinets. Christine wasn't sure what they were looking for, but they trooped on, being as thorough as possible. It became much more of an investigation than originally speculated. They were not looking for trinkets to take with them. It wasn't typical of any mourner.

"Is there something particular you're looking for?" Christine asked. "Maybe I can help. I need to go through so much still, but—"

"We want to remember her," Leonard said, looking with a stiff stare at Sylvia.

"Well," Sylvia said, collapsing in an oversized chair.

She breathed out in a gust, and Christine wasn't sure

about the appropriateness of telling older individuals to relax and take their time.

"It must be in the lockbox," Sylvia interjected. "Rose mentioned... We were looking for some evidence of a certain kind. Rose said to find it if she ever died. There was still a possibility—"

"Oh, I think I found that the other day. I didn't open it, but it's in the hall closet." Christine moved over to the closet, nervously wondering, slightly put off and apprehensive, about what these two characters wanted from Aunt Rose's lockbox. She found the key the other day right on top of it. She was waiting to open it with Uncle Mark in case she found savings bonds or something in it that should go to the lawyer. She was ready to open it now for these two old friends who were seemingly on a mission to find something.

"Can you believe she left the key right on top of the box? Not much of a safe if you ask me." Christine was trying to loosen the two up so she could figure out why they were so desperate.

"Let me see," Sylvia interjected and pulled the box from her. She wobbled over to the coffee table and opened it with a reasonable amount of shaking for her age. She kicked up a stare at Christine, apologizing. "Rose would want us to look through this first, dear."

While they opened the box sitting on the couch, Christine stood above, looking down at them. Sylvia riffled through papers. Christine found several savings bonds like she expected. She'd have to tell Uncle Mark about those right away. A manila envelope fastened with a brass clasp rested in the middle of the mess. The dust-coated envelope had dirt that gave it a more mustard color than a modern shell of the same character. A rusted paper clip held some more papers to it.

"Ah-huh," Sylvia whispered before she even opened it.

Sylvia produced a folded photo that said, "Die bulldaggers" across what appeared to be an apartment door. The black-and-white and glossy documentation spelled out a hate crime. A sharp crease bent the gloss and revealed a papery texture. The yellowing at one of the edges and a grainy look was the clue the paper held age, but she couldn't find an exact date.

Sylvia opened and showed the two others a folded note. They passed it around. The text, faded and gummy, held a few key words. Whoever wrote it had typed it up on a typewriter. The horrid note simply said, "Die bulldaggers. You don't belong at this place of work."

A few faded documents littered the container: an unreadable receipt, a list of grocery items, and a photo of what could've been June and Aunt Rose.

"This is not enough." Sylvia let her hands drop in a clump in her lap. She drew in breaths through her mouth. She had a light wheeze, but she didn't seem to know or was at least denying it.

"Can I get you some water?" Christine asked out of kindness. She wanted to know what all this meant but didn't want another dead woman in this house.

"No, I'm fine," Sylvia said. She slumped and rested her shoulders too.

"You see, honey," Leonard began to say. "Rose, well. Cops coerced her into lying about her crime." He was resting on his cane as he sat but moved it to the side of him to see the photo closer. "June, her lover—"

"I know about June," Christine said. "I also kind of know she was coerced. There were some letters I found."

"Can we see them?" Sylvia asked. "We need to see them." Sylvia didn't care how greedy she appeared. This was a just cause.

"Sure. I'll get them." Christine paused and gathered herself, not understanding what was happening.

"We thought we'd find something, for June, 'cause she's innocent. These two things might help?" Leonard framed it as a question. It wasn't going to be easy to free June either way. He wasn't in the best shape to get a case together and fight for June at this stage in his life.

Sylvia turned to Leonard. "Maybe if we drop the evidence off?" She spoke dull and even, sober, and shrugged. "Dearie, your aunt didn't go to prison because June did."

Christine didn't say a word. She wasn't a lawyer, either. She was sitting in the chair across the room. Her face flushed when they spoke. Christine had come to this conclusion already. She needed to help June. It was her duty, her responsibility. So many things would need to be done before she began.

It wasn't immediately apparent what these two pieces of "evidence" even meant. It was a hate crime. Rose acted in self-defense. It was a loose argument, but plausible. At least it established harassment. The good doctor wasn't so good anymore.

Christine filled Sylvia and Leonard in on details of her investigation, her visits to see June. They nodded in agreement when they looked at each other, almost giddy at the mischief. Christine had already started to find justice. By the time Sylvia and Leonard left, they determined Christine should take up the fight. Sylvia and Leonard thanked Christine, a godsend. They complained they had no energy, and they didn't know what to do. Christine would fill in. It became evident it was better in Christine's hands.

Each of the old friends took a piece of crumb cake with them at Christine's insistence. They left out the front door, warning her that not everybody was good in the world. Christine didn't know what to make of this piece of wisdom, only they had wanted to say something, if anything, to help her along the way. They assured her she would call them and keep them updated—and wasn't she the best person in the world to handle this.

Christine gazed over the contents of the lockbox a little closer when they were gone. Sylvia and Leonard, the scatterbrained pair of do-gooders, had glossed over several other things in the lockbox. The box itself was hardly enough to make it through a fire or stave off thieves. The thin green metal must've been fifty years old itself. The noises the rusty hinge made when opened didn't scream security.

She lifted the two savings bonds and put them to the side. She would call Uncle Mark later in the day and have them given to the lawyer. Uncle Mark might even give them to her. They were only one hundred dollars each by face value, from 1989. Some coins were on the bottom of the box, too—a buffalo head nickel and several bicentennial quarters.

The box held a birth certificate, an old driver's license, and a manilla envelope. Sylvia moved right past everything to the envelope. The records were similar to the one she had opened with Sylvia and Leonard that dated to well before Christine's birth. The folds of a stack of papers crinkled, brittle with age. The edges of the paper in the manilla envelope were sharp, able to slice because the paper was so thin and stiff. The documents included patient records and evaluations regarding Aunt Rose's time in a mental hospital.

The records detailed Aunt Rose's condition and treatment plan while at the state mental hospital. The cold summaries indicated she was delusional, among other things like anxious and easily irritated. Scribbled over notes posed she was depressive. The homosexual check box was checked, however vague the ink. The records didn't gloss over it. It stuck out front and center on the cover sheet. After treatment transferred to Dr. June Ashmore, there was no reference to her sexuality, and the records noted slight improvement.

Aunt Rose's medical records detailed her course for electroconvulsive therapy, stating the experimental procedure should be performed within two months, and a schedule for "the treatment" was devised. A note included the recuperation plan and expected results. Two parties signed next to *X*s, one of which might have been Aunt Rose's uncle.

It appeared they never carried out the treatment. The patient switched to care under Dr. June Ashmore, and the records stated, "Patient exhibits unexpected improvements relating to depressive episodes and manic anxiety. ECT is not recommended." The stated condition of "homosexual" reversed to cured. A doctor penned a checkmark next to the determination. The whole thing was silly. Someone placed a checkmark next to a term.

After another six months, they cleared Aunt Rose for release. June was her miracle. She was slated for gutting of the brain. All the psychiatric bullshit concluded a disgusting procedure would cure all insanity in a snap. Aunt Rose may never have seen her record while she was in the hospital, but Christine gawked at the ridiculousness, the waste of her years, her time. Aunt Rose knew her fate and her miracle.

Christine locked up her new house, unable to look for any other clues to the mystery. The contentious life, riddled with years of secrecy and doubt, wasn't elusive anymore. With the story unfolded, she hoped Aunt Rose didn't have all the details. If she did, the pain of each jab, each accusation, each intent at harm surely slowly killed her. All the layers perplexed the story. No one stepped back and looked at the senselessness of the facts fifty-some years later and determined the case was clear. The verdict, June's substitute for a death sentence, wrapped up in previous determinations, shut convictions, and hard sentences, came down. Yet she couldn't shake the feeling the truth should and could make this right.

CHAPTER TWENTY-THREE

PLEXIGLASS

THE FOURTH PRISON visit proved as nerve-racking as ever. Christine played a role: investigative student looking into all the details. The only difference was she didn't have an associated class. That lie, an off-white lie, was easy for Christine to tell. Now, in the same parking lot, she had come clean. There was no way around the inevitable truth. She turned herself in and had to face the consequences.

Her well-worn sweatshirt, meant for Saturday lounging, and her baggiest jeans told a different story. They wore her lie on the outside. She didn't care if the guards noticed.

A different person emerged from her car—one determined to make amends.

She matched her car, leaving behind a fake stand-up character. At the same time, her suspicions and resentment of June vanished. She opened her thoughts and feelings, letting June in as she supposed her aunt would want her too.

She brushed the window where someone had left a handprint mark from the inside. No one had been in the rear passenger side seat recently. The print was a full palm. She wasn't sure who would have put their whole palm on the window and left. The tacky film left behind only smeared. She shrugged. It must've been her. She still cared for the beat-up, crappy car.

June had mentioned her visitors list was limited. She was only allowed to add a handful of names. She told Christine she should feel lucky. Christine did. She was fortunate June would talk to her at all. The response to her letter was heartwarming as she opened it. It meant Christine could write her. Instead, here she was, having been summoned by June.

She'd relaxed into the one oversized chair at Aunt Rose's house a few days ago to read the letter. She had been coming to visit, imagining the place a different way, trying to rekindle the spirit of Aunt Rose. She wanted to tell the story of Aunt Rose in the house; a story the house had never reflected in its appearance.

The letter had come to her apartment. That was the address June had. She stuck it in her bag as if she was hiding it from Terrie. She didn't want to read it in her presence.

This relationship she had with June was still sort of a secret. She didn't want to tell all or imagine Terrie reading the letter alone after finding it on the table or her desk.

Dear Christine,

You know how I like to write letters. I'm glad, at least, to have an address to write to if I need it.

I knew your great-aunt to be a spectacular person and lover. She was my everything, as you may already know. I still talk about her to this day to the women in this godforsaken prison. But a lot of hatred brewed between us because of one incident and the slew of horrible events followed. Still, I could only hope she could talk to me again. Because of her stroke, I don't know if that will ever be possible.

I accept your apology for tricking me. It was clever if you ask me. I understand you had to get answers, and I hope you resolved things with the questions you had. I have forgiven Rose, so that is why I can come to you now. I hope you have also found it in your heart not to be bitter toward me.

Please come and visit me. I've added you to my visitors list. They should call you to confirm. I only get so many on the list, but I had some open slots. I'd like to see you, the honest you. Please bring a photo of Rose at her best, to see. I still miss her terribly.

Sincerely,

June Ashmore

Christine had never been a letter writer until recently. She didn't know how to have one-way conversations. She sorted out ideas she had in her head, awkwardly deliberated. Letters were June and Rose's life. That's how they bonded—through letters the other person had never even read. Collecting and transporting their thoughts, Christine's initial intention was to be a conduit, show them each other's side. Their lives without each other were full of heartache and remiss, but in the ether in the air that blew from one to the other, they felt love and remembrance of what they were together. Christine's intentions and hopes for an improved health diagnosis for Rose were now moot.

Aunt Rose had died over a week ago. Christine went to tell June. She deserved to know. That would be the hardest part of the meeting. Christine wanted to get it out as quickly as possible, be forthright. She had lied too much already. Bringing it up first would be the best way to show she was honest, to show she wasn't hiding anything. It was the least she owed her.

WHEN SHE ENTERED the door of the prison, she was afraid, from the first step, a guard would recognize her. She didn't make eye contact and held her head low. No one said anything as she signed in and filled out a form. She sat in the waiting room for about fifteen minutes and was led to a long row of booths. Each had a phone behind a plexiglass wall. They faced each other burdened by the impersonal nature of the scene and without connection. It would be impossible to give a hug, impossible to look head-on into her eyes to offer condolences. A vague figure emerged through a translucent pane. Christine peered closer. She rubbed some fingerprints with the corner of her sweatshirt, hoping it would somehow help.

When June entered full of happiness and excitement, springing her step, happiness reached the opposing corners of her head. Christine only imagined the opposite as she was leaving, saddened by the news of death. They lifted the phones together, but Christine was certain to make sure she was the first person who spoke.

"I'm sorry. June, I'm so sorry," Christine entered, pushing her words to the obscured figure through an impenetrable wall. She was also apologizing for Aunt Rose's death. It was so hard to hear and see. She wasn't in the same room with June behind a plexiglass cordon.

"It had to be done. I actually see your perspective," June responded to her beseeching words. "Tell me. How did you find out about me? What did she say?"

Christine only thought about the Band-Aid. Her sullen countenance was not yet visible to June. "Oh, she talked about you every now and then. She was a private person, though." Christine picked at the counter, waiting to say the words. Staving off the bad news was easy, but the feelings of remorse grew. "It was when I found a letter to you...in her closet. I fished around. I probably shouldn't have. She would probably be angry. Would have, probably." Christine teared up. A few times since the funeral, she got upset. The tears flowed easily now, drop by drop. She couldn't hold it together in this prison, where crying was the biggest sign of weakness. "Aunt Rose died last week." She picked again at the counter. Her eyes would not move up.

"Oh, no. Terrible news. I'm glad you're here though." June looked okay for someone who had loved with passion and fervor. "It's been so hard without her. I guess it's true. We'll never be together again. Doesn't mean I don't still love her. You should too." June dropped her head down now too.

It might have been out of respect for Christine's tears or the weight of her sadness. Christine wasn't sure. Regardless, Christine leaned into the empathy June was projecting.

"I know you were her niece," June stated.

"What do you mean? How could you have known?"

"Well, first of all, you look like her." June smirked. "You're her shadow. And your last name. Well, I know some things about Rose. I know who her family is. There are people in here who got information for me. I wanted to know about her, think about her. Information is a commodity in here. You want to check up on people. Do you understand?" June asked.

"I guess. I guess I...don't know why you didn't say something."

"It's complicated. Tunneled information scares people. You wouldn't have come back."

Recovering, Christine raised her eyes to meet June's. "I know you're innocent. I know you didn't do it... They harassed you. It was self-defense. Wasn't it?" Christine wanted so much for June to say it was true.

"Oh my. Yes, it wasn't our fault. But that's the way the world works. That's the way the world worked. Someone got shot, died no less, and someone had to go to prison. Even if I didn't do the shooting. I'll never get out of here. I'm stuck with what I have." Resolved to her situation, June already tried everything Christine might argue. She offered no new evidence to make any difference. "I have been through parole hearings so many times. They won't let me out. I'm sure it's bent on the defense. The precedence of my case has been an example so many times. It would look bad."

"But I have hard evidence. I know for sure. I can tell them, vouch for you. Sylvia and Leonard helped me find some things—that after Rose's death—"

"Nonsense. I'll have none of it. I'd be homeless. You know that. You wouldn't want that, would you?"

June didn't want to hear it. Her joy had dissolved not with the news of Aunt Rose but with the change in topic. The words in the rest of her sentences drifted listlessly once Christine started to talk about freedom.

Christine respected this, even though all she could think about was June's innocence, how she could help. She would help in any way possible. They continued to talk for the remainder of the time they were allowed. Christine spoke about Sylvia and Leonard and how they were crazy old gays. Their quirks and mannerisms. She and June talked about what it was to be old, to see through an old gay lens. At last, they were friends.

June talked about Rose and how much she missed her. She spoke of the relief that came with knowing she had died. She was free from constant persisting hope, the need to be with her. Somehow, June was at ease.

When Christine left, when the time was up, she promised to see June again, and for as long as she needed a friend. She would be there for her. Aunt Rose owed her. She couldn't say "thank you" and "I'm sorry," so that would be Christine's job.

As Christine left the long hallway into another room that connected to the waiting room, a guard stopped her. He grabbed her from behind by the bicep and pulled her around. Christine froze. Alarms rang trouble. Her stomach sank to the bottom and turned over uneasily. A bleak fear ran over her face as she stiffened her neck, waiting for brunt force.

"You know June, right?" the guard asked, somewhat straightening her in front of him. He didn't move to manhandle her anymore. It was as if he hadn't known what he was doing, hurting Christine, demanding.

"Yes. We're friends." Christine, delighted she could say they were friends, relaxed into the conversation. It was like they always had been and never wouldn't be.

"Well. I guess she told you—she's up for parole."

Christine's face indicated she didn't know, but June had mentioned it in their first meeting.

"She gets up every time, but I thought you should know. She's a model inmate. She's never any trouble," the guard mentioned.

"Well, I hope she gets it. She is a good person. I wish I could help in some way, attest or something," Christine said. She clapped her hands on her thighs, still nervous about her blown cover, even though the guard barely noticed the difference between law student and dedicated friend. If she could do anything, she would do it. This guard, a young, concerned, friendly face, couldn't save her. It was no use pleading her case. She couldn't do anything.

"She's been in here so long," he noted, relaxing and slumping into his left side. "That's the thing. They never know how to handle things when they leave. It's so different. She's been here most of her life. I've seen it happen. It's an utter shock."

"Yeah. I can't imagine." Christine wondered where June would go. She assumed she had family.

"You live around here?" the guard asked.

"Yeah. Not too far," Christine responded.

"Well, she'll need help. Like I said, it's a different world inside and out. Especially when it's been so long."

He let her go as she continued to pull away, still bothered by the lie, the authority. As she exited, Christine knew she'd be back to see June as friends. They had bonded. All was forgiven. Christine hoped only to know her better.

June was this seemingly simple woman she had befriended. Anyone told her story, the real story, would side with June and her innocence. Beyond the prison sentence, she was a kind-hearted woman, a woman who still held love in her heart. Everyone lucky enough to know her could only be grateful to be her friend.

Christine wanted to hear more about Aunt Rose. All of it: the juicy stuff she identified personally with and the significant LGBT history she had been a part of for so long. In a matter of a few meetings, she had developed a taste for the stories, as she had through Rose.

Yes, she would return. Bringing her kindness and her ears, her sympathy, and her compassion, she would be June's friend as much as she could. She didn't take pity on her but acknowledged the impact she could make.

Christine kicked dirt on her way to the car. She relaxed, moving toward the prison, as one of many visitors. The car had a hard time turning over in the parking lot. She might take some of the inheritance money and buy a new one if it'd be a wise idea. It was tough weighing the need for car repairs and long-term savings. So much was on the horizon; Christine was making so many decisions.

CHAPTER TWENTY-FOUR

RECEIPTS

WITH ALL OF the furniture in the corner, she cleaned, rinsed down the floors. Two dust mops leaned against the chair rail. She should've been studying. Graduation was in two weeks. Terrie emerged from the bathroom with Clorox wipes in tow. She got down on the ground and scrubbed spots of gunk rather than wash over the mess with a mop.

Christine bent over, a blue bandana pulling her hair out of her eyes. She scootched forward with her butt, moving to the next spot. Her fingers rubbed into the wood as she did her best to make the place as clean as possible. She never knew when she'd get a good clean in again, so it was worth doing it well this time.

Christine's sexiness came to the surface, gleaming as she cleaned. Terrie watched her, standing with a mop, leaning on the pole, unaware she was supposed to move until Christine told her to clean. She needed to make things sparkle.

Christine felt insecure most of the time, despite her attractiveness. She often missed the attraction when people would try to flirt with her. She became a mystery to others, all while she blocked her opportunities with her inward thinking and self-questioning.

They were excited their college careers were over soon. Anxiety spilled as they cleaned. They hoped these behaviors, incessant scrubbing and picking away at even the smallest stain, would relax their brewing nervousness. It only made them more aware they were behind schedule, and once they got back to their schoolwork, they would need to work faster. Still, they let this time be a pause, a more grounded task than studying.

The buckets sloshed water on the ground as Terrie kicked it. Christine said, "Hey, watch it." There was no need for concern. They both cared about the house.

"I know you can make it, Christine. Do whatever you want to do."

Christine explained that she was trying to decide what she wanted to do but couldn't leave IT wholly behind.

"I mean, in career world, you find your way, right? Can't you do IT for a hospital or something? If that is what you are trying to do, be helpful?" Terrie asked.

"I do want to find something more fulfilling, something that'll make a difference. Is research a field I want to be in? IT for medical research. I don't know, but I guess it's worth a try?" Christine pushed on the table with a towel, not really interested in cleaning, but more in finding out big-picture things. She would clean every week for days to come. But the trajectory of her life was at stake. She would fall into something, prepared by college and grad school or not, and would likely follow that path. Medical IT led to more medical IT; you couldn't just go into start-up programing after working with hospital technology. You wouldn't be poised in a competitive world. "I can't just apply. That's the problem. What if I get the job, get excited, and take it just because I got it, and it's not what I want?"

"You're going to do fine either way. I mean, I know what you are saying. This is the crucial point, the tipping point." Terrie tapped the bucket lightly with her toe.

Off and on throughout the day, they discussed their plans. Each had a distinct set of ideas about life after graduation. They challenged each other with Plan Bs. Neither felt more fearless, though, finding their way with a degree.

"And you, Terrie? What do you really want?"

"I don't need a picket fence. I only need you." She smiled and cocked her head. "It's fine for you to get your bearings. I mean I could go back to school follow my trajectory too, but I'm not that concerned with it. I'm concerned with supporting what you do. I want to relieve stress right now. Your stress. We'll see what's to come, but search for jobs, take your time, do your research, ask questions of employees at companies, then apply to a place you want to work, not the job. I have the hardware store, and there's no better camaraderie. That's why I don't want to leave."

"Oh, honey. This is so much for me. You—" Christine leaned in with loving eyes and a kiss. "You are so much for me."

She would be free and in the job market. Christine had sent in two job applications herself the week before. Terrie was looking but didn't necessarily think she could find something better than the people she had. Each of them gave encouragement like a seasoned, proud, nurtured partner.

Terrie held Christine in her grips on the couch in the corner. They spoke sweetly in each other's ears.

"You are my picket fence. Whatever you need," Terrie whispered. Terrie ran her fingers from the scalp through the ends of her hair.

Terrie lifted Christine's chin, pulled her head to her chest, and circled her body with her arms. The moment flashed and continued. They were resting in this place. Their wings were flapping slower and slower to land. Without the tension of time, they shed clothing, littering it gingerly, and lay naked staring at the one light in the center of a room cleared of furniture. The clothes were the only mess. This was their home.

On the couch in the corner, they clasped their bodies, their love, kept it warm and nourished it. It could disappear in an inhale and exhale if they didn't encourage it, tend to it. They lay naked, alone in a big house, trying to build a standard coupled life. They were too old for themselves. They were beginning their adult lives, and here they were settling down for the long haul.

They laughed. Commune life was not for them, and they could make a home, albeit awkwardly traditional, in Aunt Rose's house. They would get typical jobs and see where it went. The house was still Christine's, but Terrie would get groceries and pay the electric. Christine hoped she would take her out to dinner more often.

Each of them acknowledged the other in their life, continuing for the unforeseeable future. Neither of them spoke of their insecurities or questions. They let this thing that was evolving, the new house, take over their course and make blind all other tensions.

AFTER THEY PUT their clothes back on, they got back to work. The diversion, sex in late afternoon, could only last so long. Once the clothes were off the floor, they could again see the gunk and grime. Tipping back Christine's head, Terrie gave her a kiss and went back to the bucket.

"Well, who's getting the spare room?" Terrie asked. She moved to get the bucket with cleaner and water in it, dunking the mop.

"What do you mean? There are three rooms," Christine responded. She was still on her knees, working at the gunk in the joints of the hardwood.

"Our bedroom, a spare bedroom, and the third room. Who gets it?" They were practically married. Why shouldn't she get the room? It was a gesture of commitment.

"We're going to have to toss a quarter for that one." She

laughed off the comment until she realized Terrie was serious. She wanted it. "Well, we'll have to share it. Office on one side. queer-cave on the other. It's only fair."

They were having a lover's quarrel, nesting together somehow through a small argument. They would be happy here in this house, the two of them. Neither of them had questioned their relationship in a while. They had moved along blissful partners, although rattled by tensions, and dove into this new endeavor. It was a step up in their settling down.

"Maybe we can work something out." Terrie was pressing her. "You could have the whole living room or something."

Terrie turned up the eighties new wave they were listening to and rocked out. She remembered all the words to Blondie's "Heart of Glass" and followed singing a Talking Head song when the music came through the speakers. She was a musical genius by her standards. Christine moved to clean scuffs off the baseboard. Terrie was so hot when she was working, even if it wasn't with a hammer or screwdriver yet. Christine wouldn't know what to do without her.

At one point, Terrie was Pippi Longstocking and tried to scoot around on two sponges. Christine laughed at the hilarity. Terrie was an inch away from falling on the floor every stride. The day was a release from their stress before tightening down for finals. The last bit of guilt about not studying floated away as she threw a wet towel at Terrie and fell on her butt, laughing.

Terrie found a slip of paper under the table with a single paper clip attached to it. She read it, trying to decipher it.

"Hey, this is old. You can barely make out the writing. Look at this." She fidgeted with the scrap in a perplexed manner. Terrie handed the peculiar piece of history to Christine, who rose from the ground in stiff, awkward jolts.

"Hmm. I wonder if this fell out of the safe box we opened the other day."

The receipt had a similar paperclip, rusted and gunky, to the one they had found when looking through Aunt Rose's papers. Christine brought it to her face to examine the faded words and waited for a sneeze. The edges flaked off.

"You can hardly see what it says, but it looks like a receipt for something." Christine was only infatuated and convinced the snippet was important because she couldn't understand who would keep a receipt from 1968. She stiffened her shoulder and readjusted.

She examined the paper to be sure about what she was reading. It couldn't be anything else. "Oh my god," she screamed. "It's the receipt for the gun." Christine put the receipt down and googled on her phone, sweating out anxiety. After a few minutes, she glanced up, glowing. "Look here; it's obviously for a gun. It says Colt Commander. Colt Commander, the gun, duh... You don't know what this means, Terrie." She fumbled with the receipt. It bore Rose Winster's signature. Ace's Department Store. The date on the receipt was March 4, 1968, two months before Rose committed the murder. This evidence, not yet entered into the record, proved June hadn't bought the crime scene gun. The gun was one of the hanging facts that made her complicit.

"Terrie, I have to get this to the prison, a lawyer. I have to call them. I don't care if it doesn't do any good. June's up for parole. They need to see this." Christine was riled up. She couldn't clean at this point. Terrie had found gold.

After Christine had read over the receipt, articulating each word, so the letters and numbers made perfect sense to her, she called the prison. She had no clue how to go about informing the authorities. It was a long shot to try to introduce evidence. She wasn't sure if it was even possible.

She got the intake and fumbled through a conversation. They kept saying she had the wrong line. Christine kept saying to transfer her. It wasn't clear who she should be talking to, and everyone wanted to hang up on her. A records specialist had no clue what her request was. Honestly, he didn't know what his job was when she questioned him, hoping he would help her. The records specialist transferred her to a case manager. She left a message. Later in the day, after considerable house cleaning, he called.

"Look. First of all."

He knew what he was talking about. That was true. But he didn't have to mansplain so particularly, talking down to her. The screeching of dying birds entered her ears.

"You can't call and say, 'I have new evidence.' You need a lawyer to introduce things. You need to get a lawyer. You can't submit that. Do you understand?"

Of course, she understood. How long would it take to become a lawyer? How much was a lawyer? He was such a dick.

All that pretending to be a law student did nothing. The padfolio and suit, the websites she scanned before arriving, did nothing to make her more aware of the procedures of law. She was no savvier to the criminal justice system than she had been when she went on a *Law and Order* marathon with a friend a few years ago.

"I know. I was hoping I might put in a good word," Christine parlayed.

He surely had to do something. He had to put it in June's file, at least. Wouldn't it sway opinion like if she had excellent behavior? It all had to work in there somehow. Christine was sure of it.

He paused and ruffled through papers.

Even when Christine said, "Hello," to prompt him, he didn't answer.

When he finally did return to the phone, he stated, "Look. Why are you calling? She already got let out. Lucky for you. I don't have time for this. This is ridiculous. Do you need anything else?"

"Wait, what happened? Where did she go? Is there a forwarding address?" Christine gaped. She physically stuttered on her feet. She moved into the wall and rested against it to rectify her balance.

"Uh—I don't have a forwarding address. She was released. I can't give you that information anyway. Who are you again?" What a dick.

Christine hung up the phone and headed for the couch. She shrunk into the cushions, and the room swirled around her. Her face went flush and vacant. Wouldn't June have contacted her? Looked her up in the phone book? She guessed probably not. They were strangers who had met three times. Maybe June was waiting until she got settled. That must be it. Christine leaned back and collapsed inside. She was worried and excited and had so many questions. Yet helpless and without answers, she lost her endorphins.

Terrie entered with the Chinese takeout on plates. She sat next to Christine. She had heard her talking in the next room but did not know what was spoken. They sat in silence for a good ten minutes. Terrie ate, and Christine stared off into space, relieved but anxious. When she, in the end, explained the story to Terrie, Terrie nodded and agreed, offering words of happiness. It was a good thing she was free and would find her. They were friends now. Christine would be able to help.

"Would you ever get a gun?" Christine stared straight into Terrie's eyes, unquenched direct and accusing. She had waited to confront Terrie, not knowing why they had so many secrets. It would end them. There were so many reasons to ask: her safety, her honesty, her intentions. Still, Christine had not asked. She hadn't rocked the boat.

"Oh, uh," Terrie stammered.

At once, Christine was relieved she wasn't able to lie any longer. Well, it had been a lie, but it was something hidden, not spoken when it should have been.

"You know we were at the shooting range. Well, I got a gun. I've taken it to the range several times. Look. It's a given you don't like guns, but it gives me so much power. Holding a gun makes me feel so butch, like I am this strong person. I hold this command. I know you won't understand."

"Why didn't you tell me? That's a big thing, Terrie. How could you keep that from me?" Christine shed dampness in the corners of her eyes. They glossed over but did not weep.

"I'm so sorry—"

"I need you to be forthright. I need to be too. We have

to make this work, and to do that, we have to be completely honest," Christine pleaded. She stared deep into Terrie's bottled-up eyes.

In one respect, it was reassuring and comforting that Terrie didn't try to hide the truth. For once, Christine could see that she might have held it at a distance because she didn't want to upset Christine. Christine in the same respect didn't want to smother Terrie. Almost as a reward for her honesty, however much it had to be pried out of her, Christine fell into Terrie and relaxed.

"Don't tell me you didn't have the best day. We were so happy together. It was so fun," Terrie cheered. "Remember. I am here for you until you, we, find our way."

"And June was released. We got so much cleaning done," Christine responded, elated.

"I won't forget any of it, ever."

In the morning, when Terrie woke, the sun was already up, and birds chirped at a water feeder that had grown over with moss. Christine. out of the corner of her eye, watched Terrie turn the living room light off as she left. It had been on all night, their lighthouse, so they didn't get lost in this golden new house, burgeoning love. Christine watched Terrie stop at the feeder and pick at the moss on her way out the door. Christine peered out the window every morning at the same bird feeder. Her sleepy eyes opened to see Terrie picking away. Abruptly, she turned and left. Christine went into a deep sleep.

Terrie didn't even ask Christine to take her to the library, and she couldn't see Christine's one open eye watching her. Terrie held her as she slept hours ago. Now

Christine didn't want her to know she was awake. She didn't want to ruin the perfect night.

Christine woke up, stretching with yawns in syncopated movements. Graduation was once again going to consume their lives. When she was in second grade, Christine had memorized times tables every day for a month. She had such a hard time with the logical figures. The strain, time involved, scraped life off her innocent childhood, memories, play. The same thing was bound to happen now, except it was a continuous love she would not understand. Romantic decisions would have to be put on pause. She reached up, stretching. College life would vanish right before her as she studied, a mask covering her blossoming emotions.

Terrie and Christine wouldn't see each other and have time like this for the foreseeable future, until class and homework, final projects, and studying were over. Playing house and falling in love had to be left for another day. They left their careless affections in the house with the cleaning supplies. They would come back to them—all in due time.

CHAPTER TWENTY-FIVE

SYLVIA

SYLVIA ARRIVED LATE. She sat down right away on the couch, her coat still buttoned. She had something to say. Christine sat next to her and then patted her thigh. After she urged her to relax, she got up and went into the kitchen to pour some hot coffee. She returned with a deep-green coffee mug that matched the sweater Sylvia was wearing. When she returned, Sylvia's coat was draped over the couch. She adjusted her body in her seat.

"Christine, you need to hear the story. That's what I'm here for, to tell you so you know and to pass on the details before I go too."

Christine handed her the mug with a lazy smile and relaxed into the couch softly next to her. Christine was happy to listen.

"They pulled Rose out of that cold and damp prison," Sylvia said. "Inside, the people Rose talked to looked for ways to get out, tried to make trouble. In the mental hospitals, patients walked around confused, not knowing where they were. It's like they don't see anything at all. Patients tried to wander away. Some were just as happy to be there than not, numb. But when Rose was in the prison—a prison this time, you hear me—they put her with other mentally unstable people, violent people who were also criminals. It was a whole other affair." Sylvia dusted the seat of the couch. "Rose told me about it. We talked about it a lot. Rarely about June, albeit, but the trial, the events, always. They haunted her," Sylvia said, remembering the conversations she'd had with Rose. "Rose cried every time.

"The corrections officers ushered her over to a small room outside of the central prison to meet the detectives. Her movement was a big deal. The officers told her things needed to be said. 'It'll be nice to have a little freedom for once,' the officer said. Can you imagine? Well Rose did. Maybe not at that moment, but she figured it all out after those events mulled over in her head a million times.

"The detectives were both young and eye-catching. Rose could tell that much, right? Had Rose been a young straight woman, the detectives would expect her to flirt with them and fawn over their manhood and authority. They were all like that back then. You understand, honey, right?

"She knew there was going to be a request. He didn't exclusively want to tell her something. She was going to do something for him. She only wanted it to be painless.

"See." She took a deep breath, sighed. "Rose sat through the whole interview. She listened. It was going to be about June's involvement in the murder. At the scene of the crime, she declared—that's how they said it—June had told her to kill Dr. O'Malley. It was her bidding, her order to kill. That was what they had on her." Sylvia looked at the age in her hands. "Strange, isn't it? That a coercion could even be a reason and excuse to murder someone. Her spontaneous statement that June told her to do it. That was what they called the evidence. It was ridiculous. Rose did realize, eventually, that her statement was preposterous.

"The detectives, these horrible men, wanted to confirm the statement at the scene, give it more validity, even though she had since denied the accusation. This is what they told her in short direct and persuasive language. At the time, now, Rose was, I'd say, angry.

"She needed to help the investigation. That's what those detectives with the ulterior motive said. She would be the hero. Her assistance was required. So, she was there in that small room with those evil men." Sylvia grew stern, the anger pulsed in her lips.

"'Listen, Rose. Let's call each other by first names. I'm Mike, and I'll call you Rose,' the detective said. That's how Rose relayed it. They tried to be friendly. Get her on their side." Sylvia mimed the incident. Her sarcasm and bitterness were strong.

"She began with what she decided while waiting for trial

that June was not guilty. All this, but she would never, ever win. She never had a chance.

"The detective said, 'But let me get this straight, Rose. You said at the scene of the crime June told you to do it. She tricked you, didn't she?' Like that. He probably gave her a pouty face, probably treated her like a child.

"Rose only said that, no, she didn't. She was incorrect. Rose hated every minute of that interview. She felt the pressure to say what they wanted to say already, and she wouldn't let it seep in...at first.

"You see. There's this thing about what you say at the scene of the crime. Whatever you say, it's the truth. There's research on this principle. It's like your purest moment. In extreme anxiety, you always tell the truth. They call it res gestae. A person only exclaims the truth under stress, on the spur of the moment. It's proven, Christine. That's what they say, at least.

"They told Rose it wasn't going to get any easier that June convinced her to shoot Dr. O'Malley. They said she did it to save her job. They continued with things like June was going to get fired too. They said to show her love, to save her, Rose shot him.

"Rose was strong and even-tempered, especially with June by her side. Anyway, June would never do such a thing. She never wished ill will and loved Rose so much more than anything. To harm what they had, their relationship, was insanity," Sylvia said.

"The detectives said that's what June was doing. She was saving her butt. If Rose were duped, it was okay. Justice would be served. They talked about psychology and how it was manipulative. All the while, they were manipulating Rose. Those psychologists, right? The one said it was fine Rose was tricked, padded her ego. They called June a brilliant woman. Which she was, of course, but they didn't mean it the way Rose knew it to be true. More that she was diabolical.

"They said they were after the real criminal here. They said they could get her and put her away, so she didn't do what she did to Rose to someone else. They referred to another person. A new person who June might be corrupting."

"So, of course, Rose wanted to know what woman that was, who she was with."

"They gave some baloney about the way gay people are. They meant promiscuous. They said she was with a woman on the police force, a receptionist. Shirley, who was actually on the police force and was actually a receptionist. She was sort of out but wasn't political, an activist, at that time. I mean it was the sixties; everyone was in the sexual revolution. Everyone was out and proud. Well, not exactly everyone. I mean most of the people in our group wanted to keep their jobs and all. We kept in close circles. We certainly weren't activists, though." She tapped on the side of her mug. "I'm certain there were a few guys in uniform who went to the bars.

"Rose knew Shirley, Shirley from the police station, the receptionist. They had dated, yes, but everybody did. Rose wasn't jealous, but there were feelings. Anyway. At first, Rose didn't believe them because Shirley was with Maureen." She bit down and abruptly stopped.

"The detective had this photo. It was of Shirley and

June. As Rose described it, June had her arm around Shirley, and they were definitely in an embrace. With all the tension, Christine, Rose certainly felt the pressure to respond a certain way. The detectives put the pressure on her. It might've been Shirley. Rose was jealous.

"He said she'd get a reduced sentence. She'd all but get off," Sylvia stammered. "Christine, Rose took the deal. It was the fluorescent lights, she said. She hated them. She just wanted to get out at that point. She wanted it to be over.

"He fed her some bullshit. 'Has she come to see you, Rose?' All that shit." Sylvia looked out into the distance, avoiding eye contact with Christine.

"They gave her a statement. It was already filled out. It just needed her signature. With all the pressure. All the tension. Rose's fragile mental state in with all those criminals, lumped with the problem prisoners.

"Rose wasn't sure if they would let her out of the room or if they would even feed her until she signed the statement, but that wasn't why she signed it. Rose signed her life away when she made the outburst or statement or whatever they decided it was at the scene of the crime. They were going to use it as evidence regardless. This was a rare opportunity to reunite with the real world. June hadn't come to see her, you see. She was left to her own devices, and she was nothing without June. She didn't know what was fact and what she was supposed to do.

"I was there the day of the trial. It was such a sight." Sylvia lifted the back of her hand to her nose and exhaled into it. She stared off into space remembering this moment, not from what Rose had said when she talked about how awful it was, but from her own memory. "The scene, Rose's face, told all the tales.

"When she entered the courtroom, Rose's head was down. She avoided looking at June or even in that direction. With an officer leading the way, she shuffled to her spot and waited for the lawyer to call her as a witness. She was certainly prepped about what to say, but in her own words, she didn't quite know how to say it, and it showed," Sylvia said.

"She jittered from stress, and her head constantly looked to either side, but never at June. I wasn't even sure if Rose knew June was in the courtroom. She was like that before, before June, nervous.

"The detectives presented off-base accusations, lies presented as facts. Their whole prosecution used bad evidence. June hadn't bought the gun. Rose bought it herself, telling a few lies along the way to get what she needed. The receipt they produced was not the one Rose held during the cash exchange with the man at the register. Rose and June both must've figured that much. Rose didn't ask any questions. She only nodded her head, somehow off-beat when someone looked to her for confirmation.

"When Rose stood up to walk up to the stand, she didn't look over her shoulder. She avoided every glance. The two of them would never be together again. She threw the whole relationship in the trash. To be fair, so did June. When she finally did look up and stopped stammering, aiming anger at June, June's line of sight didn't waver. That's what I watched, their faces, not the bunk evidence some half-cocked lawyer spewed. Res gestae my ass.

"'Did June tell you to do it?' That's what they asked.

That question lingered until Rose answered it. She waited. Oh, she did. It was the one question they went over hundreds of times.

"She said yes with an even temper, with tensed angry lips.

"Rose said June tricked her; that's what she understood. When she began to say that's what the detectives had told her to say, she stopped abruptly and looked at the judge. He stopped coaxing her to speak. She knew what she had said. The jury still didn't get it." Sylvia poured emotion into the firsthand account.

"Rose continued with details about the gun June bought. That was a lie. That was Rose's lie that she planted. She said June gave it to her to shoot Dr. O'Malley, and that was it. The lies were all told. Her obligations were over. She met the detectives' demands and walked away with a reduced sentence. June went to prison. That was it.

"Somehow, the jury bought it. Saw Rose in her state or whatever, and it stuck with them. They were all people too, you know. And, with Rose's past. Well, sometimes it's hard to gauge her emotions, what is real. I guess. That was it."

Sylvia relaxed into the chair, and they stared at each other. A slight grin popped up on her face. They were passing a tradition, passing a torch. "Rose is in a better place now, honey. It's all over for her, but for June. Well, we'll see." She took slow, dragging sips of her coffee. As they chatted, they decided they would pool their resources. They would think it through.

CHAPTER TWENTY-SIX

CRIMINAL INTENT

CHRISTINE GOT THE call, alone, begging for a voice. The blanket of night descended, and she was straining her eyes in low light again. She reread the final two chapters of her information security textbook for the exam the next night. Information security and forensics leaked from her pores. She wasn't sure how they would fit into her career plans overall. That's why she'd saved those classes for the last semester. They were meant as part of the core overview, but Christine focused more on application development and information management. She stalled out on those two chapters, going over her future in her head, where she was meant to be, after finishing the degree. That is, she knew where her education would lead her, the type for which she was poised. She could imagine herself there, in that job, working her way up, mouse, cheese.

All the good she might do as a nurse or a lawyer was in the back of her head. She wanted something less selfish and, at the same time, personally satisfying. She couldn't imagine herself there, however. She didn't think about the alternate profession for six years. She hadn't framed her life in a hospital or law office. She didn't imagine herself turning someone's life around because they met her, making their path an easier go. She hadn't seen past the fog, the unsureness. She went to her book and reread the chapter.

She was ready for a break, so the call rang a godsend. In actuality, the message bore anything but good news. Someone's life was in jeopardy. A horrible, horrible thing had occurred. When something terrible happens, the world stands still for everyone involved. They all share the silence until someone can speak.

"Christine. It's Amy. Jesus, Amy. She's hurt. She's—" Jill was in a frenzy.

"What do you mean? Slow down," Christine said. She sat down on the spot, guessing that Jill was pacing in the room she was in. The haphazard location where Christine sat happened to be the arm of the apartment couch.

"It's Amy. She was attacked. Mugged. It's so horrible." Jill took in huge gulps of air. "I didn't know who to call. Amy asked me to call you, talk to you."

"I'll be right there," Christine blurted out, swiping her

keys off the counter.

"No. Don't come over. Amy is lying down. I don't want to create a fuss. She doesn't want anyone to come over," Jill whispered. She calmed down a bit, but everything was not going to be all right. "Should we call the cops?"

"Tell me exactly what happened. You're all scattered. I don't know what's going on."

"Amy was coming home from the library. She was mugged. Someone grabbed her bag but left it down the street. She said there were homophobic comments, the person called her a dyke and kicked her. She's banged up. Her head's got this huge cut on it. Christine, Amy thinks it was Terrie."

"But she's okay? I'm mean, for the most part?"

"She's alive if that's what you want to know. I don't know what to do. Was it a mugging or a hate crime? Christine, it was a woman's voice, a deep woman's voice."

"Well, what did she look like? You'll need that for the police."

"She didn't know and didn't see. I don't know; maybe she'll remember. Right now, she's resting. Her body's all banged up, but she made it all the way home somehow. We didn't call the police yet."

Jill was in and out of the conversation. Her voice drifted when she told Christine they had broken up last night, and she wasn't sure why Amy had come to her apartment. Jill guessed she was scared.

"It'll be all right. I'm sure. You two will be together again. It was so nice to meet you at the party. I want to do anything I can to help Amy."

A long pause ensued. Jill adjusted the phone on her cheek. "Christine, she said the person had a green zip-up hoodie. Doesn't Terrie always wear a green zip-up hoodie at night? Amy mentioned that Terrie has a green hoodie."

"Ooh. Whoa. What are you trying to say, Jill? Are you serious? Terrie doesn't even wear that hoodie anymore. She put it away. It's too hot, even at night."

"It's still cold at night, Christine." She pushed at her through the phone. "Do you even know where the sweatshirt is?"

Christine couldn't stand the drama soaked in lies. She hung up and threw the phone across the coffee table. There had to be an excuse for this. How could Jill even say that? It was not possible. Who was she to say?

Terrie's creepy behavior came forward from the back of Christine's mind. She and Amy had talked about her irksome ways several times. She had hung around outside her apartment for Christ's sake. Christine remembered when she spotted Terrie waiting for her to leave outside.

The events overloaded her wiring. As much as Christine fought herself, she couldn't come to terms with these statements. She went to the bedroom. Peering in the door, Christine moved quickly to look. She had to put the stressful events out of her mind, confirm they weren't true. She went to look in the closet for the green sweatshirt, but there it was, a green hoodie, on the chair next to the closet, splayed over the arm of the chair, ready to fall off.

She pushed everything out of her mind. She blocked out all external stimuli. There was no way. It was not possible. She would not listen to one offhanded accusation and a freshly thrown sweatshirt. This was not enough evidence. Amy was the evilest person in the world for suggesting what she did.

Christine paced, a sentry. Anyone looking in through the window would think she was obsessed, a maniac. She couldn't put her thoughts down. Even though she had no idea what to ask, she had to find out if Terrie had done this. The alleged deeds were the worst thing she ever had to confront Terrie about.

No more studying got done. Christine would fail the final tomorrow. She didn't care. It was only a matter of time before not only Terrie's world, but her world too, blew up. Everyone would ask her why and how she had committed to someone like that. And didn't she know she was like that, capable of what she had done? Well, there were some warning signs, but you never think something will happen.

WHEN TERRIE CAME in the door, Christine was upset. Terrie at once went to her. Despite Christine's crossed arms, Terrie approached her. Christine thrust backward to avoid Terrie. She did not want an embrace and she want a good six feet of distance as well.

"Did you wear your green sweatshirt last night?" That was the only thing she planned to say. Everything else would be in the moment. She couldn't think straight, but the green sweatshirt linked the incident. She radiated anger before she even heard the answer. Everyone's first guess pronounced her guilty. Nothing proved her innocence.

"What are you talking about? Why are you so crazy? What's wrong, honey?" Terrie's face lacked expression, a blank, pale register. She held up her arms and moved to hug Christine. Her eyebrows furrowed with confusion as she blinked, trying to make everything go back to normal.

"Did you wear your green sweatshirt last night? What time did you get home?" Christine was livid. Terrie moved in and out of the house lately, minding after herself, explaining nothing. She had no reason to be trusted. She was stalking Amy for Christ's sake.

"Uh. I think I wore my sweatshirt, and you know I got home at midnight. I was at the bar. Who cares? Why is it so important? Are you going to tell me what's wrong?"

Christine crossed her arms in front of her chest to avoid Terrie's hug. With a strong "No," she made herself clear. "Amy got jumped last night. Somebody assaulted her. They say the person had a green sweatshirt. They think it might be you?" She shook her head in an even, stiff pace, slow bursts. Terrie couldn't do something like this. It wasn't possible. Christine couldn't believe she was this erratic, this uncontrollable.

"Who said that? Jesus Christ, what are you talking about? I didn't assault Amy. Why the hell would I do that?" Terrie's hands shot straight up in front of her, and she stepped backward.

"Were you jealous? Are you kidding me? You'd attack someone because they were getting between us. I can't even believe I'm with someone who hit someone."

"Well, you're right there. Your relationship with Amy does make me feel left out, but I would never ever attack her.

This is way out there, Christine. Jump her? Why the hell would I do that?" Terrie shook her head at Christine now. Her shakes became more vigorous and aggressive. Her eyes slanted down, filled with their own rage.

"So, you're denying it? They're probably going to press charges tomorrow. You better fess up for whatever reason you did it." Christine stood again and paced, unsettled. She had no appetite for any more conversation. "Look, you better leave. I can't have you here." Her words ended full stop.

"Christine...I didn't do anything. It wasn't me." Terrie moved toward the door as she spoke.

If Christine believed this, which she did, it wouldn't shake. She had it stuck in her head. She wouldn't hear Terrie's words. "I don't trust you. I can't have you here. Amy is my best friend. How could you do this?" Christine slammed the door to the bedroom and lay facedown in a lump. She pushed her fist into the pillow, wishing she could fall asleep or for it to finally be morning.

When she left to visit Amy the next night, her best friend appeared in the front of her mind. If she could do anything else, she would. The security final went fine, despite her mind wandering all over the place. She barely understood how she had shown up in the first place. She had studied enough, after all. Her GPA would not suffer. But by the evening, she had a nagging feeling. If Terrie had committed the crime, Amy wouldn't want to see her. Christine was guilty by association. It was her girlfriend, her lover, who was jealous in the first place. It was practically Christine's fault.

But when she texted after she poked at leftover dinner,

Amy agreed to see her. When Christine entered the parking lot, she scanned both ways and around the corner. Terrie didn't appear in her sights. She might be lurking, ready to strike again.

Amy was banged up. She had a bruised eye and a cut across her forehead. Her wrist and arm had a brush burn, and her wrist had tape around it. She managed to exhale in a short, excited burst when Christine entered her place.

"Hi. Miss you—" Amy whispered, offering sweetness.

"I don't know what's going on. You have to believe me. Terrie... I never... She was jealous. I don't believe it," Christine said. She chewed at her fingernails and sat on the edge of the couch, facing out, not facing Amy, who sat next to her.

"So, you do think it was her?" Amy backed up her emotions.

Christine's stomach curdled with unease.

"You thought it was her, right? She had the green zip-up hoodie. She wore it that night. She told me," Christine said, tilting her head toward Amy. She let out a loose, shallow breath, trying to keep calm.

"I went to the police station today. I told them what happened. Somebody jumped me, shoved me down, called me a dyke, and took my bag. Christine, I don't present as a dyke." Christine didn't know where to go. She did think the assaulter was Terrie, but how could she say that to her best friend about her lover? "They're going to have her come down. I said her name."

Christine stared straight ahead and prepared herself. "Amy, you were right to do what you did. If you think it was her, you think it was her. Terrie has been acting secretive and strange lately. I asked her to leave. I said I couldn't have her in my place. We're over. You don't know how embarrassed I am that I didn't know."

"Christine, I never wanted this to happen. I'm so sorry. It might not have been her. It was so hard to tell." Amy didn't offer anything else.

Christine only dwelled on the chasm her best friend had created in her relationship, and Christine was here to comfort her, of all people, her. Amy grinned lightly, wrapped up in several blankets, knees tucked into her chest.

CHAPTER TWENTY-SEVEN

ASSOCIATIONS

THEY ALL HAD their robes on. Christine kept hers zipped up all day and intended to keep her look that way after they graduated. She didn't dress up underneath it. Fran wrote, "I'm Coming Home Again, Mom," on her mortarboard. Andrea's said, "$46,435." It was finally graduation, the long-anticipated achievement. People meandered to their seats in the most time-consuming way. Amy twirled her hat in circles with her two index fingers and any momentum she mustered. Jill was out in the crowd somewhere, a happy supporter.

"Yup—46,435 dollars. I make my first payment in six months," Andrea said with a humorous grin likely only brought on by the eventful day. She twirled the cap in between her fingers. She hadn't gotten a graduate assistantship like most of them. She followed a few short seconds later with "They should guarantee you a job when you're finished."

Christine adjusted her rainbow pin and straightened her mortarboard. She was happy she'd get to make smaller payments and maybe pay off some of the loans with her inheritance.

As Christine eyed the stands, she caught sight of her parents. They appeared bored, but they were there, pointing to things in the crowd and talking sporadically to each other. Despite their concessions with Christine's life, they were still her parents. They made it clear they would be that. Christine had made it. She was graduating. They were satisfied. It was going to be perhaps their proudest moment for the simple fact when she did marry a woman, she couldn't imagine her parents behind her 100 percent.

The field lawn, long and massive in its breadth, sprouted a few flowers and weeds at its edges. The grass, lush and uniform, would be covered in brown patches from skidded shoes and adjusted chairs by the end of the day. Bold, photography-worthy, blue sky clouded vision, and a sweet, warm breeze only padded the feelings of accomplishment, success, and culmination. The place and day were celebrating with them.

Christine scanned much of the area. The field held so many people she would never find Terrie. In the distance, a form grew larger. The figure had the same stature and walk. She didn't want to see Terrie. The point was to *avoid* Terrie.

Christine had this constant feeling everyone thought she was off too. She made terrible choices and should be left behind after graduation. Somehow, she had condoned Terrie, to whatever degree. She had to be as far away from her as possible, even though she needed to touch her one last time.

"We should have all come together," Fran said. She adjusted her robe, trying to smoothe the wrinkles that had worked their way into the gown when the cheap thing was in its packaging. Everyone else had ironed theirs.

"We'll catch up with everyone later. No worries," Andrea responded.

Christine wanted to find someone she was trying to stay away from, not find lost people to add to the group. She continued to look, stepping away from the group.

Terrie had been questioned at the police station several days before. A cop had called her and told her to go down to the station. With no real evidence, they had let her go. They'd keep a watch out for her. Other than that, no one had any actual leads. No one had talked to Terrie since then. No one had tried except Christine.

They had all decided, like an honest bunch in a democratic fashion, that Terrie was bad news. No one should contact her. If she approached them, they would tell her she wasn't welcome among them. Christine told Amy about the gun, and it was an issue. Amy shouldn't walk alone, and if she was with Christine, there should be a third. Amy wasn't fretting about her life. She said everyone had to live like normal. Still, she was at risk.

Christine called Terrie because she had never said goodbye. They at least owed that to each other. She didn't tell anyone she'd made attempts, particularly since she was the one spouting warnings about Terrie's behavior: what she may or may not do; how she probably felt about Amy and Christine; and what kind of temper she had. She wanted to have one last moment, one last conversation, even if that meant a yelling match, accusations, and excuses. Christine never got in touch with her. Terrie never answered her phone or texts.

Christine left two messages on her cell. The first was angry and asked about motives and future actions. She wasn't welcome anywhere near her again and she would go to the police. She railed she couldn't believe herself and the deception she lived with every day. She picked up her phone and placed it down five times in a row, unsure who else to call.

The second time Christine left a message, three days later, she was the polar opposite. She was rational and level-headed. She mentioned they needed to talk one last time. Some things she needed to say, and other things she needed to know. They owed it to each other to say a few words. The lives had been so intertwined.

"I don't know why they didn't arrest her," Fran said.

Christine scanned the room, thorough with every corner, almost leaving the group. If Terrie was out there, Christine would find her. Christine thought she would be able to feel Terrie's particular heat, her personality, and she looked for it.

"I don't know either. It's a matter of time. They

probably have to do some lab tests or have Terrie come in for another line of questioning. It's not safe with her out here." Christine shuddered, partly due to the fact she was scared of what Terrie might do, and partly because they had been together.

Andrea and Amy found Jess, which was more than Christine could do, and waved her over.

"I got a job offer," Jess told them. "My first day is in two weeks out in Boston. I have to find an apartment, move, and get settled all in two weeks. Ouch." She glowed. "Plus, I have to get the house cleaned for my aunt. She's going to rent it out again.

"You're good," Andrea said. "If I know anyone who can do this, who can make it, it's you."

Fran and Andrea didn't get their own mortarboards after everyone threw them in the air. They picked one off the ground and left. Everyone was going to meet at Vic's house in the evening, but Christine, Amy, Jill, Fran, and Andrea were heading to the downtown café to begin prepping for the night with large amounts of coffee. After stopping in and showing her face to her parents, Christine hopped in the car with Amy and Jill. They also drove her in the morning to the ceremony.

"THIS IS IT. The closest thing we'll get to being a college student now," Fran said. She rubbed the fresh stubble on the back of her head.

Andrea sat down beside her, handing her an iced coffee,

creamy with half-and-half.

"We're done. It's so over," Amy said.

Jill sat down and handed Amy a drink with a bold congratulation.

Jill and Amy were apparently still somehow involved. Christine wasn't sure what she thought of Jill. Her bubbly presence came across as dumb but sincere. She didn't get jealous. Jill urged Christine to appreciate the space from relationships. Amy and Jill didn't want to hurry into something. Terrie and Christine had rushed into something, and maybe that's why it didn't work.

"I know. It's so crazy. We will be the same, won't we?" Christine reached over to Amy's hand and grabbed it. She meant she didn't want to lose her friends.

Dawn, a friend of Terrie's Christine didn't know well, was across the room. She glanced over at her numerous times. She wasn't necessarily trying to make eye contact at first, but she did. Dawn's head bobbed a few times too. They were going to talk.

The group chatted about who put in the most job applications and how late they were going to sleep in to for the next few weeks. Surprisingly, Andrea was getting up at 6:00 a.m. every morning to practice real-life work. They all bet on how long it would be until she realized what she was doing. Fran was moving to her parents' in Seattle, and the two of them were going to date long-distance until they both found jobs, fingers crossed, in the same city.

They all agreed they'd meet for coffee dates at the café, schedules depending. Christine was going to try to pick up some odd jobs after she moved into the new house. By then, though, she hoped to have something decent, permanent. Amy was working part-time as a health care records specialist. She hoped to do something different, but it worked for her right at that moment. Jill still worked on campus at an eatery. She hoped to finish her undergrad next year. Everyone would be back toward school on weekends or if they needed to run downtown to get something.

The café owner came over and gave them each a slice of chocolate cake on the house. He wished them congratulations and stated he hoped they would come back daily. That solidified it. Everyone needed to plan at least one day a week to meet for coffee and a chat at that same café. The tentative plan was the least thing for a free piece of cake.

When Christine bussed the table and took the plates over to the trash can, Dawn was still there. She sipped coffee across from someone, maybe her girlfriend. Her safety vest spread over her chair, and she wore her construction job jeans and a T-shirt for Clyde's, a bar where Terrie used to go a lot. Her cropped hair was short, buzzed in the back, and she scratched at the stubble every so often.

Christine put the plates down gently in the bin beside the trash can and slowly peered over toward Dawn, hoping to catch her glancing. "Hey," she whispered, trying not to interrupt her conversation but edging her way into an exchange. Dawn stared at her and did not respond. She rose up and sniffed, which might've meant "speak."

"Have you seen Terrie? I want to know, I guess, where she is."

Dawn did not want to talk to her at all. She sat and stared at her, mortified.

When she spoke, prolonged and direct, she commanded attention seriousness. "Terrie left." Another obscene pause took root. "You killed her." The next break turned out to be her cue to leave. When she got up, she lifted her coffee cup, still carrying liquid to the bin, ready to say a few more words to Christine. "How could you ever think she did such a thing? Why would you ever? It's not even possible. You're shit." She glanced down at Christine's shoes. She was about to spit. Dawn and the woman Christine was never introduced to left without looking. Christine had an enemy she didn't even know about until that moment.

She watched them walk toward Dawn's bike. They both got on, and as Dawn looked back, she spat beside her. They would never be friends. She would never speak to her with kindness or any bit of composure. Christine would never find out where Terrie was, not from Dawn. She would never know her fate.

Christine slapped her hand to thighs, acknowledging the truth. Of course, Terrie had committed the act. It couldn't be any other way. Evidence appeared in every corner. She scrunched her nose, offended, bucking foolish acknowledgment of this creep Dawn and her intimidating words. It was Terrie, damn it.

She missed Terrie in a way. All this hatred that built up, boiled over, couldn't stop the feeling she had when they were together. She still cared for Terrie. She still loved her. That Terrie had left was inconceivable. Where did she go? Another state? Would she ever turn up?

Everyone huddled outside the café, regrouping. They were all going over to Vic's later, so they all said goodbye for now. Fran and Andrea both had to tend to their families. Amy might have to catch up with hers too. That was it. The bond of school was broken. They were going their own ways. As much as she wanted to slow the process, they were dispersing.

THAT NIGHT AT the party, everyone was excited and sad at the same time. Exuberant hellos and bear hugs turned into frowns and laments. Christine's perky smile melted. Friends chirped that they would see one another again soon.

Fran and Andrea took the same corner they were in the last party. People stopped by to congratulate them and talk. They were a waypoint, as Vic was at the door. Christine entered the party, this time sans girlfriend. She chatted with Fran and Andrea as regular friends do, but something was missing. It was not solely the physical Terrie that was absent but their essence as a pair. Christine was alone and now an outsider. They couldn't double date. Couples had other interests, and single people tagged along.

Fran hugged Christine. The frown had melted onto her face minutes ago because she was upset about everyone leaving, everyone leaving her for good. The sentiment was now tattooed on one of her limbs. Fran hugged Christine because she was alone and initiating a new life, at last, one that was after graduation. Fran tried to fix her up with Andrea, telling her Andrea wanted to go to another classic movie night. They had that in common. Christine didn't hook onto that one. She complained the popcorn at the theater wasn't any good. They didn't add butter. Who didn't add butter?

Christine stationed herself next to Ray, hoping for some casual conversation. Ray was a guy with intense queer energy. His face was on fire with expression every time he spoke. Words bubbled over. She had only met him in passing. Holding her party cup close to her mouth, she asked him snarkily if he had already graduated. She only realized how she sounded after she spoke the teasing words. He snapped at her. He had friends there.

Ray and Christine stood, backs to the wall, looking out, looking for someone to make eye contact with them. Christine continued to chew the rim of the cup. She seeped boredom, yawning fist to mouth. Eventually, leaning back and pushing off the wall, Ray left. He moved toward the crowd, but she couldn't see who he was going to meet. Christine was fine. She enjoyed relative silence for a bit longer. She didn't mind; no one needed to stop by and share the joy.

Christine emptied her cup, breath, and happiness, all with an exhale. She missed Terrie and wished so much that they were still together, that none of this had happened. What she remembered was they were working on their problems, working it out, making it work. They were becoming the power pair like Jesse and Sandy or like Fran and Andrea, who were able to withstand a long-distance relationship, big things.

Still, she questioned everything. Who was this Terrie person she didn't know? She went to write late at night, and they never discussed the incident. They had agreed on their relationship. If Terrie cheated, it would be over. She never questioned it. If Terrie cheated, it would mean she had left

Christine. She could've been doing anything on those late nights. Terrie's jealousy ran deep, inconceivable, a weapon actualized. Anyone with a fever over someone else, someone so innocent, was unsafe.

Terrie was a criminal. Christine had caught her stalking Amy, being sneaky and subversive. She had lied to her, driven her away when she asked questions. And the gun, there was always the gun. Christine and the group had discussed it. Terrie might come after them with a weapon, for who knows what reason.

The things Christine didn't know, the things that now ran through her head were voluminous and malicious. Terrie was capable of everything and anything, and in a way, Christine was a silent accomplice, complicit in that she could've stopped her from all of the acts. If only she would have known. She was now a single soul unattached, and sad to be alone, but that didn't stop the regret for all of it, every second they spent together.

Amy and Jill were seated at the table. Inconveniently, or potentially conveniently for them, there was no place for Christine to sit. All the other chairs were off in another direction, occupied. Christine stood and chatted. She was there for a few quick words, and then they would continue with their couple's conversation, their partner bonding.

"You want to go to a movie tomorrow?" Christine asked, almost unaware of Jill.

"Aww. Can't. Jill and I are visiting my parents. They're having a graduation party for me. You know relatives. Hopefully, I'll get some money for it." She glanced down at her plate. Jill gulped her drink and sighed. She didn't know what to say but wanted to say something.

Christine cut her off. "Oh, right. Yeah. I think I have to see my parents too. Might as well be tomorrow. I'm sure they'll be glad to know about Terrie." Christine didn't believe she had brought up Terrie. She needed to mention her as little as possible since everyone's, especially Amy's, faces went white as ghosts. Words and expressions left their bodies. "I haven't told them," Christine stammered. Amy and Jill appeared pale and lifeless, like they wanted to change the conversation but had no initiative, no idea what was possible next.

"Yeah. Amy's parents are having every extended family member you can think of over," Jill said, and everybody exhaled, thanking god somebody had redirected the conversation.

Christine could only think about how her parents hadn't planned a party for her. They were to have dinner together, eventually. While she might get some money from her parents, she wouldn't see her extended family. She hadn't even asked. Uncle Mark might come for dinner one night to see what she'd done with the house when she was finished. He offered to lend a hand in any way, but it didn't seem to ring sincere.

This friend family wasn't all she had, but they were the most she had. They paired up into mother and nonbinary father, or the other way around, uncle and uncle, or aunt and aunt. She was here with everyone she ever needed to love, but now a barrier existed, the mistake of Terrie. They must still love her. Christine demanded their attention.

Feeling woozy from shifting foot to foot, Christine made

her way to the couch. She needed to rest a bit. She sat alone again for the third time in thirty minutes. She couldn't butt into any conversation. She had nothing to say. A loaded darkness hung in the air—a girl who dated a girl who attacked one of their gay family members.

She relaxed and saddled into a comfy couch in a back room, around the corner from the action. The dimly lit lamp hid her. She wiggled her butt into a pillow and sipped. She had a seat in the stands, excellent for people watching, so she didn't need to rush through the drink. Someone may have stolen her place. It became a waiting game. She couldn't leave early. It would look like she didn't want to be with her friends. She couldn't sit alone. She'd look antisocial, and she'd drive people away. Still, she didn't want to go up to anyone and introduce herself. Why make friends at this point? She didn't want to tag onto a conversation either. Sick of being the third wheel, she wanted an honest connection.

The night drove on, and she sat in the same seat without enough initiative to get a refill. A waiting game, she was holding on to the relationships with her friends a while longer for the remaining time she was there. She was continuing to make a connection. She was fine. She was with friends, in essence, at least. Soon she would forget there was ever a person hanging on her arm.

Chapter Twenty-Eight

Cold Rooms

THE PARTY, LOUD and raucous, went on for hours, but Christine was only there for one. After Christine had settled in with her third drink and a fresh plate of munchies, her phone rang. She hurried, chewing faster to finish her food, and answered.

At every instant the last several days, she tried to shake the feeling Terrie was responsible. Terrie would explain it all. In a way, she wanted the bit of interaction, a stab at closure. But to sacrifice her feelings at this time and look for her was unthinkable. Each time the phone rang, the anticipation pined. The door smacked shut every time. Terrie never answered. In an instant, Christine both wanted the definitive answer to be it was Terrie and at the same time decided she would be livid, merciless if it was her. As she answered the call and recognized the voice, those emotions muted, and her compassion and excitement banished them from her mind.

"Hello? Who? Hold on. I'm at a party. I have to go outside." Christine held the phone tight to her chest to ward off the noise and rushed through the sliding glass door. On the deck, the rarity of this call came into full focus. It was June.

"June? How are you?" Christine, already a bit tipsy, knew at least that it was after hours for phone calls.

"Christine?" June had slow, low-register tones. Her age showed through the call. Her voice cracked, deeper than before, soaked in the rain, a wet rag of despair. "It's so much. They let me out, Christine."

"June, I'm so happy for you. All this time—this is great. I've been waiting for you to call." Christine jumped up and down to a steady beat, trying to lift June as well. Her glazed-over voice shined through, attempted to light the room June was in some miles away.

"I was going to call you. I was. I wanted to get settled. It's this place they put me in. I'm not free." June stopped her words in an instant and held her breath. She drew in rapid gasps; tears freely flowed. "I'm in a mission, and it's awful. I have no money—no way to live. The conditions are horrible. The people don't treat me well. It's worse than prison, Christine. I'm stuck for the rest of my life in what's worse than prison." She stopped short again.

June's energy related she wanted to speak, so Christine listened. Christine held the phone, clutching it, aware of the darkness of her surroundings. Only stars glistened light.

"Christine, can I stay with you? For a few days until I can figure things out?"

"June, of course. I'll pick you up now. What you did for Rose so many years ago—when she called you—I wanted to pay you. I needed to do something. This is it, June. Of course."

Of course, Christine would be there for her. To hell with this party where she stood alone—a solitary mess unable to make a connection with anyone. Scorned for her association to Terrie, destined to be alone forever, she tipped her drink and chugged liquid. June would live with her, of course.

Throwing the plate with remnants of food and the empty cup in the trash, she went to Vic and hugged her, said she had to go. She waved to Fran and Andrea and hugged Amy on the way out, giving a waist-level wave to Jill as she moved toward the door. June needed her, and Christine's ability to support her made her happy for the first time in several days.

WHEN CHRISTINE WENT to pick June up at the mission, she couldn't believe where she was. Homeless people hung around out front. They smoked, dealt drugs in grey shadows. People walked freely in and out, crossing the road. A car smashed into another down the street, and Christine slammed the brakes to stop. Her beat-up car fit in at this place, but she hid the phone cords in the side console regardless.

June was sleeping on a cot. She referred to the place as somewhere where she got mail but not sleep. She had to go somewhere else, anywhere. She talked about the hallway to her room ridden with rat shit and the expired food they gave her. She had no money, no recourse.

"They wouldn't send me to a nursing home. I'm not bad enough yet. They thought I'd be fine out here. I'd make do." June took short, shallow breaths as if she had climbed flights of stairs. No doubt, one trip up a floor for June would produce the same character of breath. She rumpled the sleeves of her shirt.

"At least I can wear normal clothes. It's the least they could do." June flipped her head up in typical fashion. She'd always kept her self-regard right in front of her.

No longer a burden to the state correctional system, now she was a burden to public assistance. She would always be a burden to someone for the rest of her life. She walked with a limp now, after only several days of cramped living. She cried to Christine she didn't want to be the feeble old woman.

Christine saved her. June thanked her over and over again. She was a saint in plain sight. June hugged her when she arrived, as they left the building with her single duffel bag, before they got in the car, and when they got to Christine's house, her great-aunt's house.

"I'm so sorry I have to do this to you," she whimpered, as they drove away. "I'm an old lady with nowhere to go. They should've never let me out."

"June. I'm happy to do it. We'll figure something out. You're welcome to stay with me. We'll figure things out together." Christine also had a tear in the corner of her eye. She didn't know quite what it was for, the cruelty of the world, the lack of help for people like June, or the fact she was helping someone she could. She was making a difference as a memorial to her great-aunt.

As they drove, they sat voiceless for a bit. June squeaked out her contentment to watch the cars go by. Christine leaned with the car as she turned down the streets and made it to the highway. She was at ease knowing June overflowed with compliments, abundantly grateful.

Strictly since she didn't know what else to say, she started a new topic. "My girlfriend was arrested," Christine said, introducing earth-shattering information. "Well, she wasn't arrested, but she committed a crime. They took her in for questioning. They didn't say she did it, though. So, there's that. She attacked my best friend. She was jealous. I'm a fool for loving her."

Christine spoke all of this uniformly, presenting the evidence as a necessary fact. June could not live with her unless she understood this information. She wouldn't be able to relate unless she acknowledged this. Christine's abrupt monotonous voice came to a stop, and June's shallow breath filled the space.

"Honey. Christine. It's okay. People do crazy things. People date crazy people. We'll work this out." June's comforting voice was what she needed. She was becoming a parental figure, a voice of reason, one that had seen the range of emotions, the world of women loving women. They would work it out together, process.

"I've been meaning to tell you something. If you love someone, say like me, what you're doing for me is love, I believe—in some way, they will show you that you love them, do something, right? Wouldn't you do something for me if I needed it?" June asked. Still, she hadn't gotten every word out. She needed to say more but didn't. Everything was a jumble, but Christine knew what she was trying to say. If you love someone, you'll do anything for them. It was so true.

When they arrived at the house, emotions quieted down. She turned on the lights. The painting was still not done. The full wall-to-wall clean was not yet complete. Christine set June up in the spare room. She brought her bag in and waited up until June got settled and ready for bed. The time, slipping past, was late, too late.

Christine curled up with a novel she had put down twenty times before. She made a cup of tea. June had mentioned on the way over she preferred tea, but all they ever got in prison was thin coffee. Christine found honey in the back of the cabinet. At that moment, some simple honey was a godsend. It was something Christine gave to make June, who had seen so many sad nights, bubble. Some things were left over from the funeral. Even though she never had honey in tea, she knew what you do, what June might do.

June was welcome in the house. She would try hard to be a good friend, a helper when she needed to be. Christine couldn't shake the feeling Aunt Rose would want it this way, despite all that had happened. It wasn't right. June had done everything out of love, and Rose had been confused and misunderstood everything. Christine would right the wrong and make sure she cared after June as June had done for Rose. No bitterness was left.

A FEW WEEKS went by, and June helped Christine get the house ready. They were planning a housewarming when they finished. Christine would host the party Vic wasn't able to organize and host. Vic had left for Boston last week, fully satisfied with an optimistic outlook. June encouraged Christine not to get jealous. She would find something soon. She was waiting on a few applications but was sure she would get one of the jobs. She couldn't leave the area now, not with June. It was her sense of responsibility. She was family.

They sat on the couch every morning, tea in hand, and talked about Aunt Rose. June talked about her gorgeous hair and her boisterous laugh, one that filled the room. It made whatever color the wall was bright and full of energy like her.

"She had so much life. She was so excited for everything." June lit up, ecstatic, and shook her head slowly. "God, she was everything." June swirled the spoon in the mug and yawned.

"This one time, she surprised me in the morning with flowers. God, I loved flowers. Something you don't get in prison. She decorated the whole place, begonias, sunflowers, orchids, you name it, and she made breakfast, of course. The momentous occasion was an anniversary. I think—our one-year anniversary. We loved each other, Christine. She wouldn't be mad at me still, would she? If she had known." June gazed down at her tea again and up through the top of her eyes, embarrassed she had asked again.

Christine didn't want her to feel she shouldn't be there. "Yes, of course. If she had only known the truth, if both of you had known you loved each other so dearly. If Rose had not thought you deceived her, cheated on her, lied to her. If she had known all those things, if she weren't forced to make a statement, you would be together. You were apart so long with no communication. If you had sat down and talked it out, everything would have been all right, even if the police wouldn't have forced her to blame you." Christine went on, determined to get through to June. They were meant to be together, meant to spend their lives together, but deceit and corruption had come between the diamond-eyed lovers, and it was too late. They would never be together. They would always be two people full of memories and love who would never get to express themselves to the other and make it right.

"I would always misplace things. I was going crazy in those days. You see so many patients, and at some point, you begin to think it's you. Anyway, she would find them right away. My glasses here. Keys over there. It was unnerving how she always guessed where things were even if they weren't hers." June sat back and adjusted her happiness. Her love for Rose and Rose's love for her was renewed by her great-niece. June was in love with someone she'd never meet again.

June took sips of tea. She had noticed that Christine bought extra shampoo and left it just inside the bathroom door. It was the kind she at one point said she liked. June had watched as Christine, unprompted, made her a sandwich and then slowly slid it in front of her. The new clothes Christine had bought for her lay softly folded on her bed.

When Christine brought up Sylvia and Leonard, she stuttered. They had been friends with Aunt Rose. June didn't know what it was like to have friends in the outside world and be ashamed, uninformed, and naïve. Despite all this, Sylvia and Leonard were delighted to snoop on June, and Sylvia organized a trip as soon as Christine told them she was there.

Sylvia and Leonard helped her after she got out of prison. They became friends by doing things for each other. Their meta group was nonetheless a community; they were "fam," as Christine said, and they were ready to be there when she needed it. Rose would have wanted it that way.

When they came over, they talked about all the people they knew. Robby, with blond hair, who was so good in the local musicals, died decades ago from AIDS. June hadn't even known AIDS. They needed to fill her in on extensive periods.

Donna, who worked at the bookstore for so many years, was bound with shackles to her wife. They went everywhere together. She died from cancer the year before. Her wife continued to live happily in a retirement home. She had friends in there and stated it was overall pretty great. Sylvia and Leonard shook their heads at each other. They never wanted to go in, they said. They wanted to be as free as possible. June nodded, looking at Christine unsurely and smiling.

For each person, they told where they were now. Most

of them were dead. The stories were something they could keep dear. Each person had their own world with their own plotline for the benefit of June. They reinforced the memory for themselves and shared it.

Sylvia and Leonard would be the thing June needed most, friends her age. June relaxed and listened, took it all in. They told her more in a few hours than she'd ever guessed from Christine. The pair shined the light of the world onto June, who had barely begun to know what living was like when you weren't behind bars.

To everyone's amusement, June didn't know some things. She didn't know about movies or TV and restaurants, basic things. She had the faintest clues. The one thing June did know, besides cards, was how to talk. And the three chatted for hours, each of them so happy to have someone who would listen.

They made plans to pick her up and go for coffee a few times a week. They all needed to catch up on a lot. They were edging Christine out of it all, as it should be. Sylvia and Leonard were so open-armed and welcoming. They only wanted to help and be friendly, do what they could.

When they left, it was time for dinner. Christine ordered Chinese, but June was going to have a sandwich. They laughed about the pair that came to visit, Sylvia and Leonard, and how they were the oddest couple, left with no one else. They had to roam the earth together and never fall in love. Life was, indeed, a tragedy.

June and Christine chatted, as cute of a pair as Sylvia and Leonard. It was nice to have someone. They both thought so. June offered to iron Christine's clothes, and

Christine decided she wouldn't have it. She didn't need another mother. They would look out for each other. They promised with a pinky shake. No matter who came along, they would be there for each other. Everybody needed somebody for life.

CHAPTER TWENTY-NINE

BEFORE — 1958

THEY GOT INTO the baby-blue Dodge Custom Royal, and June pulled the door shut with smacks right before Rose did the same, one after the other. Sunday drives were for older people and June and Rose. They were out in the open, hens let loose for a while, for once not terrified people would notice them or scared of people talking about them. They were going to a new area with fresh stares and people who wouldn't see them again, ever, until the next time they visited the town.

The wind rolled by the windows, howling through the

slight crack made to bring in the fresh air. June drove calm, cool, and relaxed. Rose slumped against the window at times and sighed. As June turned a corner Rose knew well and went the opposite direction, she felt enchanted with a sense of adventure. Their favorite town, where they were going to retire to, was to the right, but for the first time, they were going left.

Rose stuck her hand out the window and moved it up and down. June shook her hair back in response and smiled. She was driving down roads becoming familiar with the best copilot she ever hoped to have.

"I love you, but you're going to sever your arm," June said, touching her thigh. She made a quick glance over toward Rose to tell her she was half-serious and then looked back at the road.

"Oh, dear," Rose snarked. "It's not possible. My arm wouldn't reach to any sign or tree." She stared far into the farm fields they were encountering. The crops must have been soybeans, not corn or tobacco. They stretched up over the horizon until slight pink hues stopped at a thick line of trees. They guarded a house a bit beyond. "It might get slashed by a fly or gnat at best," she said as she held herself back, pulled her arm in the window.

"This is going to be the town," June remarked, her head high in the air, pleased Rose pulled her arm in when asked.

"I like Cortisville. You like it too," Rose stated. They both approved of Cortisville, but June had doubts.

June mentioned the land sprawled too much and miraculously snuggled too close to a larger town. She wanted her retirement to be as relaxed and as natural as possible in an area where you couldn't see another person for as far as the land stretched. She only wanted to be with Rose. "It's perfect. I don't need to look anymore." June waited for Rose to react, but she didn't. "Well, we have years to decide. We can't move tomorrow. Anyway, wouldn't you rather see?" June asked.

June hoped she could find a job in one of the towns sooner, but it wouldn't happen. Hospitals were few in the small towns they were looking at, and other jobs were limited, especially in a rural area, especially for women.

"As long as I'm with you," Rose entered with the sweetest possible sincerity.

No jarring events unfolded on the rides and maybe that was the allure. They liked being alone, together, talking, without people around. A long drive to the country became a lovers' moment, and they had picturesque scenery to boot.

Halfway, they pulled over at a roadside stand. The homely seller had fruit and vegetables, locally grown. "At the very least, we can get the freshest vegetables for dinners this week," June said.

"You mean we're not foolishly wasting gas?" Rose asked and laughed.

June joined her, and they picked through corn and apples. The fall-day air had a chill, but they had each other and the shelter of a car. They couldn't ask for anything more.

"You two are from the city, huh?" the roadside stand woman questioned. She rubbed her belly which was thigh-high next to June. Her apron bore a big apple. "The jam's sweet with a tiny, tiny bite." She inched them toward the mason jars with her eyes.

"Yeah, we're from the city. Can you tell?" Rose quizzed.

They tried to stand on their own in situations like this, independent from each other, sisters or good friends.

"Well, your accent is one thing. The second is we don't see many like you around here," The cashier sniffed in hard as she squinted into the sun. June and Rose knew what she meant.

"Well, it would be nice to fit in here," June asked, raising her voice to a question. "We'd like to move out here."

June took change out of her wallet with a dollar bill. Even though June tried to smooth everything over, they were oddities at best. Rose, with her handsome boyish looks, wasn't ready for the year this small rural town was living in. Fifteen years behind the actual year was about right, verified by older model cars and aging clothes. The woman might not have ever guessed; might not have known they were together. It might've been how June and Rose perceived it. Either way, they both wanted her to know, encouraged it, with hope the discussion would be over—they'd be accepted.

"Maybe, we'd like to move here or close to here," Rose stated.

They eventually wanted to be two nice women who lived across town to most people.

"Well, I don't know about that. I guess you'd have to see." June and Rose both knew what she meant. The woman fixed and tugged at her apron.

They gathered up their purchases and moved toward the car. If they relocated out here and people found out they were lesbians, they would push them around. They both wished their sexuality wasn't an issue. Maybe one day, it wouldn't be. If they had to be old maids, so be it. Anywhere, people would talk. People would find out.

They pulled into a drug store lot and got out of the car. Rose dusted off her jeans and tugged at the bottom of her leather jacket, straightening the stiff garment. Her shoulders appeared as faint bumps in the stiffness of the jacket, and the sleeves went inches past her palms. Rose was butching up a bit for June. That was what June wanted.

June adjusted her white blouse in the wind. The dirt in the dusty lot kicked up around her. "Did I see a tumbleweed? This is where we should be," June said. "We should check out the rural roads, too—to see." June's head jumped up toward Rose and her eyes twinkled.

"Of course," Rose whispered. "Truly quaint and quiet. And this cute main street is great. We do need some shops to come into and get groceries, supplies, things."

They walked down the street and peered in the window of the restaurant, the five-and-dime, the hardware store, and the grocer. They looked as they walked, but they felt apprehensive, as always, like they didn't belong. People would ogle at them for being from the city. Their thick accents were a telltale sign. That's what the roadside stand woman had said.

WHEN THEY ENTERED the restaurant, everyone glanced up: people on stools at the counter, two in a booth, and the waitresses holding coffee pots. The two older people at the booth were harmless, vaguely aware of their presence. The woman held half a smile. The two men at the counter wore heavy coveralls and stiff baseball hats. They didn't take them off while they were in the restaurant. They hung low, lurching over the table, forearms resting beside their plates, their eyes out of view. They might've been thirty years old. The bells jingled against the door as it shut behind them. They needed the flavor of the town. They couldn't live anywhere without seeing the people, seeing the places people go, first.

"We noticed you coming," the waitress behind the cash register whispered. "You can have a seat where you like." She flipped her forehead in the direction of the dining area.

June and Rose understood by her tone they weren't welcome. They were strangers at best.

In a booth with big cushions, they ate their food with the cook staring at them from the kitchen. He didn't move from his spot, alternating from arms folded, bending over the counter, to hands on counter, tensed at the elbows. He shook his head five or six times every ten minutes or so.

The customers were thinking about them too. The men on the stools peered over their shoulders and brought information back to their conversations. They whispered to the waitress. June and Rose didn't quite know what the issue was if they were out-of-towners, city folk, or queer. Regardless, they were different.

"Maybe we can, I guess, grow into it here," Rose said. She leaned in close and, as everyone in the restaurant listened, she said, "Maybe, they'll accept us in time."

June appeared nervous, and she was. All of these towns were quaint and pretty, but to find a spot where she found comfort was an unending journey. Something always wasn't right about a place, and it was usually the other people. Lately, she wanted to run away to undeveloped land, shit in a pit in the ground, and be whoever she wanted to be. She wouldn't have a care in the world. Rose reminded her of the impracticality. They'd die because they were from the city. They'd eventually go back to civilization. It never lasted, she said.

A man at one of the stools got up. The other one stayed put but turned in their direction. June could see them for what they were. Rose could not. He came with giant, pushing steps. The desperado dug his elbow into Rose's shoulder as he passed and slowed up. Glancing over his shoulder, he looked back. "Bulldagger."

Rose started toward him, and June put her hand out across the table. Rose shook her head down and toward the window to avoid eye contact. Rose wouldn't show aggression. It would kill her.

Feeling no response to his pause, his stare over his shoulder, he left out the door. The same bells jingled as the door closed. They were safe with relief. They would live to visit another town. They might even come here another day. They had years. People changed their minds. The townspeople might not remember. Those last two things probably weren't right.

"You sure you don't want to go around the rural roads?" Rose asked. She fidgeted with her hands.

If she didn't have short hair or a leather jacket, if she weren't wearing jeans, he wouldn't have bothered them. He wouldn't have thought anything of it.

"And have him follow us onto the back roads? I don't

think so," June said. "They'll be fine here in this town, without us. That's what I think."

She was right. It was best if they move on, pick another town. They would find one yet.

"We have years," June cooed. "Let's go to Cortisville and do the roads there. The sun's still out. Why not?" June's sadness dissipated. "Remember the blue house. Let's go by the blue house."

They careened down the road, and the car's carriage scraped against a big bump.

"All right," Rose said. "Back to Cortisville."

They both loved Cortisville. They had two friends there, and for some reason, they felt safe. It was larger than June would like, but they would have someone to visit. They had positive feelings about the place. It was the failsafe.

CHAPTER THIRTY

PAPER

CHRISTINE TRIED TO explain, without success, to June she was a liberated woman and did as much hard work as anyone else. June only muttered about how she could do the lawnmowing or shoveling. She wanted to be in charge of car oil changes.

June teetered on the ladder when Christine walked in, fully aware of what she was doing, and why. "Hi! Getting this light bulb changed. How was your movie?" she asked nonchalantly as if she weren't struggling with the fixture.

"June. You need to get down." Christine moved toward

the step ladder and held on to her legs for lack of something else to support.

"Get off me. I'm fine," June said. She ambled down the step ladder, convinced she had saved the household in one fell swoop.

They regrouped after June descended. "It used to be so easy for Rose, house repairs, things like that. She once fixed the starter on my car—way before the YouTube thing. She asked actual questions to actual people back then."

Christine had to let her try. Terrie had been the same way, not chauvinistic but proud of specific accomplishments. As long as they didn't have a safety issue, Christine would let June attempt any task she wished.

June, still proud, wouldn't admit it was a bad idea. She had to keep herself occupied, June said. Certain things, she was more adept at doing. She wanted to contribute.

Amy and Jill were away again that weekend. They went away all the time. Amy worked full-time at the hospital. They had upped her hours after she graduated, and Jill had a job in the hospital cafeteria doing dishes and prep. They didn't make her work weekends. They were out and about all the time. Christine hadn't seen Amy in several weeks. She hadn't yet come over to see June.

It was as if she had lost a friend. Jill was taking all of her time, and Christine was fading into the background when she needed her friend most of all. She was alone. She guessed that's how it happened. People settle down and go into their worlds, cut off from outside stimuli. They have kids and couple with other families with kids. Amy was transitional in this way.

Particularly lonely lately, Christine worked on the house, went to the movies alone, chatted with June daily, and of course, sent in job applications. She couldn't believe she didn't have a job yet. IT positions were almost guaranteed after you graduated. They were in demand. She went on two interviews, both times wearing the suit she had bought to interview June. They joked about it each time she left with it on.

Christine got a call while she was in the kitchen cleaning up. Cleaning up was usually June's job, but Christine was trying to compartmentalize and do things quicker than she had when she lived off campus. Christine was an adult now, and she didn't want June to have to always pick up after her. Andrea was on the phone. Christine wasn't the best of friends with Andrea. They didn't talk regularly. Mostly she was friends with Fran. So, when Andrea called, she knew it was something particular, something important, that could not wait until they met again. She had big news.

"They arrested someone. He was charged in Amy's case. He was charged in two other muggings too. One of the victims picked out a guy wearing a green sweatshirt in the lineup. The sweatshirt was a zip-up. Amy told the cops it was a zip-up." Andrea made pointed statements like she was expecting Christine to react. She didn't know how she would react, but Andrea solicited something, anything, so she could keep telling the story.

Her behavior, her jumps to conclusions, now became so unwarranted. Christine sat down. She leaned on the edge of the kitchen chair and hunched over. She held her head as if she had a headache, but there was no sharp pain inside her skull, only on her conscience.

Two worlds dropped for Christine. The first one was she had incorrectly blamed someone for a crime, jumped to assumptions. For that error, she would never again not ask all the questions, investigate, and think for weeks. She was at fault. She was morally responsible for Terrie's submersion into unwarranted guilt by not questioning Terrie's guilt with her friends. She had fed Terrie to everyone in bits and pieces.

The second world that went crashing to the floor was that love eternally changed for her. She had loved Terrie, felt passionate feelings, held them in her heart, and wiped them away in one fell swoop. For the rest of her life, she would question how she felt. Her love, commitment, needed to stand tests, ask questions, and persist. She would begin again to find true love, one unshakable.

"Well, it wasn't her. That's what it looks like. The mugger had one of Amy's cards from her wallet, so—" Andrea kept going on.

Christine wanted her to stop, shut up, have no more points she needed to convey. The swelling of regret was heard in Christine's voice. She made a shallow cough and swallowed down as she stared in the mirror, abhorred by what she had done. The news about Terrie made her lift her forehead, eyes darted upward. Terrie was scot-free without blame. On the other hand, Christine was the fool. She was the one who had caused so much harm.

She hung up the phone, dejected. She had driven Terrie away, ruined her connections with her circle of friends, and left her a suspect. She had never thought for one minute

Terrie was innocent. She didn't stand up for her and defend her as she probably should. She went, blind to deliberation, with the speculation of her best friend, and that left her the worst friend to her lover. She was the murderer. Terrie was gone, and Christine's friends said they never expected to hear from her again. Christine couldn't get her back.

Christine spent the next day in bed, sick to her stomach, afraid to look at herself. She had never mourned their breakup. She missed her dearly, but it wasn't over. Nothing left her hollow. Christine always hoped she'd see Terrie again and resolve everything. This was her time to mourn.

In a way, Christine blamed Amy. Amy, not herself, was the one who had twisted words, insinuated that Terrie had done it, and then outright decided that she was the one. Their relationship was as over as hers and Terrie's was, despite Amy being the one who initiated the long pause in their relationship. Christine could let that relationship go, because it was toxic from the beginning and too toxic to go back to again. Terrie she could not.

When Christine got a job offer several days later, she said yes before she finished speaking and then immediately blushed. A second's long celebration dissolved into the realization she had to go to work. She had to work every day for the rest of her life. She was not excited about the adventure, even with June at her side.

SHE HAD A steady paycheck, something to pay the expenses of the house and live off for a bit. The job paid well, and she had landed it. Dreams still swarmed her head about new and exciting careers, new paths. She toyed with the idea of law school and what was to come. At the same instant, she remembered Terrie. She wanted to rush off for a new life, a new beginning. She would leave her mistakes behind.

June got out more. Sylvia or Leonard would come over. She joined a bridge team. June had never played bridge, only spades in prison. She was thinking of volunteering somewhere. June had ideas about the library, the community center, or an LGBTQ group. In due time, she would decide. It would all work itself out.

If it weren't for June, Christine would have stayed in bed, never gotten up for work. She wouldn't have turned over in her head what things might have been. June gave her a beacon, something to keep her looking forward. The past was moving. Her life was morphing, and it would never be what it was or could've been.

Christine sat down at her small desk, the one from the apartment. She set it up in the third bedroom with a bookshelf. Some boxes lined one of the walls. Everything would be in its proper place in good time. She was at home. This was her place. She did whatever she wanted with or without Terrie. She took out a pen, one from college, and set out a blank piece of stationery. Her initials ran across the top.

Terrie,

I love you. I love you so much. There is nothing I wouldn't do for you, and there is nothing I can say to make things better between us. I was wrong, and

I betrayed you. It's simple. I want you to know three things:

We are all human, especially me. I made a mistake, and I'll regret it for the rest of my life. I won't ask you to forgive me for it because it will always be with you as well. Know I'm sorry.

I want to make it up to you. If there is any way to change the way you feel about me now, your hatred, I want to do it. I will climb mountains for you and be there to save you from a burning house—whatever it takes.

We weren't together for more than a year. Some people would drop what we had and leave and not look back. But we had something, something real, a connection. That is undeniable. Everyone argues, but we made up better. We had better after-fight sex. I do truly love you, and I can't leave all of this, all of us, without trying to make it fly a bit longer. I love you.

I don't know why I'm writing this since I don't know where you are. I'm not sure where to send the letter or who to contact. I never met your parents, and I don't know if I can introduce myself, let alone find them.

I'll be at Aunt Rose's house. You'll know where to find me. I have a friend now too, June. She's going to live with me and us if you come back to me. I'll always have a place for you here. Say the word, and I'll work on number two above so we can get to number three. We have the rest of our lives together. We can have the rest of our lives together. Find me.

Love always,

Christine

Christine sealed up the envelope and put on a stamp. She made out the return address to Aunt Rose's house, her house. She wrote Terrie's name on it without an address and put it in the drawer. She wasn't sure where it should go, to her parents' house, or left at the apartment. The act relieved her. She wrote what she had to say. It was as if she spoke to Terrie. She knew, miles away, all Christine had to offer. She'd come if she still wanted to make it work, if she accepted the apology.

June and Christine sat at the dinner table a few evenings later, and Christine told her about the letter. Christine said to her she knew, now that she said the things she needed to say, Terrie would come back. Their souls were so intertwined; they were connected so close as lovers; she must know Christine was sorry. She would have figured out they had arrested someone. It wasn't her fault, and she would return.

"I can't think of us together again. That letter stayed in the desk drawer until I got it out. She'll never read it. It's like how a person writes. I needed to get it out, say 'I love you.' I know it will never be, never can be because of what I've done," she told June.

"Do you mean you don't love her? 'Cause the difference between me and you is you still have a chance. I tried. I lost my chance. But you, you'll never know. Unless truly, it was only for you?" June remarked.

Christine paused. "It was for me. It was all about me. It always has been with Terrie. It's always been me first, my feelings over hers. This was a way for me to dwell on myself one more time. I should burn it."

"If you feel that way, honey, yes. Let's burn it. Ashes to ashes," June said. "No use waiting for something that's not going to come if it's not meant to be. You told her what you needed to say, and you are right with yourself. That's all you need. Burn it." June took small bites from her meal, wiped the corners of her mouth. "Burn it, honey."

Christine moved to the end table where she'd hidden the letter. She'd gotten it all out, all her emotions, and hid it forever. She lit a candle in the center of the table and put it over a pan. With one swift dip into the flame, it lit on fire, and charred black appeared, crept, covered all of the letter. She burned her dream about Terrie. The wish, as she blew out the candle, was they were back together, twinkling stars, lovers once again. She burned her delusion that it all had never happened. And, now, she was free.

CHAPTER THIRTY-ONE

SENT

AFTER IT WAS all over, after the letter burned to ashes, Christine went to sleep, commanding herself to start over. It wasn't so easy though. When she woke up in the morning, it hadn't started over. She was still the same person with the same feelings, the same need for Terrie.

She couldn't settle down that morning. She was on the couch and then moved to the kitchen. Chopping fruit for work lunches, she hummed oldies. She read a book for ten whole minutes. She dusted. It bit at her, her regret over Terrie. Busily, she tried to put the rampant thoughts out of her head and forget. She tried to find a place to lock away her feelings, never return to them. It was not an easy task. As soon as her chest hurt and she exhaled hard, almost weeping about her mistakes, she'd get up and move to something different. She ran away.

As she cleaned, June entered the room. She entered like she had something to say, her mouth almost speaking. And she did. Christine rushed around, moving things into particular places. She couldn't yet find where everything went. Bookends and tchotchkes had to find permanent homes. She moved the flower vase four times in a week.

"People read my letters." June blurted out the nonsense while Christine paced. "You never know when people will do that, I guess—unsent letters. They can be the death of you. I had this friend, Marty, in prison, and she cared about me. She was more sprite than me, for sure. Well, she stuck up for me," June said. "I never wanted anyone to read them. They were my way to figure it all out. It was my way to figure out why I was in prison... Why I accepted where I was. It was all for her cause I loved her. You know now, I'm sure. I talk about loving her so much." She sat on an armchair as Christine buzzed around. Her head faced forward almost as if she spoke a soliloquy on a stage. She was hazy but composed. She was remembering the past and trying to persuade Christine's future actions.

"Oh, June. You're welcome here. You know," Christine chided. She was tapping a pen against the table, wondering where to rest the useless thing. Instead, she went over, sat on a chair, and faced June.

"But listen—Marty knew people on the outside," June

said. "She could've made things right for me. But she didn't. She knew I wouldn't have wanted it. It would break me. I wouldn't have any reason to write any more letters. It was the only thing that gave me a will to live." She tapped her forearms against the arms of the chairs. Her point would never come out.

"Marty read those letters, and she broke in. She exposed my world, my true feelings. It was the most humbling thing anyone could do to me. I hated it. But, in her own way—due to the fact she interpreted the letters her way—it was good. She gave me perspective. What I'm trying to say is—I'm glad I opened up to you and shared my feelings about Rose. No one except Marty knew. Nobody else was even my friend. You have done so much for me, listened to so much from me. I'm so glad to be here with you."

"June, I'm glad to have you—to do something good, someone who loved Aunt Rose," Christine said. She got up again. They'd had this conversation so many times.

"What I mean to say is nothing is ever entirely private. Someone will always know. And...if you write it down, it's never yours. It's everyone's, anyone who reads it. It's never the intent, of course, for it to be read by anyone, just the addressee. But once you do write it down, it's a record. It means anybody can know. It's what you feel. It's what you've told the world."

CHRISTINE DRIFTED ONE more time. She checked Terrie's name, typed it into Google. She found her profile picture on Facebook. It was not public, but she was still there with her smiling face. Resting her head in her hands, Christine examined it closely, searching for Terrie to know and respond she knew Christine loved her still.

"I miss you," she pleaded. "Where are you?"

Even if Christine wanted to call Terrie, she couldn't. Terrie blocked her number. The last time Christine called, by accident, the line was disconnected, or she was blocked. She didn't know which. Terrie never fully moved in with Christine, but her lease ran out the week of graduation. She would have found a new place either way. Terrie hated what she had. She talked about it as a place, a den for mice and spiders. The plan, never actualized, was for Terrie to move right into Christine's house.

She missed the surpriser, and the way there were always flowers in the house. She missed Terrie's random acts of kindness, leaving her stumped and stuck on the words "thank you." She never repaid her more than that, Christine now reflected. Terrie's strength and open arms were gone. Her tight cuddles were fading. Christine remembered the bike ride, the way Terrie looked over her bike, over and over again. Had Christine only remembered she left her and went far ahead? Was Terrie's anger also a heavy memory? Doesn't everyone get mad sometimes? She was the woman Christine could grow old with. They both discussed it in that very house. The gay dinners supposed to last into their eighties drifted. Visions of Terrie on a ladder and Christine holding it, grey-haired with a light bulb, vanished. Images of long drives to the beach on vacation with the same oversized sunglasses still in her car faded out. Those visions of the future wavered like the air over a gasoline tank on a hot day. She would drive everywhere alone, free of the tumultuous seas of romance, free of a stable relationship, settled and at peace.

Looking down Terrie's friend's list, she noticed a few people still connected to her. They would know where she was. They would tell Christine. She drafted an email to her friend Lexi. The quick note asked if she would spy on Terrie and see where she was. She needed to find out for Christine since she had some things to say to her.

Christine drafted an email but couldn't send it. She was spying. Terrie needed to come to her on her own terms. Christine was supposed to wait. She couldn't push her way into Terrie's life. Terrie didn't want anything to do with her. She would become the stalker. The main thing Christine spent her time hating about Terrie over the last few months was her stalking other people. It was so wrong. But was she doing it at all? Christine was the one. She was invading private space, forcing herself on others without their knowledge. In a way, it was assault. Christine was poised to become the things she had come to hate most.

It was too forward. Christine couldn't look desperate, let alone creepy asking for all that information from Lexi. She was, though, desperate. She needed Terrie. Terrie would understand in the end. Right away, she didn't want to be suspicious. She didn't want to come across aggressive. She needed to hide the whole search.

Christine googled for hours looking for an updated address or some piece of information. She was too scared to call the hardware store. They knew her. She found the contact for Terrie at the library information technology office where she had worked several hours a week on campus last year as part of her graduate assistantship. That's where she and Christine had met. Her name was still there, even though she had left her position.

After lingering around for a while, reading another ten minutes of a book, and finishing the food prep, Christine took a stab at something she was avoiding. In an awkward action, she made a call to the police station that had brought Terrie in. She asked if they had her address would they give it to her. Of course, Christine should have known. They couldn't give her the address. They said to call 411. It wasn't Christine's business. She didn't deserve to know. She hung up with the police.

At wits' end, Christine called 411, but they didn't have the address either. She tried the library and asked for her forwarding address. They weren't sure what it was. They didn't have a record of it. They couldn't give out the information, or they were too lazy to look. It didn't matter which at that point. That's what Christine decided.

When Christine called Lexi, Christine told herself it was for love. It was for Terrie. Christine needed to know Terrie's contact information so she could at least apologize. She needed to offer herself to Terrie or at least make amends. She couldn't live the rest of her life with the weight of guilt on her.

In Lexi's opinion, it was weird. That's what she articulated, weird. It was evident Terrie didn't want anything to do with her. Lexi knew what had happened. When she found out the police cleared her and they caught someone else,

Lexi acted as if Christine wounded her. She was protecting the innocent.

Christine pleaded. She lost all sense of self-respect in her search for Terrie. She was embarrassed and humbled. She told Lexi how she was wrong and needed to see Terrie. Lexi bluntly said Terrie probably didn't want to see her. She couldn't give Terrie up. Christine made an analogy. She put the situation in the context of Lexi and her ex. Lexi would never get over her. Christine told Lexi if she found the definitive reason they broke up, the reason their relationship went on the rocks in the first place, wouldn't she want to discuss it with her ex, to close the book. Lexi gave in.

Terrie hadn't posted on her Facebook page since a month before the incident. Nothing was updated. Lexi did, however, know some people, and she did Christine one huge favor. Christine promised she would return information if she ran into her ex, get some gossip. Lexi said no thanks and hung up to do some reconnaissance.

The stalker to the innocent, Christine waited for the one she loved. She couldn't leave her behind. She had become the aggressor, the one breaking boundaries, and the law. She had already looked for love and found it. She needed to keep what she had. The pipe dream of becoming a lawyer faded into practicality.

CHRISTINE LEFT FOR work in the morning several days later. When she got to the intersection, she veered to the left toward their old apartment to see if Terrie was there. Spying on Terrie, the same as old times. She wouldn't be late. She got up extra early this morning and left knowing she could drive by, but not at all sure until she got to the intersection.

Christine was at an apartment door not too far from their old apartment. Her place was a row home with multi-units. Steps inside the main entrance was a unit door made of thick wood. She entered on the first floor, and the door faced a narrow hallway. A small metal slat took the mail. The mailman would drop folded pieces of paper, held shut with tacky strips, right in the door. Christine couldn't knock, even though no lights were on. Terrie wasn't home. She was always up early. She was gone by now.

Christine went and sat in her car. She drafted a letter. It was as close to the same message Christine had held over the candle those few nights ago. She felt the same way. The words were still genuine. Nothing had changed. She would mean those words until the day she died. It was the way she intended them this time. Yes, Christine was recounting her feelings, but it was for Terrie. It was for them both. The purpose, the delivery, the intent for her eyes only, the action was Christine giving love and bravery. She wrote the words exactly as she had written them before.

So many things might happen if her car didn't turn over, a chain of events. She would wait for Terrie. Ask her to help. Her tears would flow, and it would be all better again. She would be weak with her, vulnerable, so Terrie would go soft and forgive her, let her in. If Terrie acknowledged her pain, helpless, she would need to help, make the one she loved better again.

When Christine finished, she slipped the letter, without

an envelope, into the mail slot. She exhaled relief and made her way to the car. She didn't need to do anything more. Even if Terrie never called the number in the letter, her number, the number Terrie already knew, she would be satisfied. She had said what stabbed at her to say.

THE PHONE RANG six days later, on a hot Sunday in July. She snapped it up. Terrie's restrained pause before she spoke let Christine know it was her. After breathing five light, hot breaths into the phone, she spoke softly but levelheadedly.

"Christine?"

"Terrie...I'm sorry. That's all I can say."

"Can you say more? Keep talking. Things other than 'I'm sorry.' I want to hear your voice."

Acknowledgements

I owe a lot of people a lot of things. I'd be remiss if I didn't at the very least thank everyone who played a part. Support and belief in me and for this collection of words meant so much to me in so many ways. I am indebted most greatly to my wife for her encouragement and at times simple statements and ideas that resonated and carried me this far. A great gratitude goes out to Sharmin, Joe, Jeanine, Carolina, Jackie, Kristin, Chris, Emily, Jeni, Laura, Ashley, Jeanette, Michelle, Ryan, Rae, and everyone who read the whole lot, chapters, or listened and hoped with me all the way.

About S.E. Smyth

S.E. Smyth is a versatile author putting words into the world. The stories she tells are never exactly how they happened. Elusive as she proclaims she is, you can usually find her nose buried in primary sources plotting a story. Despite persisting historical references, she wholeheartedly believes she lives in the present.

She resides in a smaller sort of town in Pennsylvania, carries heavy things for her wife, rubs cat bellies, and can often be seen taking brisk walks. The household is certain there is something odd going on. She and her wife travel when the air is right looking for antique stores, bike trails, and the perfect beach. S.E. rises unnecessarily early and usually falls asleep by 9 p.m.

Email

sesmythauthor@gmail.com

Facebook

www.facebook.com/sesmythauthor

Twitter

@SE_Smyth

Website

www.sesmythauthor.com

Coming Soon from S.E. Smyth

Hope for Spring

Five blocks to the main road, in a perfect well-traveled corner outside a quaint neighborhood, I stuck my thumb out. I worked to maintain anonymity. I feared seeing someone I knew, but I had to get to the bus station. A reserved dowdy woman of about fifty-five picked me up. She did not seem to be the typical kind of person that picks up hitchhikers. Likely, she knew my mom, but she wasn't sure if I was her daughter. She may have been afraid to ask. She kept talking about her book group. "Well, Nancy says the African missionary in the book is bad for society. She totally impresses her views without stepping out of her comfort zone and experiencing their community for what it's worth. You know, I agree. If someone stepped into our neighborhood and said this is the way things are going to be, well. there'd be a riot." I nodded and smiled where appropriate. There were some "yeahs" and "totallys."

The ride to the bus station took about twenty minutes. The frumpy woman drove me right there. The destination, a recourse, however inconvenient, ended up with me getting out at the front entrance. She rolled down the window and waved as I got out and peered into the pit of the car. She said, "It was nice meeting you. Be safe wherever you're going. Are you sure that sweatshirt is warm enough?" Then she backed out and sped away, still smiling. People here were pleasant, but they were exuberant.

"One ticket for Santa Cruz, California," I said, still double thinking myself.

"When do you want to leave?" the ticket agent said.

"For the next bus," I said. When else did Ms. Cashier fucking think I wanted to go?

"The next bus is at 4:35, and it'll be one hundred and sixty dollars," she said.

I rolled my eyes; my pockets didn't have that much money to spare. I had a handful of cash over two hundred dollars. Hell if I know where I got all that. "I don't have that much. I called earlier, and they said fifty-nine." I said rolling my eyes.

"That's for a bus two weeks out. If you want to buy a ticket for two weeks from now, it'll be that much," the cashier said.

"Fine, I'll take the one two weeks from now for fifty-nine dollars," I said. Scrunching my brows together, I willed a smooth transaction. Returning home wasn't an option. I'd have to tell my parents I was leaving, or they'd ask challenging questions about my life.

I sat over on one of the seats out of view of the cashier for another hour and fifteen minutes. Over the loudspeaker, they called bus 167 to Pittsburgh, Chicago, Denver, Los Angeles, and other stops in-between. I snuck outside to the boarding area but avoided the cashier. The driver glanced at the tickets, while I bowed my head down closely at mine in my hand and nodded passengers on. I waited for ten or twelve riders to get on and filed in line. He glanced and shrugged as I got on.

The intercity bus system had some real flaws in their execution of business. I took free intercity trips in the months to come like candy. Each time, I had a different way to approach a cash-free trip. If the driver said, "No, this ticket is for two weeks from now," I would have told him I was sorry I thought it was for today. But he didn't, and I got on with a tad bit under two hundred dollars in my pocket. I held in my jeans about enough money to stay at a hotel for three nights.

NINESTAR
PRESS

Made in the USA
Middletown, DE
08 November 2022

14199080R00196